"And are you coming, too, Miss Coole?" Oliver's voice and eyes softened. His tenderness transformed him from a hearty salesman to a kind friend.

"Why, yes . . ." Lacey said, her eyes wide. "It is very kind of you. . . ."

Riley Scott stood in the shadow of the veranda, watching Oliver wooing Lacey in this manner. He did not approve of either Oliver's invitation or Lacey's ingenuous acceptance. And he was angry. He had accepted and been accepted by each person he had met here tonight—except Lacey Coole.

Now why was that . . . ?

NOBODY READS JUST *ONE* LUCY WALKER!

The Other Girl
Heaven Is Here
The Distant Hills
Sweet and Faraway
The Call of the Pines
Come Home, Dear
Love in a Cloud
Follow Your Star
Home at Sundown
Reaching for the Stars
A Man Called Masters
The Stranger from the North
The River Is Down
The One Who Kisses
The Man from Outback
Down in the Forest

The Moonshiner
Wife to Order
The Ranger in the Hills
Shining River
Six for Heaven
The Gone-away Man
Kingdom of the Heart
The Loving Heart
Master of Ransome
Joyday for Jodi
The Bell Branch
The Mountain That
   Went to the Sea
Ribbons in Her Hair
Monday in Summer
Pepper Tree Bay

Available in Beagle editions

PEPPER TREE BAY

Lucy Walker

BEAGLE BOOKS • NEW YORK

The characters in this book are entirely anonymous
and bear no relation to any living person.

Published by arrangement with the author and the
author's agent, Paul R. Reynolds, Inc.

First printing: April 1973

Printed in the United States of America

BEAGLE BOOKS, INC.
201 East 50th Street, New York, NY 10022

CHAPTER ONE

On the eighth day of March, at the fag end of a heatwave, Oliver Harding, motor magnate and man of many parts, was cruising his big car along St George's Terrace. The congested traffic, evacuating the city in the peak hour of five-thirty, brought him to a standstill at the pedestrian crosswalk.

It was then he saw Laura Montgomery.

He smiled and there was a touch of sardonic humour in his eyes.

What a lady was Laura!

Whenever he saw Laura which was too often for his peace of mind, he saw her not only in the present but as she had been in the long ago of childhood. In the musical intonation of her voice he seemed to hear again the distant and set-apart hush of that remote time.

He tooted his horn but Laura did not see him. He watched her step into the bus and the smile came back into his eyes as he admired her fine leg. Then the traffic moved forward and Oliver's great glamorous car had perforce to move with it.

If he judged his speed rightly, he thought, he could pull in behind that bus when it reached Pepper Tree Bay.

At Mill Street he turned left and then farther down the hill turned right again to follow the river bank. It had been a hot humid day and the river lay at the foot of the mount, shimmering blue steel.

He thought about Laura until he reached the Narrows, the point of confluence between the Canning River and the Swan. He slowed down to a willing crawl and let the rear traffic overtake him.

They were going to build a bridge here. First they would reclaim some of the land from the river in the bay that curves inwards to the very base of the mount. Oliver felt a certain sentimental regret about that in spite of the fact he had been one of the prominent business men pushing behind the Government to build that bridge. He had land on the other side of the river that would improve in value with that bridge but deep in his heart Oliver knew that was not the reason why he, and others, had pressed for its construction.

You can't hold back time, he said to himself. Time flowed over and about one always. The bushland must go, and the river bays too. Time was here, importunate for progress. No one liked change, and yet change was as inevitable as that flesh-borne bodies of today would be dust in the charnel chill of far-off tomorrow.

No one, knowing Oliver, would ever have dreamed he thought this way. His inner heart was disguised behind a manner that was full of surface good cheer. When he talked he spoke with the idiom of the man in the street, never in the rolling sentences and poetic flourishes of his hidden mind. He enjoyed being an anachronism that only he himself understood.

Anywhere else in the world he would have carried the stamp of his country and fortune in his build and face, in his manner, in his voice and in the loud engaging excellence of his clothes. He was lean and sun-weathered, with intelligent humorous brown eyes, a gold cap to his left incisor in an otherwise perfect set of white teeth, a voice that was on occasions too hard and on other occasions, when he spoke softly, had a rich resonance that suggested the gentle and the tender.

On occasions he wore eye-glasses, always when he attended Board meetings, for instance. Those glasses were framed in terms of Oliver's personality, for they were gold-rimmed in the latest Continental style.

When he played golf he wore the kind of expensive outlandish clothes that caused the women to smile and the men to shrug their shoulders. However, whether his beholders smiled or shrugged, not one person ever failed to notice him or failed to remember he was a rich man; a hard man, yet a man with inexplicable moments of human good fellowship and open generosity.

In short, he was a figure in the city and a potentate in the suburb of Pepper Tree Bay. He was a man whom, because of his studied brashness, some would prefer to dislike but they were disarmed by his success and the flash of his personality.

As he continued in a leisurely way around the river he thought about Laura as she had been all those years ago when they were kids in Pepper Tree Bay. Laura had been a proud head-tossing missy who spent half her life in Ireland and half of it in Australia. She hadn't fitted either place very well because she had belonged to both and yet to neither.

He, Oliver, had been the son of the church caretaker. Laura had been the niece of old Joe Montgomery, who as Rector of Pepper Tree Bay built and headmastered the school. Oliver remembered that the Reverend Joe Montgomery had given him a scout uniform in the hope of making him a boy scout. In addition he had given him the job of picking up papers in the school grounds for pocket money. Now Oliver Harding had his own son at that school and he could have bought all the scout uniforms in Perth and not noticed a dent in his bank account.

And now he knew Laura Montgomery socially and was able to have a quiet laugh at her expense! Well, not quite at her expense. He liked Laura. He just liked having a joke with life too.

He'd catch up with her in about fifteen minutes now. He liked to watch that look of startled doubt in her violet-blue eyes; the quick proud curve of her mouth and the unconscious lift of her head. She was a true aristocrat in the way she carried herself.

Oliver fell to wondering if Jewish blood ever got mixed up with the Irish. If Laura's eyes had been any other colour she could have passed for descent from the best of the Jewish tribes. Her features were Semitic though her nose was good, not beaky. A bit Roman, perhaps.

What the devil had she married her cousin Danny Montgomery for? He was a nice feller, but when you'd said that you'd said everything. A bit of a Peter Pan, if you asked Oliver. It must have been something to do with that feller Freud's return-to-the-womb theory. Danny was the last of the Montgomerys . . . as if that could possibly matter to anyone in the world except the Montgomerys. He stood for the Irish end, and Laura couldn't get really Australianised. With those looks she could have married anybody.

Well, not Oliver. He was married already.

He smiled again. When Oliver smiled things went hardly with anyone watching him. There was the very devil in that smile. That was the trouble with Laura. Oliver's smile entangled her; just as years ago Danny's golden head and beautiful Anglo-Irish accent had captured her homeward-turning heart.

Danny was thirteen thousand miles away right now and that left it a field-day for Oliver's smile.

The big car swept on past the City Baths and Oliver looked at the speedometer and the clock. At this pace he'd beat the bus to Pepper Tree Bay in spite of the fact he was taking a longer route. He slowed down again.

Suddenly he stopped thinking of Laura and began to think of Riley Scott. Now that was a feller for you, Oliver thought. Queer chap Riley, but clean, and heading for the top. He'd

7

been thinking about Riley Scott a lot lately. He, Oliver, wanted a man for the Council. He'd been down to the Yacht Club where the bigger of the business men habitually met, and sounded them out about Riley. They didn't know anything of him but they were prepared to take Oliver's word for it. They wanted things done round the foreshore too.

It was Oliver's idea to build a promenade around the river edge on the East Side of Pepper Tree Bay. Something for the community . . . and it would improve house property too; though only one or two were fool enough to mention this last point.

Riley Scott might be the man for the Council.

Oliver remembered playing about with him when they were kids. Riley had lived in some small shack over beyond the swamp in those days. Screwing up his eyes thoughtfully, Oliver conjured up the misty-edged memory of a small boy in pants that were too long for him and definitely frayed at the edge. Bare feet too. Well, Oliver thought, thinking in the idiom now, I had ragged pants and bare feet too. That didn't matter a damn.

Then he'd lost sight of the kid. The next thing Riley had turned up hiding in the pepper trees behind Joe Montgomery's church along the highway. He'd been so hungry he would have eaten the food out of Oliver's mouth, if he'd let him. Oliver had fed him and kept him hidden in the cubby house he'd built over in the school grounds while the school was on holiday. Then Riley had gone down to the river for a swim and a wash up. They'd caught him and put him back in that Home.

Well, that was nothing either, except Mrs Montgomery, the Rector's wife, had fought a legal battle. She didn't believe in convicting a child for being neglected. The details were all hazy as far as Oliver was concerned and he'd never bothered to check up on them, but he wondered if Mrs Montgomery remembered. Mrs Monty was a battler even in those days.

That was a hell of a long time ago, and it couldn't matter less!

Riley had a fine war record and that farm of his down the south-west had swum to the top on the wool boom in 1949.

Oliver didn't wonder why Riley Scott had come back to Pepper Tree Bay. Everyone who had ever lived in Pepper Tree Bay came back some day before he died.

It wasn't only the river, or the school lying like a green-fielded oasis between the Highway and the Bay; or that queer mob, the pioneering families, who lived round on the West Side of the Bay.

It wasn't the ladies who still wore gloves when they did the morning shopping, with baskets over their arms. So help me Bob, it wasn't the big riverside houses on the West Side with their Victorian furniture and their inmates, daily dying out, with their Victorian manners. Nor the click of ball on bat on the school grounds, across the way from the church. It certainly wasn't the got-rich-quick building their glass palaces round the East Side of the Bay.

It was something to do with the wide flat tree-sheltered streets leading down to the river and the fact that you knew all the faces and that the air was still and calm and peaceful. And that years ago, when you were a kid, you'd swum school races in those rickety old baths and shot duck on the swamp and shied stones at the boys in the school who wore boots and socks all the year round. And the fact that you said 'I live in Pepper Tree Bay' and felt proud and privileged and enviable.

Maybe it was just because it was the place where you were born, and it was orderly, sun-warmed and very beautiful.

Oliver wondered if the building of a promenade was the last touch of irony to the houses springing up, glassy-eyed monstrosities, round the East Side. Like putting the last circle or triangle in a futurist picture. Because that East Side would never be truly Pepper Tree Bay. Not as Oliver and Laura and Riley Scott had known it. Barefooted days of wild flowers and wild duck on the swamp.

And that reminded him. He was thinking of Riley Scott. Well, Riley Scott had bought himself a town house in Pepper Tree Bay. Properly organised, he ought to do well for the Council. Born in the Bay. That would get him the voters who never really think. A self-made man – that would get the tradesmen's vote and the Labour crowd too.

Good-looking. That would get the women. Made big money . . . that would get the Yacht Club boys and the new-rich on the East Side.

No one would get anything from the West Siders so one didn't have to bother about them. They were rich and old, and on their way out. Their Victorian furniture would be auctioned at inflation prices and their houses knocked into schools and blocks of flats . . . or something. They were too old and too tired, those people there, to go out and vote on a Council issue. Besides, if they didn't recognise a name on the list of Families-

9

First-in-the-State they would think it was a *t'other sider* anyway and stay home and play bridge or talk about one another's cousins who had married somebody else's cousins. They were a mannered lot, over there. Pity that manners had become an anachronism. The world lost something more precious than the contours of Matilda Bay when genteelism went out of fashion.

Yes, Riley Scott would be a good man.

Oliver swung his car round the right corner to meet up with Laura's bus at the right moment. The bus had stopped and Laura was the only passenger to get out. As she stepped down she showed that fine leg again.

Oliver smiled and tooted the horn. This time Laura saw him. She stood poised, one foot on the kerb of the footpath. Her hat shaded her face but not enough to prevent Oliver seeing that quick startled look in her eyes and the equally quick recovery.

He laughed quietly. Laura would never believe she showed her feelings. Didn't she know a man who ran a business as big as Oliver Harding ran one knew all about the easy friendly smile you had for all people; especially the laddies who were trying to edge themselves in at Board meetings?

And just what was he trying to do with Laura now? Edge himself in?

Oliver's smile lost its demon and became honestly friendly. No, he just liked Laura. He liked having fun with her. He wanted her to get rid of whatever it was that haunted her and stopped her from being one of the most beautiful and sweet-hearted women in the world. Maybe she needed psycho-analysis and not Oliver Harding.

The bus lumbered off and Oliver eased his car up beside Laura. He leaned across the seat and swung the outside door open.

'Get in,' he said. 'I'll take you for a ride.'

Laura had regained her composure. She rested her impeccably gloved hands on the top level of the open door and spoke to him through the open window.

'God, she is beautiful!' Oliver said to himself. 'What would she be? Thirty-something? Near forty? But that skin! That's Ireland for you. And her mother had eyes like violets. The rest of the Montgomerys had sea-blue eyes. Except Denney. Denney, the fourth of old Joe Montgomery's girls, had a touch of the violet. It must be a Montgomery heritage after all.' Oliver remembered that Laura's mother had married her cousin. And Laura herself had married a cousin.

'That's what's the matter with them all,' Oliver thought. 'They can't or won't shake off the shackles of Ireland.'

'Aren't you off your beat, Oliver?' Laura asked. Her voice was like her eyes, controlled and very charming.

'Not by a stroke. I followed you from Perth.'

That put Laura off *her* beat. Funny how the truth always knocked the other feller for the count. Laura, always so self-assured and just a little haughty, was at a loss for words. At last she found her voice.

'Well, that's very flattering of you. Did you want to see me as badly as all that?'

'Not badly. Just wanted to see you. Are you going to get in? It was a hundred and five by Levinson's thermometer in Hay Street today. Don't tell me you wouldn't like a whisper of sea air before dinner.'

'I surely would like that,' Laura said, getting in and arranging her dress so the skirt wouldn't catch in the door when Oliver closed it.

Was that the Irish speaking, or just Laura? Oliver hadn't been to Ireland so he wasn't certain how much of Laura's way of speaking was her own and how much was unconscious imitation. Fundamentally Oliver thought all Australians ought to be just plain Australians and to hell with from whence came their parents. But his ear, which knew and understood music, could not help enjoying the softer tones of northern climates.

'Won't Esther be expecting you for your dinner, Oliver?' Laura asked, looking at him upwards and sideways in a glance that was pure coquetry. An instant later she changed it to something more direct, and a cool smile. Then she turned her eyes to look straight ahead through the windscreen.

'About as much as your aunt will be expecting you,' he said. 'Do you suppose anybody south of the Capricorn will be eating a hot dinner tonight?'

'It is hot,' Laura agreed.

Oliver noticed the changed nature of Laura's glance at him. Now why, he wondered, did she do that?

'Ever been up there behind the school house and looked down on the Bay?' Oliver asked.

'Years ago,' Laura said.

'The public never sees that scene,' Oliver said. 'That's why I want to build that promenade.'

Laura was not interested in the civic progress of Pepper Tree Bay so she did not take him up on the subject of the promenade. Instead she glanced again at his face and saw his absorption in the school grounds.

'You really love that place, don't you?' she said.

'Who wouldn't? I cleaned up the raking papers from it when I was a kid. I played marbles with every one of those Montgomery girls behind the scrub. I kissed my first girl where that box tree is. There used to be bushes there.'

'Who was she, Oliver?'

Oliver was watching the traffic on his right as he made ready to swing into the Highway.

'Esther,' he said between half-closed lips. 'She was ten and I was fourteen.'

Esther was the first and the last. He wouldn't say anything about what went on in between. A man did not kiss and tell, if women did. He wondered what Laura's record was. Don't tell me anyone with a mouth like Laura's was satisfied with one . . . and that one Danny Montgomery.

If I was a mick I'd cross myself, thought Oliver. That Danny was a good chap all the same. Every time I look at Laura and want to have a laugh at Danny I feel lousy. Danny's like one of those pale-skinned pommies you think a mouse would scuttle and they go out and win V.C.s and crawl into Japs' camps without batting an eyelid. Give me the pommies every time when it comes to a fight, thought Oliver. He remembered that rosy-cheeked kid priming his rifle while they were waiting for the Japs to come down the trail up there in Timor. Cool as a cucumber. And not even feeling he was a hero. Which he bloody well was. Nineteen, and about to die; and knew it. All he himself had lost was his right hand. Well, what went for a right hand inside that leather glove on the steering wheel was as good as anybody else's two hands. So what! But that kid was dead and the important thing about that was he hadn't even known what fear was. I'll take the pommies, thought Oliver.

'We're not very communicative, are we?' Laura's voice broke his line of thought.

'That's friendship for you,' Oliver said. He did not turn his head but his easy smile curved his lips. He narrowed his eyes as he drove up the hill because he was driving straight into the setting sun.

'If he wasn't so good-looking,' Laura was saying to herself. 'But it isn't only that. There's a sort of magnetism. One can't get away from it. Those eyes of his . . . There's a power behind them.'

She rested back in the silence that was between them. She

put up her hand and lifted off her hat and half turning threw it on to the back seat. At the top of the hill they felt the breath of the sea. It touched Laura's forehead gently and sweetly. It was like oil on a burn. Rest after a long day. Mercy.

'Oh . . . that's lovely,' Laura said. 'As soon as one comes over the hill the air changes.'

'I thought you'd like it,' Oliver said.

'Shall I take your hat off for you, Oliver?'

She glanced at him, suddenly embarrassed. He might think she thought he was unable to manage the car with that gloved right hand of his. It was too late to take back the words. Laura bit her lip. Oliver grinned. He knew what she was thinking.

'Thanks a lot,' he said. 'And light a cigarette for me while you're about it, will you?'

Laura took his hat off and then put a cigarette in his mouth. She had to lean forward, close to him, to put the lighter to the end of his cigarette. She squinted a little as she did it and wanted to prolong the ceremony because she knew that in an instant Oliver would take his eyes off the road and meet hers. There would be that sardonic smile in them. She kept her eyes on the lighter as she brought it away from Oliver's mouth to light her own cigarette. She knew he knew she was running away.

'That right hand of mine can do everything but one thing,' Oliver said. 'But thanks a lot, Laura.'

She didn't ask him what that one thing was. Oliver wondered if she knew.

Actually it was his left hand that did two hands' work but the right travelled along. It made do, except it couldn't feel the peach-bloom warmth of a woman's flesh. Funny how he missed that. Funny, too, how he kind of hankered after it. He'd got most things beaten in his life but he could not beat the longing, when his left hand slid gently up and down Esther's arm as they lay in bed at night, and dreamed it was his right hand. It spoiled pleasure.

He swung along the waterfront and turned quickly to brake into the lookout half-circling above the yellow beach.

The suntan fanatics were lying on the beach in swarms. The water was crawling with swimmers.

The sun was blazing down the western sky with colours that had the wrath of God in them. In a minute the red ball would sink behind the sea and the colours in the sky would hurt because when they lost their wrath they'd have a changing beauty one wanted to share because one could not hold them, and keep them, and take them home and put on the dining-room mantelshelf to look at whenever one liked. Or feast on in the loneliness of the night.

And the night was lonely.

Must be the middle-aged manic-depressive period, Oliver thought. Do men get it? He felt better when he thought in his second personality idiom.

Oliver smoked his cigarette, using his right hand just to show he could do it. He leaned back in the right-hand corner of the seat and looked at Laura now. She had a Roman profile. That was it. Must have been some Ities, not Jews, mixed up with the Irish sometime. The skin of her cheek and her long curved arm was glorious. He just might put out his left hand, in a minute, and touch it. It had been at the back of his mind when he saw Laura get in that bus. There, a long time.

Laura caught the edge of his smile then she turned her face back to the sea. Suddenly she slumped back a little in her seat. It was as if energy, the life fire, had waned in her. It was a defeated gesture.

This ocean always defeated her. It was over it that the family had come and gone over the years When they were children she had come here with her cousins to watch the ships bringing back her father . . . or Danny. Over it she had come and gone three times now. At least she had come three times. She had yet to go back.

'You know . . . in Ireland,' she said to Oliver, 'when some-one crosses to England we say they have "gone over the water". The Indian Ocean's a bit big to call "water".'

She's thinking of Danny, Oliver thought. Wonder what she's thinking of him. She's not in love with him now, if she ever was. He thought about Danny himself. He remembered the fair-haired boy with the impossible accent climbing the back fence of the Rectory to eat figs with him. He also remembered the impossible clothes. A black cutaway suit and somewhere in the background there'd been a top hat. Golly, it was funny then. That must have been twenty-three years ago.

'Why did Danny go to the war?' Oliver asked. 'He didn't have to go. The Irish weren't in it, were they?'

'Danny's kind was in it,' Laura said. 'They were first in it and last out of it.'

By golly, she was right! Danny had been Royal Navy re-serve, or something. And he was a year in it after all the rest of the reserves had been demobbed. A queer crowd, the Irish.

14

Suddenly he knew that left hand of his wouldn't go out and touch Laura's arm.

He was a funny feller, Danny, but he'd fought seven years of war and he didn't look the kind that had a day's fight in him. Tall, slender, fair, with careless eyes. Addicted to shabby clothes when on holiday, and somehow managed to look the polished gentleman in them. Guess he was made of the same stuff as that kid up in Timor. You just couldn't ever see it . . . that was all.

Oliver leaned forward and turned the key in the ignition.

'Well?' He turned his head a little to smile at Laura. 'Feel better for that breather?'

'Yes, it was lovely. Thank you for bringing me.'

He swung the car round and began to drive slowly along the sea front. The moments that might have mattered were over now. They could return to worldly things.

'Do you ever remember a boy called Riley Scott, when we were kids? Used to live somewhere over by the swamp?' Oliver asked. 'I can't quite remember where myself, but I think I once saw the house. A dump of a place.'

Laura shook her head.

'Should I remember him?'

'Not particularly. I just can't find anyone but myself who does remember him then. He's another of these self-made fellers, like me.' Oliver laughed. 'Only better-looking.' When Oliver laughed he sometimes got a crackle into it. It made other people want to laugh as well as shudder.

'Talking about being self-made is like boasting,' Laura said. 'You either do it to make someone else feel uncomfortable as if they've suddenly found themselves in a company of frogs, or you do it to slap yourself on the back. Which is it?'

Oliver smiled but the smile never quite reached his eyes.

'Remind me to stop boasting next time I start,' he said. 'Riley Scott means nothing to you?'

'No. Why should he?'

'I'm going to back him for the Council. When you put your weight behind a man you want to know what everyone else thinks of him, or thought of him years back. You've got to get the whole picture. Then you've got the answer to every question — you've got a spike for every gun.'

'Why should there be questions and guns? Can't the man stand on his own merits?'

'Laura, my darling, civic politics is the jungle law. Would we be mixing our metaphors?'

'Go on. Tell me some more about Riley Scott and the jungle.'

Laura couldn't have cared less about either. This, to her, was vapid conversation that had to fill in the half-hour it would take Oliver to drive her home. She would only listen to enough to hear the cue when she had to answer or ask a question. Oliver made her suffer enough by just being Oliver without having to suffer his enthusiasms over petty politics in Pepper Tree Bay. But maybe they mattered to him. Perhaps he wasn't just making conversation. Already Laura had forgotten the name of the man he was talking about.

'He's a great feller,' Oliver said. 'You ought to know him now if you didn't then. He's made a lot of money since the war and now I'm going to make him spend some of it . . . on Pepper Tree Bay.'

'And your own money?'

'I'm not the advertising kind,' Oliver said. 'Don't you worry, Laura. I put my hand in my pocket but as it's my right hand I can't feel it, and it doesn't hurt.'

'Go on about Riley Scott – is that the name? Which is he? Irish or Scots? With a name like that he ought to be a civil war on his own.'

'Probably pure Australian, which is the same thing as civil war. New independence versus ties with the old country. I'm just going to get the boys to back Riley Scott for the Council, that's all. When my crowd back a man they've got to have every angle on him. Like *Life* or *Time* magazine, they got to go right back over the path he's come till they get to his mother's maternity hospital.'

They swung round the corner past the school. The shadows had gone with the dying of the sun. The world was all one colour except where the magpies were black spots on the school oval. The trees stood in a stillness so complete they might have been silhouettes on a vast canvas. They drove past the church, the Rectory, the little bungalow house where Oliver had first known Esther. She'd been a little girl with yellow curls, a face like a doll's, and lace on her pants. Funny how the street was changed and yet unchanged. They'd put a fancy front on some of the houses and built on the vacant blocks. But the pepper trees in the Rectory and the lilacs in the street were still there.

Suddenly Oliver thought of old Williams and his cab. He laughed.

'What now?' asked Laura curiously.

'That old cab used to stand outside the station. Used to wait

16

to bring old man Sawkins home. Or if not him then Billy Thomas and even the Reverend Joe Montgomery. Old Sawkins and Billy Thomas always used to get off the train reeling drunk, but Williams was waiting for them. People used to see him drive past just at that hour and they knew he'd picked them up off the station and stacked them on board and was taking them home. They didn't have to look at a clock when they saw Williams drive past. They used to say, "There goes Williams's cab" and they'd look at one another and shake their heads. You remember, don't you, Laura?'

'Yes,' Laura said, suddenly sad. 'I remember,' She also remembered the evening when Mr Williams had driven her, with her cousin Theodora, up the hill that she and Oliver had just driven down. They were looking for Sylvia, Laura's sister. And they found her lying in the sand-dunes overlooking the ocean. Sylvia, too, had gone to watch over that ocean for the ship bringing Danny from Ireland. But her heart had always been weak . . . and she died. Up there alone, looking for Danny to come back.

Laura also remembered the day when Sylvia had had one of her heart attacks and Oliver had helped carry her home. She wondered if Oliver remembered. How she had hated him in those days! Just a nasty barefooted boy who threw pebbles at her ankles and jeered at her way of speaking.

Now she was driving beside him and hating him for a different reason. She hated him now because she couldn't escape him.

How do you love a man you hate? Was it love . . . this thing that was an agony but which made her heart nearly turn over when she saw someone who looked like him? Queer how a motor car sold by his firm driven down the street by an absolute stranger was invested with a power of magic and a power that wounded.

Brown eyes, a square forehead, a firm jaw and a mouth that when it smiled showed strong even white teeth. Six feet and broad shoulders, with tawny-brown hair. Not an unusual type and she saw him often in his fellow men here and there. The likeness caught at her heart and then made her feel a pain at the back of her head.

Yet what was there about him to have this effect on her? Why should she let him get under her skin? What did he *have*?

Just his smile and those brown eyes and something that came from him that touched you yet which you could not feel.

He couldn't be in a room without everyone knowing he was there. That was her only consolation. Others . . . everyone . . . felt that magnetism.

How did Esther endure being married to someone who belonged to everyone else?

Nobody who had got as rich as Oliver could be really good. If she had admitted anything different she couldn't have gone on hating him. If she didn't hate him then she'd love him. And dear God . . . she couldn't love Oliver Harding. She would always see the guttersnipe in him, and she would always feel the bully in him. Laura didn't fall in love with people like Oliver Harding. He didn't fall in love with people like Laura Montgomery. He just liked spiking them like butterflies on a pin.

She supposed this Riley Scott of whom he talked was another who had climbed like himself. Oliver was going to make him work to keep his place up there with the boys at the top, the business men who held the purse strings of the State.

Get up near Oliver and you'll have to pay for your fame.

Laura knew she thought bitterly, and probably unfairly. She had to think that way to keep herself sane.

2

Oliver parked the big car in the garage beside Esther's smaller one. He went into the house by the french door on the side verandah. Esther was sitting upright in an armchair, her legs crossed and the telephone receiver in her hand. As Oliver came in she put it back on the cradle, and stood up.

'That was Jack Levine,' she said. 'I heard you coming. I thought you wouldn't want to start talking on the telephone just now.'

'You're dead right. Pull out the plug, will you, darling? I don't want to hear the telephone bell for an hour.'

Oliver threw his hat on to a chair and walked across to the cocktail cabinet. Esther rested one hand on the mantelshelf and watched him. He took a bottle of Scotch whisky from the cabinet, then a water jug from the small refrigerator camouflaged behind a polished jarrah panel.

'It's been a bad day,' she said. 'Another century.'

'A stinker. Here's your drink, honey. Mild for you, powerful strong for me.'

'Do you feel that way, Oliver?'

He took a drink then leant forward over the glass in his

hand and kissed Esther's forehead. She was as cool as she looked. Her skin was as good as Laura's but it took a lot of time and money to keep it that way in this country. Her eyes were a soft childish blue and her mouth was still lovely . . . like a doll's mouth.

Esther was tall and looked elegant in her simply cut pink linen dress. She was very fair and her hair curled naturally at the temples.

Oliver looked at her slim manicured fingers as they clasped the glass he had given her. Nothing ever ruffled Esther. There was never a hair out of place, never a wrinkle in her simple but beautifully cut dresses. She designed and made them herself.

'John home?' he asked.

'Yes. He's doing his homework. Struggling with long division of algebra.'

The room they were standing in was long and narrow, furnished in the modern style. The easy chairs were upholstered in gay colours and the honey-coloured legs and arm rests matched the wood of the wireless chairs and the cabinet. Esther called it the sun-room and Oliver called it the loaf-room. It was pretty in a gay coloured way and the wide window along the south side gave a panoramic view of the Bay. The whole effect, because of the river view and the modern furniture, was of colour, blue and gold.

'I paid income tax on twenty thousand last year,' he said. 'And I never learned long division of algebra.'

'No, dear,' Esther said. She was still standing in the same position at the mantelshelf, beside the chair where the telephone table stood. 'You were born in the motor-car age. John was born in the nuclear age.'

'Not in it, my love. Into it. Aeroplanes dotted his date line.'

'Have you had a heavy day, Oliver?'

'Mm. Have you pulled out that plug? I don't want to hear the telephone.'

'It's out. Shall we have dinner at seven?'

'I've got to get cracking on that phone about half past seven,' he said.

He wondered why she stood there behind him like that. She was standing quite still. Was there anything odd about that? Oliver tried to remember if Esther often stood quite still in a room when she didn't have to do it. He couldn't remember.

He felt tired as the devil. What had made him go for that

blow to the ocean with Laura? It lost him three-quarters of an hour's rest. Without that rest he couldn't put in the evening's work.

Esther had looked pretty, and cool, and calm, when he walked in that french door. Wonder what it would be like to come home to one of those slatternly women who had the day's cooking down the front of her dress? Hair all over the place. Esther was always the same. And she was cool, cool, cool. But he couldn't feel coolness with his right hand, only the left. Always that fact haunted him.

Oliver put his empty whisky glass down on the floor beside his chair. He leaned his head on one hand and looked through half-closed eyes at the river. He heard Esther go through the door to the kitchen.

Oliver's eyelids dropped over his eyes. He'd have to come to grips with Harvey in the morning. Harvey was a good executive but he'd never make the top level. Too tensed up. He wasn't as good as he thought he was and a sense of injustice was already unnerving him. You can't put a fellow up on to the top step who'd bust himself, and the works, wide open. So what do you do? Make a heel of yourself and tell him the second stair is his level? And make him sour for life? Blokes like Harvey reach a point in life where they go berserk or go sour. Well, he, Oliver, would have to see him and settle it once and for all in the morning.

I wonder where Riley Scott put in those two blank years? I got the whole raking story but something doesn't add up. The dates don't add up. Maybe he's just forgot. I couldn't remember myself how old I was when I did what. Riley was a good fellow and it didn't matter what the hell he did with two years that Oliver couldn't find. It's just you've got to have the whole record ready for anyone who wanted to get into competition for the votes.

Laura's eyes were deeper than Esther's. Wonder what haunts her? . . . And her mouth! Moody, passionate . . .

Oliver's eyes closed. He dozed.

After dinner young John went back to school to rehearse his part in the chorus of *The Mikado*.

'Pile up the dishes,' Oliver said. 'Maybe I'll do them for you. Maybe, some day, I'll really get round to doing them, Esther.'

'You have another cat-nap, Oliver. You need it.'

'Look, Esther, money can buy someone to do those dishes. Why don't you get someone in? I don't care what I pay.'

'I just couldn't put up with anyone, Oliver. In the war we

had to go without servants. Then afterwards they weren't available. Now you can get them, but apart from charging the earth they're more bother than they're worth. I've been too long without help. I get nervous about telling them to sweep under the benches and not leave dust behind the canisters. I just haven't got the knack. Besides, if you do tell them about the odd corners they pack up and go, and you've got to get someone else. Start again.'

'You sound like Miss Smart down in the typists' room. She pays a senior typist more than a university lecturer gets and the service she gets in return includes the mistakes that are part of the efficiency level these days. Well, I guess I'd better plug in the phone again.'

Oliver went into the sun-room, sat down in the blond-wood armchair and plugged the telephone cord into its socket. He lifted the mouthpiece and dialled a number.

'That you, Dick? . . . Yeah – me, Oliver. Listen, do you want a good second-class executive? I've got one for sale and he's a hundred per cent okay. Good chap . . . What? . . . Yes, that's right. It's Harvey. I'm not going to give him Tomlinson's job and it's going to break his heart . . . Look, that job gave old Tom ulcers and a heart attack. Harvey wouldn't stand the racket . . . What? . . . No, I don't want to get rid of him. You know that. He's a decent loyal servant of the firm. I just want to give him a let-out if he can't take it when I tell him tomorrow. You got over five thousand employees there and you're screaming for trained executives. Harvey'd be a gift. Give him something with a prestige angle, and let him loose on your country sales. You might raise his salary a bit too, or give him commission or a bonus. He'll earn it . . . What? You'll sleep on it? Of course you will, you old snake, but I'm not selling you a pup. You think him over . . . You will? Good. Now I'll tell you what. If you think along my way I want you to call him up or see him some time between nine and ten tomorrow morning . . . Don't bring me into the picture. You know how to handle it. Make it look as if you're asking his advice about recruiting a top executive. It'll give him something to think about. I'll see him round eleven and tell him I'm not giving him Tomlinson's job. I'm leaving him where he is more valuable to the firm than up on the policy-making level. If he can't take it, your job will give him an out. Incidentally, if he can take it, I don't want to lose him. He's a good bloke . . . You'll sleep on it? Okay. And tell you what. I need a bottom-grade accountant on the ground floor. If you've got someone you want to pass up, let me in first, will you? I don't care if he's got a chip on his shoulder so long as he can keep the books. I'll pass him on if he gets the grizzles here. Meantime I'll get something out of him . . . What? . . . Tomlinson's job? Listen, boy, in a big show like yours you ought to wake up. The tops have got to be trained men these days. I'm bringing someone over from Melbourne who's done a university course in business administration . . . Okay, Dick! Don't say I didn't give you a tip. Why don't you send one or two of your promising young men across there? . . . Listen, I'm touching your crowd for a hundred pounds for the Maimed and Limbless Soldiers. Pass the box around, will you? . . . Of course I'll get something out of it, you old snake. Ever know O. Harding do anything for nothing? I'm due for another cork hand some day.'

Esther came into the room as Oliver indulged in one of his crackling laughs. He lifted up one eyebrow at his wife then turned his mouth back to the phone.

'Okay, Dick. Just don't let Harvey know I'm in the picture, that's all.'

He put the handpiece back on its cradle and took out a cigarette and lit it.

'That's one off my chest,' he said to Esther. He leaned over and dialled another number. 'That you, Ethel? . . . Can I speak to Clarry? . . . Yes, O. Harding.'

He hung on and watched Esther as she sat down on the other side of the room. She crossed her legs neatly. Everything about Esther was neat. Her ankles . . . her shoes. Wonder what she paid for her shoes? He'd never asked her. When she bent her head like that the lashes lay on her cheeks. Wonder why she liked sewing the way she did? That embroidery stuff she did was fabulous. Knocked everyone over sideways when they came in.

'That you, Clarry? . . . Just checking on the collectors for Friday's street appeal. You got enough? . . . Good. The tins can be picked up at eight o'clock from the Parish Hall. There'll be a Red Cross man there to parcel 'em out . . . Yes, Esther's in on it. Bet she collects more than Ethel.' His laugh crackled out again. 'Listen, if they want to know what Unesco is, tell 'em it's what would've happened to their own kids if the Japs had got through the Timor line. And tell'm I stopped the Japs single-handed at Timor. They kept the other hand for a souvenir. Okay, Clarry. See you Friday.'

He hung up.

'Guess I'll give the phone a turn now,' he said. 'I'll let it ring me.'

The words were hardly out of his mouth when it rang.

'Hallo, hallo!' A smile spread itself over Oliver's face and he leaned right back in the armchair. He put his feet up on the small occasional table that stood a little to the left of the chair and he dropped his voice to dulcet tones. 'And how are you doing, sweetheart? . . . You're doing well? Good for you . . . What . . . So help me Bob I forgot.' He put his hand over the mouthpiece and spoke across the room to Esther. 'That party's on Tuesday. Did you remember?'

Esther nodded. 'Of course I did. It's our party and our house. I wasn't likely to forget.'

Oliver turned back to the telephone.

'Good job you rang, Theodora. I forgot I was giving a party. Esther didn't forget though. Good old Esther . . . You're coming? . . . The whole gaggle of you? . . . Good. Got a new dress for it? . . . You sure should, Theodora. It'll be a good party.' He broke off into a roar of laughter again. 'That's why it'll be a good party. When I forget a thing I turn it on in case I forgot something else . . . All right. Be seeing you.'

He hung up.

'I'd better check the caterers, I expect.'

'I have done so already, Oliver.'

'Well, there's one person I've got to check. You can't because you don't know him yet.'

He dialled another number and helped himself to another cigarette while he waited for an answer.

'That you, Riley? . . . You all set for Tuesday night? . . . Good. I want the fellows to meet you that night . . . By the way, what year was it you went saw-milling down in the southwest? . . . You'll look it up? Just like me. I can't remember what year what happened . . . Anyhow, how's things? . . . Good . . . Good . . . Good! Well, see you on Tuesday night, if I don't see you before.'

As he hung up the receiver he saw Esther's reflection in the big mantel mirror. The light caught the bloom on the skin of her arm as she reached forward to take the small silver scissors from the work box. Oliver had a quick memory of Laura's arm lying on her lap as they'd sat up there looking over the sea. He'd nearly touched Laura's arm. He had intended to do it. He had meant to let his hand, his left hand, glide over it . . . up it . . . to that soft throat and the curve of her chin . . .

The telephone rang. He picked up the receiver.

'That you, Harvey? . . . What? You sold thirty cars to Evanson and Sons? . . . Man alive, have we got thirty cars we can forward? . . . You left a let-out clause on delivery times? . . . Thirty cars! That must be your record, Harvey. Good fellow! Listen, Harvey, I want to see you eleven o'clock in the morning. Can do? . . . Good.'

He hung up. Esther, looking up, noticed there was a sombre look in Oliver's eyes.

'God,' he said. 'He sold thirty cars in one week. I'm not going to *break* his heart. I'm going to *mangle* it.'

CHAPTER TWO

Mr Coole on his seventieth birthday bore, as ever, all the hallmarks of the landed nobility. He had a smooth oval face with a narrow square brow, a hooked nose and pale grey eyes over which the lids drooped, in the manner of those who in another country could claim centuries of noble blood as against Mr Coole's original yeoman stock and two generations of Australian squattocracy. He was tall, straight, and proud in his bearing. His mouth, thin-lipped, turned down at each corner, thus giving to his face, along with the drooping lids and hooked nose, an air of superiority and disdain. His hair was thin and grey but there was no baldness.

People in Pepper Tree Bay old enough to remember said he did not have that dour disdainful expression when a young man. He had been serious with a stern countenance, probably had little sense of humour and had bent himself, as his father had done before him, to turning out of the semi-desert country one of the finest sheep stations in the north of the State.

It was his father who had first built the stone and brick house on the West Side of Pepper Tree Bay as a town retreat from the forbidding heat of midsummer in the north-west. That was in 1880. It was he himself who had added to the landed resources of his family by taking up a substantial block of grass and forest land in the deep south-west.

While the Cooles, father and son, worked unremittingly and with great energy for themselves they watched their fellow settlers do likewise . . . or throw in the sponge and return to whatever country their family had originally stemmed from.

24

In all cases they came from one of the three countries of the British Isles, for the west coast of Australia was colonised originally and exclusively by Britons. A handful of cheap labourers in the form of convicts were sent to help them after the colony had been established twenty years, but, except for this, the Cooles and their kind had made their fortune and built a nation themselves.

In 1950 Mr Bernard Coole remembered the hardship much as one remembers pain that is past. He remembered it but he suffered it no more. He was rich, he owned three homes and for the last two decades his word had been law around that part of the Bay where settled and foregathered others stemming from the families who had wrung wealth from the some-time colony.

This group, until most of them died, lived in an exclusive Jane Austen society on the West Side of Pepper Tree Bay. Their houses were good and solid and were furnished with pieces brought from England by the first generation. They sat, ate, and talked as kinsmen in the British Isles of an earlier generation sat, ate and talked. Their manners were as period as their furniture and, except for what the hardship of the early days had done to them and to their appearance, there was something of an old world graciousness to be found in their way of living in Pepper Tree Bay that was as alien to other communities in the country, as if these people were of a different race altogether.

Yet in spite of this inviolate walled way of living, the denizens of the West Side controlled the State affairs from behind the scenes. They had vested interests stemming from the early days in now-flourishing enterprises. The public felt the pulse beat of their hearts through the newspapers on whose directorates they sat; in the Legislative Council which they dominated; in the big insurance, trustee, and real estate companies in which they invested . . . and in the land, a good deal of which they owned and so could choose to whom they would sell.

By the time it came to the third generation, the exclusiveness was breaking down. Mr Coole, however, was nearly the last of the second generation, that which had seen the city grow from a swamp to a thing of beauty on the banks of a lovely river.

Mr Coole, bereft of sons by a war, was left with one daughter to console his age. Lacey Coole was not so much the darling companion of his shortening days as his servant. In her

25

late teens he had protected her from *t'other-siders* and new-comers as he would protect a treasured thing from vermin. In her twenties he protected her from fortune hunters. The result was that Lacey Coole knew no people who were not her father's people . . . and a good many of them were her father's vintage.

As her own contemporaries married and her father's contemporaries died, Lacey, now thirty, was left to the last resources of domestic occupation. She listened to her father discuss testily the political headlines in the newspaper over breakfast. She listened to her father castigate every jumped-up nohoper and newcomer whose name found its way into print. She listened to her father's description of what Stirling first and Forrest last had decreed for the State. She listened to him describe acidly the neurotic self-interest in health in which, he thought, his few surviving contemporaries indulged. Then when he was ready for the day's events, dressed in his slightly Edwardian but perfectly tailored suit with its immaculate shirt and hard butterfly collar, the hard-brimmed Homburg hat, she drove him in his Riley car to his Club.

If he was lunching at his Club she returned for him at a quarter to six in the afternoon. If he was not lunching there she called for him at fifteen minutes to one. She was thirty years of age and she would not have been one minute late if she had been keeping an appointment with the archangel Gabriel.

When she made an occasional sortie to an afternoon tea in her own stretch of Pepper Tree Bay, from four o'clock onwards she let her left hand lie on her lap so that she could see her watch without anyone noticing she was doing anything so unmannerly.

On a day in late summer in 1950 Lacey was driving her father seven miles round the Bay to his Club in the city.

When they reached the cross-roads by the old stone church and the Grammar School . . . which Mr Coole still referred to as Dr Montgomery's School and to which he feigned ignorance when he heard or saw it referred to as the 'Grammar School' . . . he suddenly said in his dry, cultured and not unattractive voice, 'Drive round Queen Victoria Drive. We'll go the river way today.'

Lacey put out her hand to give a turn signal and waited for the Highway traffic to let her through.

'Drive slowly, Lacey,' her father ordered.

Lacey could not remember a previous occasion since the war

had deprived him and the nation of the species 'chauffeur' when her father had deviated from the Highway. He gave no explanation now and she would not have dreamed of asking for one.

As Lacey never exceeded thirty miles an hour it was difficult to know what her father meant by 'slowly'. She had already reduced her speed to twenty-five and the road was virtually empty. She cruised now at a sombre twenty miles an hour.

She apprehended her father was watching the river side of the road and guessed he was wanting to see some particular point. But she would not have asked him.

They were round the East Side now . . . the place where the new bright white houses stood sparkling in the pristine splendour of their many-windowed walls.

'Common! Trash!' Lacey knew her father was referring to the houses. She also knew that they might be common but certainly not trash. They were paying upwards to fifteen thousand pounds to build pretentiously here on the East Side of the Bay. Most of the land was taken up but there were a few vacant blocks left.

'Pull up beyond that garish monster with the oleanders in front,' her father said.

This she did, and without any explanation he got out. He drew his walking stick after him and walked round the front of the car on to the grass verge. He stood looking at the foundation stones of a new house which were being set out on the last of the vacant lots with a river view. Then, using his walking stick as a weapon, he walked forward to where the work was going on. As he walked he thrust aside a stick here and a stone there with the iron-capped tip of his stick. He did this with the gesture of one casting aside rubbish invested with the personality of impudence. It was something that stood insolently in his path.

Lacey while she waited looked at her own face in the rear-vision mirror. She had good clear grey eyes and a well-cared-for skin. Her nose had something of her father's aristocratic length but it did not curve at the tip as did his. Her forehead was square beneath the cap of dark brown curly hair and her mouth was generous though it was a little sad. Lacey Coole was not beautiful but because of the guileless yet frank expression of her eyes, the sweet mobility of her mouth, she had a lovely face. She deliberately smiled at herself now to pull upwards the corners of her mouth. She did not want to develop the disdainful droop of her father's mouth.

She remembered her mother and what a lovely mouth she had had. Lacey was always pleased when someone commented on her likeness to her mother. It was not only because her mother had had a delicate face with kind eyes and a charming mouth but because Lacey had lost her. The world had never been the same since.

She saw her father leaving the workmen now and going farther towards the river bank. He stood looking out over the Bay as if looking across its mile of diamond-dancing blue water to his own house on the far side.

Lacey left the car to stretch her legs. She was of medium height and looked a little taller because of her slimness. She pulled in the belt of her blue tailored linen dress by one hole and then patted down the creases. She leaned into the car and took her cigarette case from the glovebox. On two points only had she ever won an issue against her father. She did not wear a hat . . . and, so long as he was not about, she smoked cigar- ettes.

When the hat struggle had been on, Mr Coole had dis- covered he could not see so well from his passenger's seat when Lacey wore a broad-brimmed summer hat. So he asked her to remove it. That was the end of hats. She smoked, but never near him. So he said nothing.

She lit a cigarette now and leaned against the bonnet of the car and watched her father.

Presently she saw a tall well-dressed man get out of a Humber car that he had just driven up, and cross to speak to the workmen. He did not seem to notice that her own car was where it was, nor that her father was standing on this block, his back to the road, and staring out over the river.

Yet the man had an air of authority with the workmen and they stopped working and attended to him. Their previous manner of indifference changed now to deference.

Lacey idly wondered who owned this piece of property. This man with his open suntanned face and clear directive manner? Or her father? Lacey knew well enough that her father could condemn the houses round the East Side as garish, modern and vulgar . . . and at the same time finance the building through one of his company investments. It was one of the paradoxes of his attitudes that did not give her much thought. She was used to them. But she was not used to workmen, except for a curious uplift of the eyes, taking no notice of her father and then giving their attention to a man not known in the *Who's Who* of Pepper Tree Bay.

Presently Mr Coole, still thrusting his stick forward and occasionally tossing aside another intruding and insolent stick or stone, descended a little down the river bank. He bent and peered away to the left where a rocky promontory put a period to the Bay and around which the water of the river came down from the watershed in the Darling Ranges, flowed through the city and on serenely towards Pepper Tree Bay and finally the sea.

He had almost forgotten what the Bay was like when he was a boy. Only when he was away from it could he remember. It had been all virgin country along the foreshore then. Only on the West Side had there been habitation . . . the same houses that stood there today, many of them.

He stood now where he thought Forrest must have stood when he was wondering where to set aside great bushland tracts in the form of a national park so that posterity might see what Captain Stirling had first seen when he landed in the *Parmelia* in 1829.

On his seventieth birthday this thought had been with Mr Coole all day. When he was ten Sir John Forrest had put his hand on Bernard Coole's head and said . . . 'Well, son, this will be your land when I'm gone. See you look after it.'

He hadn't done too badly, he thought. He'd kept 'their' hands off the river and off the river front. Even these yellow-bricked, glassy monstrosities of houses that were going up were well back off the bank. Nature had helped him there . . . the banks were sandy and steep. People had had to build back to give firm foundations for the products of their fetid imaginations.

He'd missed out on this particular block of land. For the first time in years Firmingham had sold a block on the river bank without giving Mr Coole first option. He would take Firmingham to task for that. Meantime he wondered why the transaction vaguely worried him. He didn't want the land. He had enough. It was Firmingham making the transaction that caused a faint foreboding. It was almost as if Firmingham thought there were other interests; other people as important as Bernard Coole.

When he, Mr Coole, had made enquiries at the Titles Office he had discovered the land had gone to an unknown person. A newcomer? A jumper-up? Man by the name of Scott. Riley Scott. He hadn't come into the colony before 1880. There'd been no Scott in the colony in 1880 for whom Bernard Coole could not account. In moments of aberration Mr Coole still called the State of Western Australia in the Commonwealth of the Dominion of Australia . . . the colony. The year was now 1950 but Mr Coole's social laws preceded 1900.

He turned round and climbed back up the bank. It made him short of breath and gave him a sharp pain in the chest. It was almost as if someone imperative had knocked at the door of his heart. He again had a moment of misgiving, but it wasn't as sharp as the misgiving underlying his wonder as to why Firmingham had not referred an available block of land to him . . . Coole. When Firmingham got back from the Eastern States he would see him about it. There were ways of bringing pressure to bear on people like Firmingham.

The tall, striking-looking man had been going round the foundation stones with the foreman. He now left him and walked with a quick easy stride back towards the car. It was only ten yards away from where Lacey leaned against the bonnet of her own car. Over the short distance his eyes met hers. There was the faintest hint of a salutation in them. No more than was correct for two people interested in the one project but who had not met. In that one minute Lacey read the mild authority in his face and the quiet inflexibility of will in his intense blue eyes. He was good-looking in a way that was different from the men of the land-owning and pastoralist class as she knew them. This man might be a business executive . . . or a professional man. He wore his well-tailored clothes easily and the briskness of his step made her think he was a city man.

She read the licence plate on his car as she threw her cigarette butt down and put her heel on it. It was a country number. Her father's car bore the north-west road board lettering of the sheep station district her grandfather and father had pioneered. That was a small snobbery on her own part as well as that of her father. It was like a banner to the world . . . the only break in a habit of reticence in manners, the only publicity given to a name never allowed to appear in the columns, social or civic, of the press.

He got into his car, shut the door with a slight bang and drove away. Yet something delicate hung in the air about Lacey's head. Something made her heart contract, then beat again quickly.

Mr Coole paid no attention to the departing Humber or the tall man he must have seen. And he made no comment. Neither did Lacey. She did not ask her father what his interest had been for she knew he would not have told her. She did not know how much money, how much land, how much anything her father had. He never discussed his affairs with her. Everything in the house in Pepper Tree Bay was bought on account. including the food, and her father paid the accounts by cheque on the thirtieth of each month. He paid her dress allowance into her bank account on that date and on that date the only actual money changing hands in the house was paid to the housekeeper as wages.

On one occasion the housekeeper had asked if she might be paid weekly and Mr Coole, without looking up, had replied, 'You will be paid on the thirtieth of the month.' The housekeeper had not asked again. She was an efficient commonplace woman who knew she was in a 'good place'. The food was luxurious, even during the war, since it was sent from farm and station; there were no children; and labour-saving devices had been installed in the kitchen and laundry. The housekeeper had no relatives of her own and her sole interest was a cataloguing of the social occasions and personalities of Pepper Tree Bay. To this end she kept a scrap book of newspaper cuttings. Amongst the housekeepers . . . a thinning race . . . and the tradespeople she had a certain prestige by virtue of her intimate knowledge of the inside working of the Cooles' house. Only in this way could people's curiosity about the big house enclosed by wrought-iron fences and shrubberies be assured. Much as tourists in London would like to know what goes on in Buckingham Palace so visitors along the waterfront of the West Side were intrigued by the silent enclosed dignity of Meenon, the Cooles' house.

'To the Club,' Mr Coole now said, composing himself, but without loss of a certain upright dignity, in the seat beside Lacey. He probably hadn't the faintest idea that he gave this order now to his daughter in exactly the same tone of voice that he had been used to give it in the days of chauffeurs.

When they arrived outside the Club premises Lacey spoke for the first time.

'Will you be home for lunch, Father?'

'Not until dinner time today. Call at the usual time.'

As Lacey drove the car away he walked with a stiff-legged gait up the steps of the Club. Inside, a servant took his hat and stick in the manner of relieving royalty of a crown. Mr Coole was unaware of the fact that this particular servant was able to convey this pleasure in the same manner to every member and visitor entering those doors. Mr Coole's sole reaction, quite unconscious, was to feel like royalty.

Usually he went straight to a certain corner seat and looked for the current magazine dealing with the pastoral industry. But today, his seventieth birthday, just as the route to the Club had to be different, all things had to be different. He saw a group of three men sitting at a table talking to one another. He walked across to them.

'Vernon,' he said to one of them, a man much his own age but more rotund, more complacent about life and what life was doing in Pepper Tree Bay.

'Ah, sit down, Mr Coole. You know Richards and Browning, of course.'

Mr Coole by a nod of his head signified he did know these men. Actually he knew them very well. Being younger, they had always stood up for Mr Coole. Now they only half rose. Mr Coole said nothing but he put their sudden lapse in manners down to the fact they had only . . . or at least their parents . . . had only come into the colony about 1900. They were likely to be affected by the contagious bad manners of the post-war carelessness in such things.

'There was a paragraph in the paper this morning,' Mr Coole said. 'Another mention of a bridge across the Narrows. I trust you'll put a stop to this sort of nonsense before it goes any further.'

Mr Vernon smiled.

'Do you mean the newspaper paragraph or the bridge, Mr Coole?'

Mr Coole regarded this remark as some kind of unhappy witticism. He did not choose to remember that there had been occasions when stopping a newspaper paragraph had been as important as stopping the construction of a major bridge. Vernon, being a superior kind of journalist, liked to play on words. Mr Coole regarded Mr Vernon in this light because, though he managed a newspaper and held a considerable vested interest in it, he did not own a station in the north-west or a large farm in the south-west. He was therefore a journalist only.

Mr Coole leaned back and signified to the steward by a lift of his finger that he would now take his usual morning coffee with a dash of '07 brandy.

'After the '18 war,' Mr Coole went on, ignoring Mr Vernon's witticism, 'the young fellows came back with a lot of ideas. The enthusiasms of youth and that sort of thing. They gave us trouble for quite a time. Just as well to be on the lookout for unwanted outside advice and knock it on the head in the first instance.'

The three men exchanged glances in a way that did not

imply they were doing any such thing.

'Apart from the bridge which is a State affair, and you know the chaps in the Assembly, Mr Coole, there are a few other ideas floating around over which the State would have no control.'

This was Alfred Browning, a member of the Legislative Council. He was thirty years younger than Mr Coole and had in his narrow blue eye a kind of waiting interest that meant he was adept at trying out other people's attitudes without conveying his own.

His words brought a sharp reaction from Mr Coole. The latter turned his head and looked at the speaker under his drooped lids.

'And what do you mean by that?' This question in this voice would, not so long ago, have put a man on his mettle. Mr Coole did not notice that the Member of Parliament had no such reaction now. Alfred Browning was a man who liked old Bernard Coole. He respected him. What's more, he revered him. But he was dated . . . too reactionary. Trouble was he still had the big pull in some quarters. He waited now until the steward had set down Mr Coole's coffee and gone through the elaborate ceremony of pouring it and waiting for a nod of approval from Mr Coole.

'There's a bunch of young fellows round there in Pepper Tree Bay talking about building a promenade from the centre through the east to the promontory, then west along the riverside. The public, they think, should see more of the river. At the moment the public is precluded by the building of houses around there.'

Mr Coole put down his coffee cup.

'Utter nonsense,' he said. 'They would have to get rights.'

Mr Vernon watched Mr Coole.

'They're talking about getting them.'

'Who from?'

'The Council.'

'I'll settle that.' Mr Coole did not proceed to elaborate how he would settle that.

The idea was obviously fantastic and impracticable. Money, land, public goodwill? Things too hard to get.

But the matter had disturbed him for he forgot the subject that had preoccupied him all around the river drive and which had brought him across to speak to the three men. The bridge across the Narrows.

'Who are these jumped-up fellows who think they can tinker

33

with the Bay?' he asked caustically.

The third man, a colleague of Mr Vernon's, now spoke.

'Oliver Harding's at the back of it. You know, the motor man. But he's got an up and coming politician in Scott. Riley Scott.'

'Riley Scott?' Mr Coole's drooped lids drooped until they almost covered his eyes. The corners of his mouth seemed to sink down until his mouth was no more than a line drawn in the shape of a bow. 'Who,' he asked in a cold acid voice, 'is Riley Scott?'

'Youngish chap. Bit of a newcomer to the political scene. I believe he's bought property round the Bay.'

Mr Coole picked up his coffee cup and said no more. He watched the other three men and listened to their talk. It was all about riverside promenades and an ambitious man called Scott who would be front man for Oliver Harding.

When Mr Coole finished his coffee he excused himself and went across to his usual corner seat. He sat looking out of the window across the river for a long time. He felt uneasy in the pit of his stomach. Perhaps he should not have climbed that river bank this morning. Too soon after breakfast. But it wasn't the climb. It wasn't even the block of land, or the mention of Harding and Scott and their schemes. It was something to do with little things that had been going wrong all the morning. Those workmen on that block. They'd turned their backs and gone on with their work. Of course they probably didn't know who he was. There had been a time when every man in the vicinity of Pepper Tree Bay had known who he was. Underneath this was another unexplored thought. Supposing they *had* known who he was? That man driving away in the Humber. He must have seen his, Bernard Coole's, car with its number plate. He hadn't bothered . . .

Here in the Club. Vernon, Browning and Richardson; What had been wrong with their manner? They had not felt he was withdrawing his approval of them when he withdrew his company? Or had they? He sensed they were relieved when he moved away and that they were now talking about him.

Once when he knew clubmen were talking about him, he knew they were talking of his exploits, his importance, his wealth. They spoke of him with the awe of envy or admiration according to what kind of men they were.

Mr Coole sat in his corner and now read the daily paper. He had skimmed through it over the breakfast table. Now he would study and digest it.

No line, no matter how near the bottom of a page, escaped him. He scanned the list of donors for an old-age benefit. Oliver Harding's name leapt out of print and stabbed him. A thousand pounds. That was the trouble with these fellows. Anything to get themselves into print, and didn't they know they were whittling a stick for their own backs? Any man worth his salt should be able to look after his own old age. What were insurance companies for? Take away a man's incentive to work for later years and you took away his capacity to work hard. A penurious old age was the just deserts of those who hadn't worked hard enough. How'd this Harding fellow get on with his motor business when his labour worked half pace for double the money, and didn't have to worry about old age?

Mr Coole was always reading and hearing about charitable organisations. They angered him. Today they did something more to him. He couldn't stand this Harding fellow. A jumped-up racing-mad motor mechanic. No background. If he was in the colony (and by this Mr Coole meant Oliver's *family*) before 1900 then he'd been the spawn of indentured servants. More likely had come in with the riff-raff after gold at the turn of the century. All the same the fellow had worked hard. From nothing he'd got to something substantial. Where were his wits that he didn't see that if others had done what he'd done himself there'd be no occasion for old-age charities, let alone pensions? And didn't he read his own income-tax account? Didn't his income tax pay for the handful of incompetents congenitally incapable of looking after themselves?

He attended a Board meeting in the afternoon. The agenda showed nothing more than routine stuff but Clarkson while on the contracts budget had mentioned something facetious about the Narrows Bridge.

'They're going to bring an expert out from England,' Clarkson said with a smile that ridiculed the idea.

'What do these fellows know about Australia,' Mr Coole said testily. 'It's all talk. Something to fill the newspapers.'

Nothing more was said but Coole wished Clarkson hadn't brought the subject up.

Interfering with the river, even if it got no farther than print in the paper, was an annoyance.

Lacey was outside the Club at exactly quarter to six. Her father came out at fourteen minutes to six and got in the car beside her.

'Drive round the river,' he said.

Lacey supposed the river was well on his mind today. Twice

in one day. It must be that block of land.

On the East Side of the Bay the yellow foundation stones stood in neat order on that block of land. The workmen were gone now but the Humber car was drawn up close by.

The tall man was standing looking over the day's work. Lacey noticed her father kept his eyes directly to the front. Perhaps it hadn't been the block of land that had brought him round the river after all.

As Lacey drove on she wondered about the tall man and the Humber car. His face had impressed her. And his eyes had met hers. Men of her age were married or about to be married. If they were younger they had eyes only for the young things who were beginning to wear their hair tied in pony tails.

Lacey liked the pony tails. They added youth to what was already sweet youth. She had held her hair back with her hands and looked in the mirror. At thirty you can't try fashions as revolutionary as that. But if she had been younger . . .

At the back of her mind she knew that even if she had been younger her father would never have allowed it. Nor any man to look at her, with or without the pony tail.

When she went to her room to change her dress for dinner she stood looking at herself as she stood in her petticoat before the long mirror.

She pulled in her stomach and straightened her shoulders. She ran her hands down the slim curves of her sides. Shoulder-length hair had been the fashion right through the war. She had begun to cut hers inch by inch . . . so that her father wouldn't notice. She wondered if tomorrow she should go to the hair-dresser again. And supposing she had a face massage?

Her skin was good. Her mother's skin had been lovely and perhaps her own would stay youthful, like her mother's, well into middle age. Yes, she would have a face massage, but she would go to some salon where no one from Pepper Tree Bay would recognise her. She was afraid they would laugh at her but actually they would have rejoiced. Lacey didn't know how much her own people in Pepper Tree Bay were sorry for her, in spite of her home and her future fortune. The shield of her pride prevented them getting through to her with their pity. The proud carriage of her head gave her dignity and distance from those who would have liked to love her.

When she had dressed she stood at her window looking over the Bay. A mile or so away, on the opposite side, would be that block of land.

He must be rather a nice man, she thought. He would have

smiled if she had let him, just a good-mannered smile. But he hadn't walked past her unnoticing.

Funny how many people there were in the world and she didn't know who they were. The streets of Perth, for instance, were full of them. The only people she knew were those who were friends or neighbours in Pepper Tree Bay, or whom she met on those occasional long drives to the north-west station or the south-west farm. Even they were mostly connected with people in Pepper Tree Bay. They, and the tradesmen.

At the turn into the Highway the women were leaving the Parish Hall after a meeting.

The Women's Aid Society, Mr Coole thought scornfully. Why weren't they at home looking after their husbands and their children? Good-doers! Nosey parkers!

Mrs Tishmore put up her gloved hand to keep her hat in place. A gust of wind had swept down the hill and fluttered the skirts of the ladies. She saw Bernard Coole drive past with Lacey at the wheel of the car.

'We ought to get Lacey in to help,' she said to Mrs Roundell. 'She has nothing to do but drive round in that car. I don't approve of young women doing nothing.'

Mrs Tishmore was inclined to stoutness. Her lace collars, strings of pearls and her wide-brimmed bedecked hats lent her the air of a full-blown rose. She was extremely able and for that reason the women generally left her to organise their occasions for them. She had given her own adult life up to civic affairs and as she had just said, she did not approve of women who made no contribution to community needs.

'I don't know how you're going to get her in,' Mrs Roundell said waspishly. 'Apart from being father-ridden she is wrapped up in herself.'

'I don't agree with you at all. Lacey has just never had her eyes opened.' Mrs Tishmore took out a notebook from her over-large and businesslike handbag. She had to bow her head at an angle to keep the wind from drifting under the brim of her hat and lifting the whole thing from her head. 'I'll make a note of Lacey's name now. We must find someone who has contact with her.'

Lacey had bought herself a Dior New Look dress. She put it on and examined herself in the mirror.

'They're all wearing them,' she said to herself.

She turned sideways and self-consciously lifted out her

breast to observe the full rounded line that curved away and then turned gracefully in to her waist. She smoothed the palms of her hands down and over that curved line. Suddenly there were tears in her eyes. There was a knock at the door and she brushed them away.

'Come in.'

'It's just me, Miss Lacey. Why, you *do* look different! Has your father seen you in *that* kind of dress?'

Lacey relaxed her back and stood, her shoulders hunched. Self-consciously she strove to hide from the housekeeper's questing eye the gentle curves of her breast.

'Father's not interested in *dress*,' she said shortly. 'Did you want anything in particular, Mrs Simmins?'

'I thought I'd go up and see my friend Miss Martin for an hour or two. Will you get your father's Milo for him?'

'Yes, of course. Do go off if you want to, Mrs Simmins. You have the extra back-door key, have you?'

'Oh thank you, dear. You know, that's a very smart dress. Were you thinking of going somewhere special in it?'

Mrs Simmins loved to have a little titbit of news for her friends Mr and Miss Martin. The smallest item about the inmates of Meenon intrigued Miss Martin. Mrs Simmins had an idea that Mr Martin, sitting endlessly puffing his not very clean pipe, liked to know what was going on too. Not that he'd ever say anything, or *ask* anything for that matter. He wouldn't have to ask a single question. His sister, Miss Martin, would do all the asking.

'Oh, I have one or two engagements,' Lacey said carefully.

'It looks like an afternoon dress. Would it be for afternoon tea parties, Miss Lacey? Or is it in the evening you are going out?'

Lacey, who did not wish now to admit she had no social engagements at all, regretted the small idle lie.

'Do you think it would look too dressy, or too ultra, for a Women's meeting?' she asked. 'I really ought to go to the Women's Aid. I haven't been for ages. I promised Mrs Montgomery I would do something for their street stall next month.'

Mrs Simmins was quite sure the dress would astound, if not shock, the ladies. It was very *ultra*. It would show them that, by being extra-fashionable, Miss Coole was superior and not afraid to look superior. In this respect she would do credit to Meenon and all members of the household down to the weekly gardener.

'Of course you must wear the dress,' she said. 'Mrs Montgomery would like it, I know. You ought to see some of the clothes that eldest daughter of hers wears. Mind you, she always looks nice . . . but just a bit too smart, I'd say. And how are all those girls? All married now, but of course they are older than you. They say Denney's married *twice*.'

'Yes, I expect she is. I wouldn't be surprised if they all married twice,' Lacey said.

Her dress was over her head now and she was not thinking of Mrs Simmins. She was thinking about five girls in one family and that they were all married while she, the only living child in her family, was not married. Then there was the cousin Laura. She was really beautiful. Perhaps it was living in a crowd that brought about the happy gregarious state of affairs with the Montgomerys. There were so many of the Montgomerys. They made a vocal clitter-clatter wherever they went. Something like the Luton Girls' Choir when they raised their voices in unison. But they were interesting. No one was ever dull when the Montgomerys were around.

Mrs Simmins, making the right kind of noises, to which Lacey did not listen, said she 'would be off now' and went out of the room. Lacey did not hear the door close for she was thinking of that vociferous kind of life those other girls led. It made the silence of her own isolation on the West Side sound more hollow. If she went to the Women's Aid, Vicky Montgomery, now Mrs David Browning, would be there. Perhaps she, Lacey, would ask Vicky to come and have tea with her. She would offer Vicky the flowers and some pot plants for the street stall.

Lacey's spirits rose as she hatched her little parochial plot. It would be something to look forward to. Something to do. And the Aid money did go to deserving people. Yes, she would give them a generous donation.

All this because she had a new dress that needed to be worn; a housekeeper who needed a social itinerary for her mistress; and it was a golden day when someone had reminded her of a family that married often.

The next morning Mr Coole ordered the car for a short business visit to the Terrace in Pepper Tree Bay. 'Ordered' was the word for that was his manner in making use of Lacey.

'I want to call in at the Bank,' he said. 'You can wait and then take me into Perth to the Club. I won't need you after that until the usual hour this evening.'

That, Lacey thought mildly, would allow her the time to go to the Women's meeting. She must go to the Aid for somehow she felt committed to it since she had mentioned it to Mrs Simmins. She also felt committed to wearing the new dress.

'Why not?' she asked herself. What would the ladies think, and say?

She had no idea that the ladies were impressed by the fact she was Miss Coole of Meenon, never mind what she wore. She had no idea that ladies of Pepper Tree Bay, who were even afraid of addressing her at all, and then only as 'Miss Coole', went home and said, 'Lacey Coole was there today. She's really quite a nice-looking girl. I've been telling her for years she ought to take office on the committee. But of course half the time she's up on the station or down on the farm.'

Certain types of people received a certain type of social prestige by being able to speak of Lacey by her given name.

She was able to bring the big car to the kerb immediately outside the Bank so that her father had only a few paces to walk to enter the main door. Nevertheless, he took his stick. Mr Coole never moved anywhere without that stick. It was a badge of office.

At the counter he asked the receiving clerk if he might see the Manager. Although it did not occur to him that the Manager would do anything but dismiss what other clients or business he had on hand and see him at once, nevertheless Mr Coole sat down on the one upright jarrah chair in the main office, folded his hands on top of the handle of his stick and watched clients enter and approach the various counters.

Years ago people glancing at him knew very well his identity. He had been a figure on the landscape. He was well aware that they had said to one another in undertones, 'That's Bernard Coole . . . big house round the river. Rich as Croesus. Bit of a power behind the throne where business and politics are concerned.'

This new generation looked twice now because it was unusual to see a man well dressed in the fashion of two generations ago. They probably had not before seen, in this country, a hard winged collar and the severe homburg hat, unless they had seen Mr Coole formerly. It was not only the oddness of his dress that struck people. It was the immaculate cut and appearance of that dress and the cold well-bred face. It was immediately and potently clear that Mr Coole was a man of substance and a man aloof, arrogant, important.

The clerk, a slim young man, came quickly from the Manager's office.

'Mr Radford will see you almost at once, Mr Coole,' he said with the carefully polite courtesy of his training. 'He is just seeing a client out of the side door.'

Mr Coole nodded his head but said nothing.

A tall man, somewhere between thirty and forty, entered the Bank by the main door. Mr Coole thought vaguely he had seen him before but he was not particularly interested. It was the athletic build of the man that attracted his attention. He had height and broad shoulders, with an easy graceful way of moving. He was striking-looking with the straight classical features that ought to mean good birth. His eyes, a very dark blue, had a quick intent way of glancing from face to face. He was a man of purpose, Mr Coole could see that.

He walked to the counter behind which the teller stood and put his hand in his inside breast pocket and drew out a cheque book. As he stood at the counter and filled in the cheque form he spoke to the teller.

'Is the Manager busy? Could I see him for five minutes?'

'I'll ask him, Mr Scott. As a matter of fact I think Mr Radford would like to see you. He mentioned that if you came in . . .'

'Good.'

He waited, the cheque form in hand, while the teller turned and spoke to a clerk sitting at a calculating machine in the office area behind.

'Scott!' he thought to himself. 'Where have I heard that name? Common enough, when you come to think of it.'

At that moment the Manager put his head out of his office door.

'I won't keep you a moment, Mr Coole. I have an appointment. Sorry to keep you waiting.'

He did not wait for Mr Coole's acknowledgement of his remarks but looked at the other man and smiled.

'Come in, Riley,' he said. 'I can fix that matter for you with a simple signature.'

Riley! Riley Scott!

Mr Coole saw himself a member of that four-man group in the Club yesterday and Vernon – or was it Richardson, the Member of Parliament? – had said, 'Apart from the bridge there are a few other ideas floating around . . . Oliver Harding is behind it . . . Riley Scott, an up and coming politician . . . bought a property round the Bay . . .'

Mr Coole knew where he had seen that man before. Yesterday morning when he had stopped the car to get out and look at the block of land Firmingham had sold without consulting him, that fellow had got out of a streamlined Humber car and gone over to talk to the workmen. Mr Coole had deliberately turned his back then because he'd known that man was the owner of the block and the house now being built.

A curious sensation pervaded the whole of Mr Coole's upright body as he sat in the Bank. It began in his diaphragm and spread outward and upward and concentrated in his shoulders and his head. For a moment he felt pain and then dizziness.

A minute later he was his calm cold self. The unprecedented thing had happened. The Manager of the Bank had invited someone else to enter before Bernard Coole. He had been required to wait, while this man, this Riley Scott, had entered the Manager's Office first.

Firmingham, who in thirty years had always given Bernard Coole the first option over saleable land in Pepper Tree Bay, had sold this Riley Scott the block without any reference to himself.

Oliver Harding, that jumped-up motor mechanic who was rushing up big blocks of business buildings in the city itself, was behind this man.

The sequence of events began to add up.

Yesterday was his seventieth birthday. The workmen had not acknowledged his presence. Those men in the Club . . . surely there had been an absence of their usual deference! Today the Manager invited another into his office first.

Suddenly a pang of fear shot through Mr Coole. His hands on the walking stick were suddenly weak and without feeling. The stick, earlier so firmly planted on the floor, slipped. Before he could recover it it fell to the floor.

At that moment the Manager's door opened and the man, Riley Scott, came out. He was only a few feet away and the stick had fallen across his path. He stooped now to pick it up. Then a curious thing happened. He put out his hand and before he touched the stick his hand seemed as if it had become frozen in the air.

The teller watching the little scene was puzzled. Riley Scott's eyes were fixed on the handle of that stick. He remained for a long mysterious minute in the bent position, his hand forward to take up the stick and his eyes on the handle.

Then suddenly the scene came to life and Riley Scott completed the movement. He lifted up the stick, holding it half-way down its ebony length, and handed it, the handle first, towards Mr Coole. Over the stick their eyes met. Riley's eyes were blank. He did not smile or utter a word. Mr Coole's eyes were cold and haughty. He nodded a bare acknowledgement.

Riley Scott went through the swing door out into the street.

The two tellers exchanged a glance and the one who had cashed Riley's cheque shrugged. The other spread his hands. It was patent that something had happened, but neither had any idea what. Clearly Mr Scott and Mr Coole were strangers to one another.

Riley saw the long car against the kerb with Mr Coole's daughter sitting at the driver's wheel.

Lacey, who had been expecting her father to come out when the glass door moved, saw Riley. This was the man who got out of the Humber car where the house was being built round the Bay. Lacey felt a curious excited lifting of her heart.

Oddly enough his eyes met hers in a long searching look. Her heart contracted. He remembers it was me, she thought. He remembers seeing me yesterday. She started where she sat in the car, for the terrified feeling that he would pass on and she would never meet his eyes again laid hold on her.

As he turned and walked towards the Humber car that was parked higher up the street she watched in the rear-vision mirror. He swung his car keys in his hand.

Then she was filled with a strange nostalgic regret. She knew he would not turn, or wait. She bent her head and took her handbag from the dashboard box. She fumbled in it for her handkerchief and a cigarette. Her hands trembled as she lit the cigarette. She forgot her father might come out at any moment and see her smoking . . . and in a public thoroughfare.

Oh no! she thought. Oh no! Sudden and bitter disappointment replaced the upsurge of excitement and the ebb of regret. She grieved in advance for something she did not comprehend.

Mr Coole left the steps of the Bank and remained standing on the footpath. He looked up the street. Then, as Lacey watched, he straightened his shoulders and walked forward towards the car firmly.

She must have been dreaming. For one dreadful moment she had seen an old, old man.

As he got into the car she looked at him curiously. No, he was the same as he always was. His smooth well-shaven face showed few wrinkles. His iron-grey hair was as it had been for nearly as long as Lacey could remember. Only his hands, resting on the handle of the stick which stood upright between his feet, were old. The veins stood out like little raised rivers and on the backs of his hands were large brown spots on the blue-grey surface of the skin.

'I want to go to a house in Bannister Street,' Mr Coole said. 'Drive slowly when we get to it. I don't quite remember which house.'

'Bannister Street?' Lacey wrinkled her brow. Was there such a place in Pepper Tree Bay? She had never heard of it.

'Drive along the Highway to the swamp road, then turn right. I'll tell you when we come to it.'

Lacey moved the car slowly forward to take the right-hand swing from the Terrace into the Highway. Already she had forgotten she had thought for the flash of a moment that she had seen in her father a very old man. Other matters were troubling her thoughts. One was the man who drove the Humber car. At least it was not him so much as herself that troubled her. That sudden upsurge of feeling. Hadn't she learned long and long since she could not hanker for the moon. And how disgusting it was that all she wanted was a man to stop and smile and speak to her. And if he did would she be content?

Lacey knew what all the implications of that feeling were. She would like what other girls of her own acquaintance and generation had got. She didn't want to be lonely. If she tried to nail down the feeling it was something to do with the soft touch of her mother's hand on her forehead when she had had typhoid fever: and the way nice old Mr Thoms used to run his fingers through her hair and say, 'Hallo, Curly Top! Whose heart are you going to break today?' And the time he said at the children's Christmas party, 'Look who's won the peanut hunt! The prettiest girl in Pepper Tree Bay.'

Lacey's father said Mr Thoms ruined his children and let money pour from his pockets. But Lacey had cried when he died. Dear, nice, kind Mr Thoms. Oddly enough, Lacey often thought of him when she thought of her mother.

It was odd that after thinking of the man with the Humber car she found herself thinking of her mother and Mr Thoms.

'Turn right here and it's the second street on the left.' Her father's didactic thin voice interrupted her thoughts. 'It's a short street with a steep hill. I think it has a blind end so look where you're going.'

Lacey turned into a narrow street of small narrow-fronted houses, most of which were wooden. Odd, but she had never been here before. She had never seen the houses. They were

44

very small and must belong to poor people. But they were clean and neat. It was a very clean and neat little street and the pepper trees lining it shaded right across so that it was like driving slowly through a green arch.

'There,' said Mr Coole. 'That house with the striped blinds on the left.'

Lacey was almost at the fence of the house when he spoke. She braked carefully and put the gear stick into reverse. The hill was quite steep and the house was more than half-way up it. What a queer place for her father to be visiting! It must be something to do with business. She was sure her father didn't know anyone who lived here.

Mr Coole got out of the car, drawing his stick after him. He shut the door, braced himself to an upright bearing and stood looking at the house.

It was a single-fronted brown wooden house with an iron roof that had recently had a new coat of red paint. The red, green and yellow striped blinds sheltering the tiny verandah were fairly new. The colour was garishly bright against the dull brown of the wooden framework.

'Turn the car round while you're waiting for me, Lacey. You'd better drive up to the top and turn there.'

He was still looking ahead at the house as he spoke. It was only the high dry quality of his voice that enabled the words to carry clearly to Lacey.

Lacey carefully released the handbrake as she adjusted the gear to bottom and crawled up the hill to do as he had bidden her.

At the top she turned and coasted down to the house where her father was at that moment being admitted by an elderly woman with a black dress, a print apron and grey hair severely knotted back behind her head.

Lacey set the handbrake and took out a cigarette and lit it.

She was aware that blinds and lace curtains moved in the two houses alongside which she was now parked, and that children had come out on to the footpath to stare. She wondered why, and then reflected that perhaps a big long car like this did not often park in this street. In fact, such a car had never entered the street before in the memory of the inhabitants. Those who saw it peered curiously between the curtains.

Mr Coole had been admitted by Mrs Firmingham, very astonished, yet with an astonishment edged with a touch of subservience and a dash of suspicion. Mr Coole had never in living memory visited Mr Firmingham in his own home. He had business dealings with Mr Firmingham. She knew that. Mr Firmingham occasionally spoke to her of them. But in the home? Mr Firmingham did not have business dealings in the home. He had a small single-fronted shop in a corner of the Terrace on the blind windows of which was painted

NOAH FIRMINGHAM
AGENT

The shop was small, obscure, humble, yet within it most of the valuable land . . . shops, houses and river frontages . . . in Pepper Tree Bay had changed hands. Always to Mr Firmingham's great profit.

A good deal of the time, as on this morning, the shop door was closed and the agency had a dusty deserted unrequired look. Mr Firmingham's clients had to await on *his* time for the simple reason that Mr Firmingham owned so many of the rent-producing homes himself and had paid rates on wide stretches of the vacant land of Pepper Tree Bay since the beginning of white man's time in the colony. Mr Firmingham had inherited the one-time miscroscopic business from his father. And all his father began with was several acres of river frontage and innumerable unwanted blocks of vacant land all around the swamp and along the Highway. He'd got them for a song in the colonial days. He had managed to live and pay his rates by dint of being rent collector for the shops in the Terrace. From rent collecting he had risen to landlord status by the simple and cheap purchase of one or two of the shops in the bank depression days at the turn of the century.

From that starting point the present Mr Noah Firmingham had continued. Up and on and out. He owned more land than Mr Coole. He probably had a bigger bank balance. He could have sold out the whole Terrace and revolutionised the town. He could have rendered small families homeless and more well-to-do families financially embarrassed. He could have put up a school or a hospital or a civic library. He could almost have paved Oliver Harding's projected promenade along the fore-front of the Bay with gold.

He lived in a little brown house in a neat but poor street and had not changed the suit of clothes he wore daily for three years. Only his boots were good and frequently renewed. He needed them that they might carry him on his daily rent-

46

collecting stretches.

What this man was worth today to Mr Coole was information only. The land round the Bay . . . and Mr Coole had intimated to Firmingham before that he would buy any block up for sale on the East Side provided it had a river view . . . was now sold. To Riley Scott. Mr Coole would not show his anger though presently, if the occasion arose, he might ask for an explanation.

At the moment he did not want to know why that block of land was sold to Riley Scott, but he did want to know who Riley Scott was and whether he owned any other land in Pepper Tree Bay. He wanted to know how much land Oliver Harding owned in Pepper Tree Bay. In short . . . just how powerful, if at all, were these two men.

Mr Coole did not explain to himself why he was interested in the present and future of Oliver Harding and Riley Scott. It had something, perhaps everything, to do with his seventieth birthday and the intimations he had had on that day of his waning authority in Pepper Tree Bay. It had a great deal to do with the fact he had a genuine proprietorial love for the great expanse of river that lay beneath his own house on the West Side; and a rigid belief that he, having lived longer, knew what was better for posterity than newcomers and upstarts whose parents had not arrived in the colony at the same time as his own parents.

It had everything to do with the comparative youth, strength and agile bearing of a man to whom the Bank Manager had this morning given precedence over himself, Bernard Coole. This had never happened to Bernard Coole in his life. He had always gone in first. The affront had been like a slap in the face and Mr Coole had never had his face slapped. Joe Montgomery had once called him a stubborn fool but Joe Montgomery was a clergyman, an educated man and a slightly eccentric Irishman. It could be passed over.

But upstarts? Newcomers? T'other-siders? To think they could pass by or push around the men to whom the State belonged; who were here first.

Mrs Firmingham had not taken Mr Coole's hat from him so he now placed it on the occasional table beside the armchair in which he sat. He held his walking stick upright in front of him and rested his hands on it. He did not lean back against the chair.

When Mr Firmingham came into the room he did not stand up or offer to shake hands. Mr Firmingham did not expect it.

47

CHAPTER THREE

Whichever way I, Theodora Montgomery, looked at the parish of Pepper Tree Bay I could divide it into two sections. There was old Pepper Tree Bay with its park, its shops lining the up-grade of the Terrace, the churches – four of them – spaced along the Highway and the road to the river. This core was flanked on the west by the riverside homes of the pastoralists and on the north by the swamp and the small people who scratched a half-acre of sandplain country with a cow or two and a dozen fowls.

The other half of Pepper Tree Bay, the new half, stretches today in rows, half-moons and a winding parade of suburban houses; those right on the waterfront being bigger, better, more costly and less attractive than the smug established dignified homes of the firstcomers on the West Side.

The residents of this new half, the East Side of Pepper Tree Bay, barely belonged there in spirit at all. They drove their big cars to Perth when they wanted to buy a pound of green peas or a new hat. The only part of Pepper Tree Bay they shared was the river. They had not been born there nor brought up there. They had bought expensive riverside sites and built houses in the spirit of competition rather than in the hope of immortality.

Their children did not swim against one another in the baths as we had done – they went to the ocean in one or other of their parents' big cars. They never sat beside the children's prams in the sprawling shady park and they did not know for whom to vote in the Civic Council elections and on the whole forgot to vote on polling day.

Looking at Pepper Tree Bay another way . . . there were the ladies who went shopping up the Terrace wearing gloves and wide shady straw hats as I remember our parents had done. And there were those who slopped up there in flat-heeled shoes, hatless, and a shopping bag hanging bulged by their sides. In quite a number of cases the latter were more wealthy than the former . . . but they were *newcomers*.

There were those who went to church and those who didn't. There were those who knew the detailed history of all the old families, rich or poor, educated or uneducated, of Pepper

Tree Bay. And there were those who sadly knew nothing of these charms.

Summed up, you might say, as my mother and all my family would say, there were those to whom Pepper Tree Bay belonged, and there were the newcomers over whom we gently sorrowed.

It was this gulf that Oliver Harding set out to bridge with his idea of a riverside promenade.

Oliver, like my family, had been born in the Bay and when he had begun to climb the ladder towards affluence he had been amongst the first to buy land and build a home around the East Side. In those days the East Side had been a lovely wild stretch of bushland where we used to walk on Sunday afternoons to pick wild flowers. It is more than twenty years since the wild flowers have all gone.

Oliver knew the river sites would one day sell at booming prices but he did not know until he came back from the war that the people who would buy them and build on them wouldn't know about Pepper Tree Bay – other than the glorious look of it.

Most of us thought that Oliver's scheme was scatter-brained, except that Oliver had never done anything scatter-brained in his life.

Though one wanted to laugh, and say 'Impossible . . . and we don't understand the people anyway,' there was a niggling doubt at the back of one's mind. Oliver, though we would never have admitted it when we were children, was always right.

And Oliver had a way with him.

When he said he wanted to give a big party and gather together all the interested people to set off his idea with the bubble and effervescence of champagne, we smiled and nodded our heads and agreed to come. It would be a good party, anyway.

Oliver did dabble in wealthy business men and flourishing medical practitioners, and – who knows? – he might be able to make them think of something else besides just the 'look' of the sparkling Bay. One could never assess the limits of Oliver's abilities.

Of course there were those who said Oliver was heading for the glory road himself. Or maybe it was just a mention in the New Year or Birthday Honours list.

But we who knew Oliver knew differently. Behind his brash façade, his quick authority and that crackling laugh, was a man

49

with a heart both soft and sentimental. You could sometimes see it in his smiles. Others said that when you've made as much money as Oliver Harding had you could afford to be sentimental.

In spite of our agreeing that Oliver was an open and an honourable man we also privately thought he had a degree of low cunning. He was inveigling us all into his promenade scheme without telling us truly and in detail what it was all about. He would make us commit ourselves openly and innocently and after that we would be in it up to the neck. It was a wonderful way of pulling in the dilatory and those with only half a heart. He must have learned the technique in speedway politics or business circles. We were far too innocent and inexperienced to know what Oliver was about.

Thus Oliver had come on a Saturday afternoon when we were all gathered at Mama's house . . . 'The Nunnery' as she was prone to call it . . . and caught us in his net.

'A promenade?' Mama said. She loved to be in on something new, something to battle for. In less than a minute she had taken enthusiasm out of his mouth and made it her own. 'A splendid idea. Now let us see . . . who can we see on the Council? We could get after Mr Rathbone . . . he'll do something for me if I ask him . . .'

'You leave that to me, Mrs Monty,' Oliver said, laughing as if it was all a joke and not something he had set his heart on and an enterprise that would split Pepper Tree Bay in two and bring the proud head of Mr Bernard Coole down into the shadow of the grave.

Oliver did not know, at this time, anything about Mr Coole's knowledge of or reaction to enterprises in Pepper Tree Bay, but he knew the kind of things that happened when personalities became involved and dignity was staked.

'I'll see Rathbone in due course, but I want to get my specific plans ready. Timing is a great thing in these ventures. For the present I want the girls to come along and mix up with some of us on the East Side and get going a kind of corporate spirit in Pepper Tree Bay. When we've got the unity and the spirit we can get people working together.'

'For heaven's sake,' I thought. 'Imagine Oliver getting people together and keeping them together. How could anyone do that in the Pepper Tree Bay of today? We are all so different . . .'

And he'd called us 'girls'. We were all near our forties. But were we? How old was Gerry? I never could remember how old were the two youngest because they were so far down the scale from me. They'd both been widowed too. That was quite incredible when one came to think of it. Widows and grandmothers had always seemed to me when I was a child to belong to the same age class. Therefore instead of being young and charming and utterly attractive they ought to have been up in Mama's age group.

Oliver was telling Mama something about his promenade.

'Riley Scott is going to start it off,' he said. 'He's building one at the bottom of the bank along with the building of his house. That'll be the first brick in the edifice.'

Mama, of course, thought Oliver's promenade would be a little concrete patio at the foot of his garden, too, and possibly something to the east and west of the baths and the jetty. Not for a moment did she, or we for that matter, envisage the reclaiming of the jagged inlets in the Bay, the dredging of the shallows, a drive that would follow the bank of the river from Perth six miles away to Fremantle, another eight miles by winding river and inleted bay to Fremantle and so to the sea.

Not for a minute did we envisage engineers and dredging contractors and bridge builders and town-planning experts from overseas. We were incapable of thinking in millions, anyway. We thought of a few hundred pounds, a pretty vista from Oliver's house over the Bay and a nice party on Tuesday week.

When Oliver had gone we fell to telling one another of the fearful things he had done to us when we were children and what an utter wretch of a boy he had been.

'But Danny liked him.' Mama said. She had to stop biting her bottom lip to say this, for Mama was now busy doing a piece of tapestry work and when she worked with her hands she bit her bottom lip. My father had tried to stop her doing it. We had all tried to stop her doing it.

I remember when she used to mix the fowls' mash . . . way back all those years when we lived in the Rectory . . . and carefully added shell grit, chocolate block and cochineal. 'Because,' she said, 'next Sunday is Easter Sunday and the fowls will lay the Easter eggs . . . chocolate ones, sugar icing ones and ones with blue and pink ribbons round them.' Instead of watching this wonderful mixture and taking a hand at stirring, I would watch Mama's face because she would bite her bottom lip as she stirred and it gave her such an air of concentration and general busyness. I would try to do it, too, and once when my father caught me watching her and doing it he said, 'There you are, Helen. Look what you've done! The child has caught that dreadful habit. Next thing is you'll all have cancer of the mouth.'

Ever after we all tried to stop Mama doing it. But we never succeeded and she hadn't got cancer of the mouth yet.

All that was so long ago. Another life, surely?

Mama stopped biting her bottom lip in order to say of Oliver, 'But Danny liked him,' as she dug her needle firmly into the canvas on her knee.

Danny, away over there in Ireland, was Laura's husband. And Laura was in love with Oliver. Or was she? Was she really? Or was it just a something indefinable between them that might be mistaken by the onlooker for love.

And Oliver? What part did Oliver play in a situation like that?

Laura was our cousin and years ago when she had lived in Australia she had invested some money in motor company shares and she also bought land. Those things had all stood still as far as the market was concerned during and after the war. Then when the controls came off they boomed. Laura had come back to Australia to see what she would do with these investments. She had met Oliver again because he was now the greatest shareholder in the motor company in which Laura held shares.

She was staying with Mama now, but this afternoon that Oliver had called she was out.

This was a little intriguing too. Had she been out on purpose? Was this part of the hole-in-the-corner, under-cover, backstairs indignity of married people having love-affairs with other married people? Was it sordid and painful as well as disturbing?

These were labyrinths into which one's mind would not penetrate. To Denney and Gerry it was a bit of a joke . . . but then how would they know about the pain of it all? To Vicky it was something about which Laura ought to be severely spoken to. To Mary? Perhaps Mary was absorbed in the legal aspect of it . . . of Esther's point of view, if Esther knew anything about it.

To me, falling in love was a painful thing. The stars were not worth the shadowed places. It was better to be comfortably married with a warm fireside and a good companion. One didn't have to worry about love any more. One just had it the way one had porridge for breakfast and occasionally the best fillet steak for dinner. Then one woke up one morning and knew this peaceful ordered existence *was* love. The other had been stardust, and as silly.

Why did Laura always seek . . . seek . . . seek? She had always been like that!

'Yes, it was a queer combination,' Mama was saying. 'Danny was such a polished other-worldly sort of person and Oliver such a rough naughty boy.'

'I suppose each liked the best in the other,' I said. 'Anyhow, Danny always liked queer people . . . and queer clothes . . .'

'Queer?' almost snorted Denney. 'I thought you were always Oliver's champion.'

'Yes, that's true,' I said. 'But then he wasn't queer to me. But he ought to have been queer to Danny. He was so *different*.'

I wanted to change the conversation desperately so that everyone would stop thinking about Laura's love-affair . . . if it was a love-affair.

'This Riley Scott,' I said. 'Who is this Riley Scott? His name keeps cropping up all the time. I never heard of him. Oliver said he was born in Pepper Tree Bay.'

Everyone either shrugged or shook her head. Only Mama went on sewing, her head bent down. Her teeth stopped grasping her bottom lip for quite a long time.

'Oliver said he's to be at the party,' Gerry said. 'As if it's important for us all to meet him at the party.'

'He's building a house round there,' Vicky said in a slightly exasperated tone as if we were all dull and had no business to question Oliver's arrangements.

'Besides,' said Vicky, 'he wants everyone to come. Everyone. He wants us all to come and bring our friends. He said so, I'm going to take Lacey Coole. It's time Lacey came out of confinement round there on the West Side. In fact I'm going to take Lacey in hand. I met her at the Aid meeting last week.'

This statement, delivered in Vicky's best oratorical manner, with her head at a haughty angle, had an effect. Vicky had a nice head with naturally curly hair which was always cut and dressed with style. It had taken me roughly thirty years to discover that Vicky's neck was a shade longer than the average and it was this that made her look as if she carried her head so well and gave her the slightly haughty look. She wasn't really haughty at all. She just had a lovely slender neck.

'Lacey Coole!' we all echoed.

'What on earth would Lacey Coole do at a party like Oliver's?' Mary asked with great calmness.

'She's an absolutely charming girl,' Vicky said, again using the didactic tone. 'All that she needs is to be wrenched away from that diabolical parent of hers. I'm going to do it.'

If Gerry and Denney smirked it had nothing to do with Lacey Coole but everything to do with Vicky's propensity for rediscovering old friends who needed her immediate attention. She would ardently devote herself to those needs and in those directions for months to come.

I did agree with her, however, about Lacey's diabolical parent. The way that girl was little more than a well-dressed chauffeur for her selfish old father!

But would she go down with the smart matrons of the East Side? And more important, would they go down with her? Lacey was a sheltered confined person who had never lived out of the Edwardian age. Her bearing, her manners, her speech were as period as her father's furniture round there in that great old mausoleum of a house on the West Side.

But she did have an air!

Yes, as I thought of it, it just might be a success. Her name, to begin with, would create the right effect. Coole was not a name in Pepper Tree Bay to be played with idly. There was a little sneaking snob in the heart of every woman with social ambitions and something told me that even if Lacey had had a hare lip and wore sackcloth most of those people round the East Side would be pleased to be in her company, even if they were too nervous to address her. And she didn't have a hare lip, and she dressed well.

Knowing Lacey, it was paradoxical that anyone would be nervous of addressing her. In fact it wouldn't be Lacey herself of whom they were nervous but of her name and her father's long-established position.

'Yes,' I said, suddenly on Vicky's side. 'Bring Lacey.'

Then Laura came in.

She had on a junior navy-blue linen suit and wide-brimmed cherry-coloured hat that made her look enchanting. One didn't mind being fortyish when one looked at Laura. One made up one's mind to go home at once and do something about one's face and hands and dress. Also, one reflected that all this inter-marriage in a family was a beneficial thing in Laura's case. She had inherited all the best physical features from all sides of her much intermarried family. Her mother and father were cousins and she herself had married another cousin.

Barty, my son, was five and a half, and besides the blue eyes that could only be equalled by Laura's in the family, he had nice podgy legs with dimples in the knees.

He was lying prone, resting his chin on his elbow and gazing peacefully into the water. One understood from the expression of benign complacence on his dear, round, blue-eyed face that he was in entire accordance with whatever it was the water world was doing and saying down there in the green and blue and golden shadowed depths.

He took no notice of me at all except to raise his head once and point to a tall man standing on a rocky pile, his hands in his pockets, watching Barty.

'His name's Riley Scott,' Barty said, then put his chin back in his hand and returned his attention to the water world.

So this was Riley Scott . . . the man who was putting the first brick in the promenade! He was watching me and there was a faint smile in his eyes as if he was waiting to see if I minded his acquaintance with my child.

No . . . on second thoughts, it was not that. There was something about the man that touched a faint chord of memory. He was tall, broad-shouldered, and his face was strong, with a good firm jaw and hard blue eyes under a square forehead. The wind had ruffled his hair and his throat was brown where it thrust up out of his white open-necked shirt. He wore a plaited kangaroo belt round his dark-grey well-cut pants.

There was a hint of recognition and of irony in the half smile in his eyes. I smiled back at him, then I knelt down beside Barty to look into the rock pool too.

Riley turned and walked away, climbing over the rocks to the sandy beach. When I looked up he was going round the promontory that fenced off the East Side from Mama's little beach.

I turned my attention back to Barty. He took no notice of me at all, for whatever went on there beneath his eyes was infinitely more beguiling than anything I had to offer.

Besides being given to gazing in rock pools, harbouring rock crabs and caterpillars in his pockets, he was given to talking with his angel. I first knew about the angel when I saw Barty walking down the street, talking. In my ignorance I thought he was talking to himself.

'I are not,' he had said with considerable dignity. 'I are talking to the angel.'

'What angel, Barty?'

'My angel.'

I thought the angel must be someone in long white robes with spectacular wings who hovered round his head and guarded him, but Barty indignantly corrected me on the misconception too.

'He is another fellow like me. An' he walks home with me. An' I talk to him.'

Whenever I saw Barty's lips moving and that beautiful fatuous smile on his lips and his left hand gesticulating in the air I knew the hour was sacred. Barty was not on the earth . . . he was talking and walking with angels.

I sat down and watched him as he gazed in the water. That smile wrung my heart for I remembered another child, oh, so long ago, who used to watch the people in the leaves of the old gum tree that stood in front of the Rectory and who peopled the castles in the clouds with creatures of her own fantasy.

'Oh, Barty, Barty,' I said sadly. 'You too!'

'Come home, Barty,' I said, and I would have liked to add, 'and talk to your angel in the bathroom while I get the dinner,' only I dared not. So many educationists and radio speakers were frightening me about this 'bad thing' of letting a child deal in fairies and fantasy. I hadn't ended up in a lunatic asylum . . . yet. But who knows? And I dared not expose Barty to the risk.

So I took him home and put him in the bath and went outside and pretended not to hear his voice as he talked, for then I wouldn't know about the angel. And I wouldn't have to do anything about it.

I decided I didn't want them to do anything about the foreshore either until Barty had grown up and didn't want to play with sunlit pools of water any more. Or keep rock crabs. Oliver, and this Riley Scott, could play with bricks and mortar at the bottom of their own gardens, but not around Barty's Bay.

Mary and Denney and I went early to Oliver's party in case Esther needed some help. Esther had said she now hadn't any idea how many people were coming. Oliver had been asking everyone and anyone and had lost count of names himself. A good deal of the time he'd seen someone he knew, or who knew him and he'd smiled and lifted his hand and said, 'By golly. Just the person I want. We're having a party on Tuesday week . . .'

Not many had known what the party was about but that was half of Oliver's cunning. 'Let's have a party' had been the spirit of his invitation to those not in the inner secret.

56

The night was as beautiful as a March night can be in this part of the world. It had been a warm humid day with the trees standing still and people walking about their affairs with a tired droop to their exhausted bodies. The long, dry, pitiless summer had taken its toll by the middle of March. People were ready to sit down and look at the river and say 'Ah . . . isn't it beautiful! So peaceful!'

What they meant was that they were tired and the brilliant starlit sky and the quiet calm light-reflecting river touched their jaded spirits with its ineffable peace. At the end of the day . . . beauty and peace.

Inside the house Esther had arranged her modern honey-coloured furniture so that it left great cleared spaces in the hall and the long lounge and the sun-room. Except for the odd chairs along the wall, the flowers and the ornaments on the mantelshelf, and the wall to wall blue carpet, the lounge had a ballroom effect with its spaciousness, its mirrors instead of pictures and the deep wide window that embraced the whole of the river view.

On either side of this great window double doors stood wide open on to the cement verandah that overlooked the Bay. The whole of that wall, which was really the width of the house, consisted of that window and the two glass double doors. One couldn't have escaped the river if one had wanted to do so.

On the verandah, now lit with streamers of coloured lights, deep chairs were arranged in groups around small tables on which stood ash trays and little bowls of nuts, dried fruits and pretty savouries. Out on the lawn there were more tables encircled with gaily coloured easy chairs. A partly shielded light hung in the boughs of a great old red gum so that a radiant glow hung over everything. Between the gum tree and the side fence was the swimming pool. It was a shimmer of lights reflected from the house, the tree, and the stars in the sky.

It was all very costly; and very beautiful.

There hadn't been anything to do to help Esther, of course. One really knew that because in her quiet calm way she was the perfect organiser. But one liked to offer to help and one knew that Esther liked the offer, even liked that small bevy of advance guests upon whom she could pretend to lean if something went wrong. Nothing ever did go wrong with Esther's parties.

We stood now, a small group, excited in anticipation, at the end of the room and laughed about Oliver's 'collection' as we already, and before they came, called our fellow guests.

The maids, hired for the occasion, were coming in now to put plates of savouries around the room for the convenience of the guests. They moved the vases, exotic with hibiscus flowers of all colours, thinking they were generally improving on Esther's impeccable arrangements. One shifted a chair by two inches and another took a plate of nuts from one table and exchanged it for one of another delicacy in another place.

When they had gone Esther came in and put everything, beginning with vases, as it was before. There was a small frown between her brows, and her red lips, so like a doll's painted lips, made a small moue. We all smiled as we watched her. Esther knew where everything, to the inch, should be for the most artistic effect.

Esther was pretty in the way that very feminine women can be pretty if they have fair curling hair and naturally red lips. There was something soft, endearing, about her . . . except perhaps her calmness. It was so enviable, and possibly misleading.

'Do you know anyone called Riley Scott?' she asked, coming towards us.

'Barty does,' I said. 'He all but introduced me on the beach. But he went away too soon.'

'We're all agog to meet him,' said Denney. 'One hears his name round every corner these days. I can't imagine why. Is there something special about him?'

'Yes, quite,' said Mary unexpectedly. 'He's building quite the biggest house on the Bay. And he lived in Pepper Tree Bay as a boy.'

Esther and I both knitted our brows and it was clear neither of us remembered. Denney was looking at Mary with indignation.

'This is the first time you've said you know him,' she challenged.

'I don't think anyone asked me before,' Mary said lightly. 'Anyhow, Mother remembers him.'

'Oh, does she?' we began in concert.

At that moment Oliver came into the room. He stood poking the forefinger of his left hand into the hair above his left temple. He beamed on the room.

'Looks like it's going to be a good party, eh?'

His right hand hung helpless by his side. At least what went for his right hand, beautifully gloved in fine brown leather, hung there helpless.

He looked round the room and through the open doors to the lighted verandah and the glowing garden beyond. He had an air of pleasure anticipated. He nodded his approval of us, the little group at the end of the room. He liked his old friends around.

Suddenly the first guests were arriving, and Oliver went with his quick purposeful stride into the hall to meet them. Esther stood in the doorway of the big room. She greeted each with a smile of pleasure and delight as if each appearance was totally unexpected and a great compliment to herself. Her face, fair, oval and with its parted red lips and the look of surprised happiness in her eyes, gave an unexpected light and shade effect to her gentle beauty.

Oliver, as soon as he sighted a new arrival, would laugh as if something first-rate and very funny had happened. He would hold out his left hand to shake hands and this would make an odd and wholly individualistic gesture of it. Then he would haul the newcomers away to get a drink and talk to someone Oliver wanted them to talk to. All the time he gave an impression of great good fellowship, and that the new arrival was the most important person yet to come.

The women all wore their loveliest, softest dresses. Their hair had been beautifully set in rows of waves, and ears, necks and arms sparkled with brilliants. The war had been long and sad and this was the reaction to the *ersatz* dressing of those days. Besides, there was something compelling about the masculinity of Oliver that commanded its exact counterpart in the opposite sex. Oliver had one standard for every woman. She should look feminine and well-dressed, and there wasn't one of his female acquaintances who did not wish to have her most becoming hat and dress on when she met Oliver in the street. There was no question of trying to beguile him; merely acquit oneself in his presence.

Denney's husband came in and she immediately left our group, still at the end of the room, and went out into the garden with him. Almost at once you could hear her laughter and her husky voice as together they found immediately a group of friends to whom Denney could immediately begin to relate her latest experiences. Nothing ever happened to Denney that she could not turn into a funny story. She always found a group of listeners.

Other people came, then Vicky arrived with her husband and Lacey Coole. Vicky was dressed right up to Oliver's standards in a blue faille dress with an enormous rhinestone brooch at her neck. She could wear long dangling earrings because of her slender neck and this she did. It made her head small and neat and showed off its excellent grooming. Her husband, David, immediately joined the select group of Oliver's cronies in one corner. This group stood about easily, a glass in one hand and a cigarette in the other, and one knew at once that this was the inner circle. They were the men with whom Oliver was plotting about altering the shoreline of the Bay, and building a breakwall, a promenade and a drive road . . . though we didn't quite understand these ramifications at the time.

Lacey looked charming. In spite of a dress cut in the very latest lines . . . the Dior New Look . . . she managed somehow to convey that slightly old-fashioned air which really was more an air than an appearance and it made her look distinguished in some intangible way. A lifetime amongst the very best, most exclusive people, had left its mark on Lacey and she carried it unconsciously.

She turned her head as Laura came in behind them. They spoke together a minute and Laura lifted her head and her glance went round the room.

As Vicky, with Lacey beside her, came towards us I could see Laura pause as her eyes, across the room, met Oliver's. He raised a glass and smiled at her but he made no attempt to come forward and greet her personally.

Esther said, 'Oh, Laura!' and shook hands with her. Esther smiled her pleased child-like smile but Laura as she returned it looked troubled. Then she dropped Esther's hand and came with Vicky and Lacey towards us.

I waved a cigarette-laden hand in a half circle.

'Do you know everyone, Lacey?' I asked.

She had a manner of unconsciously controlled ease.

'Not really,' she said. 'I expect I'll meet them presently. But it's nice to see you, Theodora, and you, Gerry. How is Mrs Montgomery?'

'Very well indeed,' said Gerry, unconsciously imitating Lacey's correct and polite manner. 'How is your father?'

At that moment Gerry must have realised she had adopted Lacey's voice and Lacey's tone of address because a colour rose in her cheeks and she was making an effort not to meet my eyes. It was one of those dreadful moments when the Montgomerys might have got that childish and irrepressible complaint – the giggles. I was quite certain that Gerry was capable of ending her well-bred enquiry about Lacey's father by adding, 'Why don't you put arsenic in his porridge?'

Vicky was aware of this and she looked at us coldly. Somehow I agreed with Vicky's unspoken comments. There were times when we were not even to be tolerated by ourselves.

'Let's go into the garden,' Vicky said. 'It's so absurd to stand in an overcrowded room on a night like this.'

As we moved towards the verandah door Oliver waylaid us.

'You must have something to drink,' he said with command. 'Now what are you going to have? Vicky?' Then his eyes rested on Lacey Coole.

Vicky remembered she had brought Lacey along because Oliver had said bring anyone who lived in Pepper Tree Bay along. Good heavens! Vicky's manner seemed to say, it's impossible they've never met! She introduced them. Oliver laughed and shook hands, then cupped his left hand under Lacey's elbow and said, 'Come over to the bar and tell me what you want to drink.' All the time he did not once look at Laura, nor she at him.

We were held as a group there by the bar, with Oliver in the centre, laughing but carefully passing the right drinks to the right people and seeing that everyone's cigarette was lighted at the very moment when that person first took the cigarette in her hand. It was then, when he lighted Laura's cigarette, they really looked at one another. Right into one another's eyes.

I turned away because it hurt, for over by the door Esther, her smile and quick eager look still doing duty, was shaking hands with someone else.

It was Riley Scott. I immediately forgot Oliver and Laura.

He came in the door of the big room and for one moment stood there immobile.

He had a naturalness of personal dignity. I could see him better now than I had seen him on the beach because I had then bent over Barty's rock pool and he had turned and gone away almost at once. He was slim and quite tall with dark-brown hair, with good firm regular features that were almost classical. One felt he was not so much himself as a whole family line. This was strange because later I was to learn he had no family at all. Or none that anyone knew of. He had an easy grace as he walked forward and though his physical appearance and the way he bore himself took one's immediate attention it was his eyes that struck one. They were of an intense blue, dark yet with a kind of light behind them. They were very intelligent and seemed to speak of a concealed courage and a faint weariness. Yet for all this they were alert. It struck one that they perceived at once the meaning behind whatever was said to him, and that in a matter of principle they gave quarter on no point. Altogether his appearance made one think he was attractive and yet there was a hard streak edged with bitterness that was not to be tampered with.

He impressed me enormously.

In that minute when he stood there glancing round the room, Oliver finished the ceremony of lighting Laura's cigarette and looking in her eyes. He looked up and saw Riley Scott.

'Excuse me,' he said suddenly.

He threaded his way quickly through the groups standing about. He held out his left hand to Riley in that characteristic gesture of welcome and his voice could be heard right across the room.

'Hah! There you are. Well, how are you, feller? Come and have a drink. Golly, I didn't know I had so many friends. Look at 'em all . . .' And his laugh crackled out so that everyone turned round and smiled because although Oliver's laugh was hard it was infectious and good-natured.

Oliver came through the room beside Riley and leaning across the bar that had been set up at one side called for a scotch and soda.

'Soda, feller, is it? Or water?' he asked, turning his head and beaming on Riley, determined that Riley should have exactly what he was inclined to have.

'Water,' Riley said firmly. 'If it's not too much trouble.'

'Too much trouble?' shouted Oliver. 'There's water everywhere. A whole river full of it if that is how you feel.' And he laughed again. He put the glass on the bar top and then handed Riley the bottle of whisky in order that he might judge his own strength. 'Now come on . . . freeze on to that,' he said almost impatiently. 'There's a whole host of people I want you to meet.'

He turned to our group first because this was the one from which he had so hurriedly torn himself.

As he made the introductions a strange thing happened, for Lacey Coole had gone quite pale. There was a small table at hand and she put her glass on it a minute after Oliver had announced her name. Then she opened her vanity bag and took out a lace handkerchief. She dabbed her lips delicately with it. Over her hand and that tiny piece of lace her eyes were helpless and shy.

Riley glanced at her with a cool diagnostic look as if he wanted to penetrate to something beyond what he saw in her face and eyes. His glance was longer than it needed to be when

62

several of us were being introduced and while I was telling him that Barty had already introduced us on the beach. His eyes went back to Lacey's face and then, perhaps because she was looking down now at her hand, he looked away with an air of finality that said he had discovered what it was he wanted to know.

Lacey's eyelashes lay, a frail, even curtain, on her cheek. Then she turned her attention to Laura and spoke to her in her quiet, calm, rather attractive voice.

Whatever had passed between them, if anything, was over.

Then Oliver took Riley's arm.

'Over here,' he said. 'There's some fellas I want you to meet over here.'

Laura watched them go and one knew her eyes were on Oliver but Lacey went on quietly talking to Laura who was not listening and to Vicky who was interjecting with contributions of her own.

The crowd in the main reception room was now drifting out on to the verandahs and lawns.

Nearly everybody knew everybody and it was like the party of an enormous family. When strangers were introduced in a group they soon became absorbed in that group because the talk, the laughter and the exchange of anecdotes went on uninterrupted.

Vicky walked about with Lacey Coole and if there were those who were surprised to meet her here at Oliver's house they in no way showed it. It was only when she had passed on and the eyes followed her that one knew the name Coole had made its impression.

'That girl . . . Miss Coole . . . Her father is Bernard Coole, the chairman of half a dozen directorates in the city. Or he used to be. I remember my parents used fairly to quiver at the mention of his name. Got a huge place round the West Side. You must have seen it . . . right on the corner of the River Drive and Hakea Street. There must be two acres of land around it. Worth a fortune . . . Well, yes . . . I did mean the land but old Bernard Coole too. The house is called Meenon, the same as their station in the north. I believe their farm down south also has the name.'

Twitter, twitter, twitter.

Yet when those same eyes met Lacey's eyes they were veiled and polite and cautious and the lips said 'How-do-you-do?' as if Lacey was a stranger well met at a party.

Others said . . . 'Oh, Lacey Coole? Haven't you met her

before? Quite a landmark, you know . . . the Coole family.'
And these same eyes when introduced were also veiled and
polite and cautious and the lips refrained from saying 'Miss
Coole' because it would divulge the fact the owner had no
right to say '*Lacey* Coole'.

And Lacey . . .

Shy, but not showing it. Correct, but easy and natural with
it. Haunted by her sense of astonishment that all these people
lived in Pepper Tree Bay and she did not know it; yet saying
nothing about living there herself because she was ashamed of
her own isolation.

Lacey, with one beautiful shod foot on the doorstep of another world, with no idea how to make an entry, yet making
a perfect one because intuitively she followed the rules of good
manners and they led her safely over all the traps.

Lacey, thirty, unmarried and who did not allow herself to
think of such things because they had been put away long
since. Love, courtship, marriage, might have been, for Lacey,
the imps that had been pushed back into Pandora's box and
the key turned by her own father.

Yet tonight, I am sure her heart had quivered. Something
like hope afraid had sprung into her eyes when Riley Scott
came into the room, and when she, Lacey, had recognised
what had caused her heart to beat so quickly she had lifted her
head proudly, and quickly turned away.

Making quite a different circuit of the verandah and gardens
was Oliver with Riley Scott by his side. Before the evening was
half over Oliver had unobtrusively introduced Riley to everyone present and it was clear that everyone present was suitably
impressed. Very few, as yet, knew the purpose behind Oliver's
presentation of Riley Scott. Those who did know remained
unobtrusively in the background. Their contribution to the
'cause' was loudly to proclaim that this evening was a hilarious
success and it must be done again. Often. What about your
turn next, Bill? You run a party on that patio of yours! We'll
all come. Hey, say! We'll all come, won't we, fellas? Bill's
turn next. Let's all keep together now we've got old Oliver
bringing us together like this.

They would have one gathering after another and, quietly,
the group would consolidate itself into a pressure group behind
Oliver and his schemes. Tomorrow in the clubs or over the
bar in the beer garden the idea would be consolidated into
concrete plans.

The two people impressed into that service on this night

who did not know where they were going or what it was all about were Laura Montgomery and Lacey Coole.

Laura was drawn into it by Oliver's passionate command.

'You're in, Laura,' he laughed, his arm along her shoulder. 'This day four weeks hence . . . at Bill Ogilvie's house. All you girls are in. How about bringing Mrs Monty?'

He'd called us 'girls' again. Well, after that who could refuse?

'And you, Miss Coole?' Oliver's voice and eyes softened. He came down two notes to reach somewhere near the level of Lacey's pleasant voice. The smile in his eyes softened and she felt the touch of a certain paternal tenderness that transformed Oliver from a hearty brash salesman to a kind friend.

'Why yes . . .' Lacey said, her eyes wide with the surprise at how easy it was. 'Yes, thank you very much. It is very kind of you . . .'

Riley Scott standing at that moment in the shadow of the verandah creepers watched Oliver wooing Lacey in this manner. Because of the shadows his face was little more than a white blur with dark pools for eyes, yet one was certain he did not approve of either Oliver's invitation or of Lacey's ingenuous acceptance. He had accepted and been accepted by each person he had met here tonight. Except Lacey.

Now why was that?

CHAPTER FOUR

Mr Coole took lunch at the Yacht Club on the second Monday of every month. His father had been a foundation member of the Club and had taken the small boy Bernard along with him on the historic occasion of the opening. The young Bernard, not yet able to swim, had been on that day nominated for membership by his father. He was now, in the days immediately following his seventieth birthday, not only the oldest living member but justly ranked, in his own right, a foundation member.

The first Monday in the month was Members' Day at luncheon time. On that day no visitors were brought into the Club. Members lunched only with members and the activities of the committee were milled over in the restricted public light of members' opinion.

In the last ten years Mr Coole had decided these occasions were not for him. The technicalities of sailing troubled him but he did not realise this. His attitude was one of cold dislike of the newcomers whose faces and often names he failed to recognise. By lunching on the second Monday instead of the first he was emulating the ostrich as far as Club affairs were concerned.

He was able on this one day to perceive from the notice board, when he looked at it, what was afoot. It gave him the feeling of partaking in affairs, though he was no longer really interested.

The lunching on the second Monday was more a rite and a habit; a gesture to demonstrate he still paid his subscription and was historically a responsible and senior member. He was there to put things to rights should necessity arise.

The Club secretary, a salaried officer present at all times, and the stewards and servants played out their parts in this kindly farce. When Mr Coole arrived there was the decorous kowtowing in the bar lounge or the bathrooms. The secretary always made it his business to come forward, shake hands with an air of pleasure and a slight deference that was really all good manners and not servility. In other words, in view of Bernard Coole's historic rôle in the Club's life, he was kind to the ageing man.

Before entering the dining-room he had looked at the notice board. It bore the names of three prospective members together with their nominators and seconders. No one looking at Mr Coole's face when he read their names would have seen any change of expression. Yet two names struck a lash at his heart. These were the names that had struck a similar lash when he had opened the Sunday papers on the previous day and read that Mr Oliver Harding, the well-known motor magnate, had given a large party at his home on the East Side of Pepper Tree Bay. In the list of guests mentioned there had been Mr Riley Scott and Miss Lacey Coole.

Mr Coole that morning had said nothing to his daughter. He had folded his napkin up and left the breakfast table. Neither Lacey nor the housekeeper had perceived at any time on that day that something had happened to Mr Coole . . . that the pain that had affected him on his birthday had struck again.

It was the fear of the pain returning that had prevented him from speaking to Lacey about her presence in Oliver Harding's house.

Today as he prepared to enter the Club dining-room on the second Monday of the month, as he had done for ten years, he had read on the notice board that Oliver Harding had nominated Riley Scott for membership to the most exclusive Yacht Club on the river. His, Mr Bernard Coole's Yacht Club.

At the fish stage the secretary, Mr Ellison, arrived. The usual courtesies were exchanged. Mr Ellison enquired after Mr Coole's health and they both commented on the weather. Mr Ellison informed Mr Coole the Club had a new chef in the kitchen and he would personally be grateful for Mr Coole's comments when lunch was over. He hadn't any doubts as to what they would be, as the Club had been lucky enough to get a Continental man who had come in with the influx of post-war migrants to the country. He came from one of the very best restaurants in middle Europe.

As he turned to leave, Mr Coole indicated the folded page from his notebook.

'A memorandum for you, Mr Ellison,' he said. 'I would be glad if you would take it now.'

A little surprised, the secretary picked up the note. Good manners prompted him to take it away unopened.

Mr Coole remained at his table through three courses and for his coffee. He sat with his face to the view and his back to the room so there was no question of anyone exchanging nods with him. As a matter of fact it had been many months since Mr Coole had recognised a face amidst the host of strangers. He was content to feel that all knew who he was and there was no occasion for him to know them.

As he left the dining-room the secretary, who had been watching for him, came hastily out of his office.

'Mr Coole. If you'd be so kind as to spare me a few minutes? You can quite understand I am anxious to see you in connection with your memorandum.'

Mr Coole's drooping lids drooped another fraction of an inch. This was the only indication that he was not quite himself.

He nodded now and the secretary stood aside for the older man to enter the office. He followed him hastily and placed a chair so that they sat side by side, at a slight angle, looking towards the window and the river view. Mr Coole was not a man the secretary interviewed across a desk.

'If you don't mind my saying, sir,' he began at once – it was quite clear that he was the one who was agitated – 'your memorandum has disturbed me. I wonder if you understand,

67

sir, that a negative vote from a committee member or a foundation member blackballs a man? I do not wish to challenge your opinion, sir, but I must admit to you this is very embarrassing. You see, Mr Harding is a very consequential member of the Club. The man for whom you wish to cast a negative vote is Mr Harding's nomination . . .'

He was hurrying on, saying far too much. Mr Coole's silence invited him to hurry precipitately as he now was doing. This action, vetoing the nomination of a man of Oliver Harding's position in the Club was of earth-shaking consequence. Mr Ellison was struck all of a mess in contemplating it. Of course, Mr Coole was not quite in touch with the activities of the Club. He couldn't possibly understand the significance of blackballing a nomination put forward by Harding. Harding, financially, *was* the Club. This was the gist of what the secretary in his stumbling but respectful argument said.

Mr Coole remained silent and apparently unmoved. When Mr Ellison paused, waiting, hopefully and anxiously, for comment from Mr Coole, he received none. The silence persisted.

Again Mr Ellison plunged into words. Finally Mr Coole spoke. He looked at the secretary out of grey eyes that were faintly rheumy and infinitely cold.

'My vote stays as I have indicated,' he said in his precise well-bred objective voice. 'I have not the slightest intention of changing it.'

There was a minute's silence broken by the sound Mr Coole made as he rose from his chair. His words and his manner of rising indicated he did not intend to give any explanation. Neither did he intend to reconsider his action.

The secretary dropped his hands to his sides. He accompanied Mr Coole into the hall and saw that he was suitably presented by the steward with his hat and stick. He bade Mr Coole an embarrassed farewell and retreated back into his office so hurriedly he almost impaled himself on the sharp corner of the square polished jarrah desk.

He fell into his chair and reached for the telephone. He dialled a number.

'Harding Motors Ltd? . . . Is Mr Harding in? . . . Listen, young lady, you put your knitting down and dial every number in the firm and failing finding him inside, dial every number in Perth likely to reach him. Tell him to phone me back immediately . . . WGO199 . . . Tell him it's the Archangel Gabriel and the business is just as important as the Book of Judgment.'

He hung up. Only then did he slump back in his chair, draw his handkerchief from his pocket and wipe his brow.

'That will let hell loose,' he thought. 'What the devil has got into the old fool's head now!'

At exactly half past two Lacey was waiting outside the Yacht Club to drive her father to his Club in Perth.

Again, on this day, he varied his route. Instead of driving a short distance round the river, then cutting into the Highway he told Lacey to drive him through King's Park and pull up at the lookout over the point where the Canning River joined the Swan.

It was at this point, the Narrows, the new bridge was to be built. Already world experts on town planning and bridge building were converging on the State to deliberate with the Government.

At the lookout Mr Coole left the car and walked to the edge of the cliff sloping down to the river road and the sweep of water beyond. At this point, the confluence of the two rivers, there stretched below Mr Coole a magnificent sweep of water.

Here they were to build that noisome bridge. He stood, both hands resting on the dingo-headed handle of his walking stick, and looked down on the sight.

Lacey remembered her father standing that way on the block where the new house was being built on the East Side of Pepper Tree Bay farther down the course of the river. She felt a pang of compunction for her father. Never before had she known him stand and stare like that . . . much like a man might gaze on a beloved sight which was about to pass from his view for ever.

As he came back to the car she felt an unexpected tenderness for this austere personage. His cold haughty face did not now intimidate her.

'You do not like the idea of a bridge there, Father?' she said as she released the handbrake and let in the clutch.

'Not any more than I like you hobnobbing with people like that Harding man. What were you doing in his house?'

Lacey, still in the wonder of feeling pity for her father yet not understanding it was pity, failed to catch the climate of his words.

'Oh, it was a lovely house. Very modern. His wife . . . you know her father . . . she was Esther Hillman, Mrs Riccard's protégée . . . is the loveliest thing imaginable. I went with the Montgomery girls.'

The mention of Mrs Riccard's name undercut Mr Coole's

icy wrath. He couldn't imagine for a single instant how a protégée of hers would come to marry a common fellow like the Harding man. He had forgotten what the circumstances were about Esther's adoption. Esther's father had been a school-master and if Mr Coole's memory did not betray him altogether, the man had had a break-down or some serious illness. Mrs Riccard was not a woman he had either known well or liked; but she had had position and wealth. She had been admitted to the hierarchy of Pepper Tree Bay. Her name could be ticked off on the right list, as it were. A peculiar woman, if he remembered rightly, a very peculiar woman. Peculiarity, however, was not a bar amongst the original families of Pepper Tree Bay. Take the Maynard-Arnolds. They had had a son who gained a Victoria Cross and another who was an idiot.

'It must be fifteen years since any of the Montgomerys could claim to be called *girls*,' he said drily.

Lacey smiled.

'We all do that, Father. Even old Mr Reynolds at the corner speaks of his sisters as "the girls" and they're all over sixty, aren't they? I expect Miss Susan and Miss Mary speak of him as "that boy"!'

She laughed rather deliciously but Mr Coole was not a man who appreciated laughter. He preferred his daughter to drive in silence and give her undivided attention to the road.

He put up a barrier of solid silence himself, and Lacey made no further attempt to explain her delinquencies.

She did not recognise them as delinquencies. She enjoyed Oliver's party more in retrospect than she had actually enjoyed it on the occasion. When she thought of it now she remembered the beautiful modern room with its great expanse of window, the softly-lit verandahs and the people, so beautifully and smartly dressed, strolling about the lawn with a big tree and its shielded light in the background. She could hear again the soft muted tones of the small orchestra that had been playing in the corner.

It wasn't that things had been beautiful and unusual to the eye but it had been a different kind of society from that which she had known. People had been bright and uninhibited. Their clothes were different, though not necessarily more expensive than the clothes of the ladies around her own part of the Bay. The women had worn daring hair styles and their ears and throats and wrists sparkled with the loaded rhinestone jewellery that was evidently so fashionable just now. Vicky Montgomery, who was really Mrs Browning, had worn gold kid shoes the heels of which sparkled with diamanté trimmings. Lacey, who loved good shoes and wore good expensive shoes herself, had never imagined anything as fairy-tale as Vicky's shoes.

Beyond and outside all these delectable memories was that solitary one that encompassed the figure of a tall man who had looked at her with strange blue eyes. It was the stranger . . . the man who had got out of the Humber car to look at the new house being built around the Bay; and who had looked hard at her as she had waited for her father outside the Bank on Saturday morning.

At Oliver Harding's party he had looked twice and then turned away.

Each time that memory sprang unbidden to Lacey's mind she put it quickly and fearfully away. It was ten years since the last man had called on Lacey Coole. He was the last of a short line of those who had grown up side by side with Lacey on the banks of the Bay. One by one Mr Coole had frozen them off.

'Fortune hunters,' Mr Coole had said within his bitter-rancorous heart.

Lacey who had no idea what her father's fortune was . . . or even if he had one beyond what it cost them to live the way they lived . . . had no idea why the list of her friends' brothers and cousins had dwindled . . . except that one by one they had married someone else. If she dared to think of it herself she thought quite simply that where love was concerned she had not been a chosen one.

It would be wrong to say she had resigned herself to this fate. She had simply put a fate that implied any alternative way of living aside. It was not, evidently, for her.

Quite often, however, when she sat on a Victorian cedar chair in a drawing-room of Victorian dimensions, surrounded by the now-grown-lovely-with-age vases and brasses, and listened to the sound of Sarah or Gwendoline or Arabella over the sweet sound of the children outside; or the more poignant sound of a husband talking to another husband from the deep cane chairs on the verandahs, a regret that she, too, had not been chosen touched her heart.

It was on those occasions she went home and stood before the mirror, or bought herself a new dress or a new hat. She had no idea that people thought she was well-dressed and proud. It was her pride, people who did not know the circumstances of Mr Coole's domestic life said, that kept her aloof from the social joys of a mixed society.

She had no idea that, because of her *pride*, people on the fringes of her own society were afraid to address her. She had no idea that these same people always looked twice at her ... the second time from behind ambush as it were ... and envied her her position, her wealth, her home and her slender proud delightful appearance.

The last of the young men had called, been rebuffed by Mr Coole, then gone away and married someone else long since.

Obscurely Lacey was afraid to let herself think of the tall man with the intent blue eyes who had looked twice at her, and not from ambush, at Oliver Harding's party. Yet he, more than the light in the tree, the laughter on the lawns or Esther's impeccable taste in house decorations, made that party seem in retrospect to have been something rare and exotic and wonderful.

Lacey drove her father to the Club and when she left him there she drove home the long way round the river drive past that new house going up a few blocks farther east from Oliver Harding's house.

Without conscious purpose, before she came to the block, she slowed down. When she saw the Humber standing there, its door open, her heart contracted. She stole a glance sideways.

He was standing, his back to the road, talking to the contractor. As Lacey put her foot on the accelerator, her heart rose in even time with the quickened rhythm of her own motor engine.

She felt, vaguely, as if she had been to a party all over again. An Oliver Harding party ... and not a drawing-room party on the West Side.

She drove the car into the driveway of Meenon and left it standing under the Moreton Bay fig-trees at the side of the house. Late in the afternoon she would have to go back to Perth for her father.

She let herself in through the side door into the billiard room. It did not occur to her to think that never in living memory had she seen billiards played in that room. Never had she seen the top taken off or the green baize of the playing top exposed.

The housekeeper heard her footsteps in the passage and came from the kitchen regions to meet her.

'There is a telephone message for you, Miss Lacey.' Her narrow eyes looked their curiosity as she fumbled purposely in her apron pocket for the slip of paper on which she had written the message. Lacey always felt that that curiosity of Mrs Simmins had an undressing quality.

'Ah . . . here it is,' Mrs Simmins confessed as if it had been an effort to find the piece of paper so obviously living in solitary confinement in that pocket.

While the search was on, and the undressing eyes had watched her face, Lacey had stood looking at herself in the mirror of the hallstand. She made a play of pushing her hair into place.

Mrs Simmins, watching her face in the mirror, saw the light in Lacey's eyes and felt a certain rising of her own spirits. Something was doing where Miss Lacey was concerned. Something was doing. Being at Mr Oliver Harding's house, for instance. Mrs Simmins did not know of anybody who lived on the West Side visiting or being visited by Mr Oliver Harding. She had read it with indignation in the social news in the Sunday paper. Her indignation was due to the fact Miss Martin would ask her about it and she, Mrs Simmins, did not have an adequate answer. This would put her to disadvantage with her friend.

She looked at the piece of paper, now holding it first close to her eyes as if she was short-sighted, and then at a distance as if her ocular sight was the opposite.

'Vicky Browning,' she said with emphasis. 'No Mrs or Miss or anything. Just Vicky Browning. She wants you to ring her up when you come in.'

'Oh . . .' said Lacey. Mrs Simmins noted carefully the pleasure in Lacey's voice. 'Vicky Montgomery,' Lacey said with a laugh. 'I never can remember what those Montgomery girls call themselves now they're married.'

Then she laughed again because she remembered her father had said it was fifteen years since any of them might call themselves *girls*. What would Vicky be? Good heavens . . . she would be forty-something. The others would all be younger . . . but not much.

'She didn't leave the number, I suppose?' Lacey said, picking up the telephone book. Somehow she had to give Mrs Simmins an excuse for standing where she was instead of going away.

'Yes,' Mrs Simmins said, again examining the paper first near her eyes and then at a distance, 'WG2407.'

Lacey was on the point of lifting the telephone receiver. Then she changed her mind. She felt an unexpected irritation at the crowded feeling Mrs Simmins gave her standing there, so close to her, in the hall.

She had always liked Vicky Montgomery but just now Vicky wore an extra interest almost like an aura. She, too, had been at that party. She, too, had been where the tall man had been. She was invested with the charm of his presence and must bear it as an added charm to herself. Lacey did not want to ring up Vicky with Mrs Simmins standing there beside her. She wanted to go away and hug in privacy the talk she would have with Vicky because whether it was about ships, shoes or sealing wax it would have the enchantment of being with someone who knew, had spoken with, Riley Scott.

'I'll ring presently,' she said. 'I want to do my hair. It's quite blown about, isn't it?' Then with a manner so forced it was immediately suspect before Mrs Simmins's vulgar curiosity, she added, 'Mrs Browning can wait.'

She pressed the switch on the telephone that connected the line through to the study . . . a gesture not missed by Mrs Simmins . . . and went to her room.

'What would Vicky be wanting?' Lacey asked her reflected eyes in the mirror in her room as she did her hair, forgetting she had done it in the hall a few minutes earlier. Lacey was incapable of lying. She had said she was going to do her hair, so do her hair she must. 'It'll be something like "Have morning tea?" or "How did you enjoy the party?" of course.' Still, it would be nice to talk to Vicky.

Again that invisible scintillating thread tightened and strengthened. Vicky knew that man . . . talking to her would be almost like talking to him. Well, not quite, of course. That was absurd. But . . . oh well, she had enjoyed that party. The man, of course, had nothing to do with it at all. She wished to goodness she would stop thinking about him. He hadn't been anything but rude when she came to think of it. That morning in the Terrace when her father was in the Bank he had looked at her as he passed the car with something that could have been cold antagonism. Except, of course, he didn't know her so he couldn't possibly feel antagonism towards her. It was probably the way the light had caught his eyes turning the dark-blue into something cold and grey. He had looked at her twice at Oliver Harding's . . . but that was all . . .

Lacey, her arms uplifted to do her hair, tried to bring back again any expression that might have been in his eyes as he had looked at her. She could not remember any . . . except there might have, there just might have been, a hint of curiosity. Yet under that curiosity there was something else. A

74

faint bitterness? But how absurd! He didn't know her. How could he have looked at her any way at all!

Her own panic had prevented her from looking at him or letting him really acknowledge that brief introduction. There! She was thinking of him again. It really was too tiresome. She could have no possible interest in a stranger she had met in Oliver Harding's house. If he had been anyone she or her father had known, or known of, he wouldn't be a stranger.

Mrs Simmins had left the kitchen door and the hall door open. She was folding down the sheets, and hearing Lacey's footsteps cross the hall she came to the doorway, still with a sheet half-folded in her hand. She completed one more fold as Lacey dialled the number, then unblushingly she bent her head sideways in order to hear more easily.

'Yes, Vicky. It's Lacey . . . Oh, it sounds awfully nice. I'd love to come . . . What is that? . . . I never really know. It depends on Father. You see I have to get him from the Club . . . Oh, I've always done it. As a matter of fact, Vicky, I *like* it. I like driving and it gives me a job in life. It's a sort of job that's a pleasant duty, if you know what I mean . . . I'll know on the day if I'm free. He always tells me in the morning if he'll need me. I'm sure I will be free though. He never does ask for me during the afternoon . . . only in time for dinner . . . What is that? . . . The promenade? It sounds a splendid idea to me and I'd love to be in on it. Thank you so much for asking me . . . I'll ring you on Wednesday morning . . . By the way, thank you very much for taking me along to Mrs Harding's party. I enjoyed it ever so much . . . I met some very interesting people . . . Oh, yes, I did enjoy it, I assure you . . .'

Some interesting people! As she said that, Lacey's heart beat a little faster. Of course she couldn't possibly ask Vicky about *that man*. Just saying 'interesting people' enveloped him in spirit. It brought her that short distance nearer the direct question, nearer the object of her enquiring mind.

Mrs Simmins withdrew to her kitchen table and the next sheet.

So it had been through the Montgomerys Miss Lacey had gone visiting round the Bay! Well, that gave her something to say when Miss Martin raised the issue. And the Montgomerys were always a fruitful topic of conversation over the knitting. They were a weird lot, they were. Mrs Montgomery had gone nursing when the Reverend Joe had passed out. Brought all those five girls up too. Made quite a job of it. Three of them had professions, so they said. Mary was the clever one. A

75

lawyer and all that. Not that she, Mrs Simmins, approved of young women becoming doctors or lawyers. Going into sordid places like morgues and the law courts. A man's job it was. A woman's place was in the home too.

Now take Mr Coole. A magistrate he'd been in the old days . . . and Pepper Tree Bay had been a place with law and order. You didn't hear in those days about children stealing motor cars or breaking into houses. Soon as a young fellow started anything like that Mr Coole and the other magistrates had clapped them into prison or a Home or something. That was the end of too much trouble from the larrikins in those days. Even if they only stole a few apples out of the orchards the magistrate told the local policeman to clap them into jail overnight. That frightened their wits for stealing out of them. Out of their parents too. If you asked Mrs Simmins it was the parents' gadding about that caused all the trouble. Like those people on the East Side.

What was it Miss Lacey had said on the phone about a promenade? Now what promenade could that be? Something Miss Lacey would like to be in on. Well, Mrs Simmins would have to bide her time and ask Miss Lacey when she was in one of her chatty moods.

Funny person, Miss Lacey. Sometimes as chatty as you liked. Sometimes so quiet you'd hear a mouse squeak . . .

2

At four o'clock on the same day Oliver Harding sat in the office of the secretary of the Yacht Club.

He sat at the side of the desk table, his coat off and his shirt sleeves rolled up. He had a pile of papers before him and more strewn about the table farther afield.

Mr Ellison sat perspiring in his proper seat. Like Oliver he would have liked to take off his coat but it wasn't worth the scramble of getting into it every time a member came to the door or one of the servants indicated he was wanted in the lobby or bar lounge.

Oliver leaned back in his chair. His gloved right hand lay on the table beside him and he brushed the fingers of his left hand through his hair.

'That looks like the ruddy lot,' he said. 'We've combed through the constitution, the regulations and the ruddy history of the place . . . and we can't catch Coole out anywhere. Nothing can stop him blackballing Scott if that's the way he wants it.'

76

'I'm sorry, Oliver, but it looks like it to me.'

'He's always been financial, you say? He's never forfeited membership by defection in subs?'

'No. And even if he had you couldn't say he'd come back in as an ordinary member because there would have had to be a committee minute on it. Even if he'd missed a period paying his subscription he would have regained his membership, in the terms of his original foundation membership, when he did pay his subscription. You can't scrub him on that count.'

Both men sat, exasperated and thoughtful.

'I wish to hell I knew why,' Oliver groaned at length. 'What's biting the old fool?'

'I did ask him. I did not get an answer. Perhaps if you were to approach him?'

Oliver shook his head.

'Not at this stage,' he said. 'Never give your hand away until you have to. He's moving behind the scenes and that's my line for the minute. He's got nothing against Scott. I'll vouch for that. Scott's as square as they come.'

Reluctantly Oliver's mind went back to that day long ago when he'd come across Riley Scott, a young boy, behind Joe Montgomery's Church on the Highway. He, Oliver, had been eating a thick doorstep of bread and squashed figs. Riley Scott's eyes had nearly leapt across the short distance and devoured the slice for him. That's how Oliver had known he was hungry. He'd handed the bread over to the other boy and it had gone down in one gulp.

His face was dusty and stained. Back now, after all these years, it suddenly occurred to Oliver they had been tear stains. He was barefooted . . . but so was Oliver. That didn't matter. It was Riley's feet that had mattered. They were black with dust and here and there a brown stain showed where sticks or stones had cut them about and the sand had got mixed in with the blood. The boy had walked miles through the bush to get back to Pepper Tree Bay.

Oliver had fed him on figs and bread scrounged from his own mother's limited resources. He'd shown the boy where he could sleep in a cubby house he'd made with the Montgomery kids in the bushes in the school grounds. The school was on the long summer vacation.

For two nights and three days Oliver had succoured the runaway boy there. Then they'd found him while he was swimming in the river to get the dirt off. They'd shot him back in that Home.

Riley Scott could never have let on who helped him in those three days of freedom; otherwise Oliver would have been in trouble too.

That was the bond! Honour among thieves!

Sitting in the secretary's office in the Yacht Club, Oliver gave a hollow laugh.

'He was as square as they make 'em,' he said reminiscently to Ellison. 'He got orphaned and shot in a Home. Well, Coole can't hold that against him, and if he bloody well does I'll drag Old Man Coole off his pedestal if I have to crawl in the gutters for stones with which to pelt him.' He looked up sharply at Ellison. 'There isn't a man or a woman living who hasn't done something . . . some one thing you can hang on to him if you want to get him, and pull him down.'

The secretary looked at Oliver in surprise. He'd known all along that under Oliver's urbanity . . . his hail-fellow-well-met air of hearty friendship to all . . . there was a hard streak. It had to be there or the man wouldn't have made the success of himself the way he had made a success. He was a self-made man and was proud of it. He had to have something extra and something tough to do that.

But this sharp tone and the hard brittle light in his eyes? Ellison might have guessed it must be there, but he'd seen no evidence of it in Club affairs and Club activities. There was something worse than murder in Oliver Harding's eyes now. There was a certain ruthless will-to-power that would not count the costs, even after the event.

Ellison cleared his throat.

'You say every man has done something. Some one thing you can hang on him. Is your Mr Scott the exception? Has Coole got something on him that you don't know of?'

'Listen, I know that boy's book from the first page to the last full stop and including the semicolons.'

Did he? Weren't there two lost years in the chronological tale? God dammit, he'd have to ask Riley about them. He just hated digging a fellow's history out of him when the fellow had had the rotten spin in the early days that Riley Scott had had. It was like rubbing it in that a fellow didn't quite make the grade. Father did a bunk, mother only half mast as mothers go. Brought up by a grandmother until shoved into a Home. And on top of that what the hell did you do with two years before you were timber felling down there in the karri forest?

Oliver shook his head.

'Ring for the steward,' he said, 'and let's drink. I'll have a double scotch.'

'You know what?' Oliver was saying. 'Riley Scott's got one of the best war records in this State. Commando tactics off Garden Island. It's still too early to write the history of that unit but, boy, when it is written . . . Yes. He got a couple of medals out of it but that was chicken feed to what he ought to get.

'And that farm he's got down there. Practically carved it out of the forest himself, in between felling and sawing timber for the State. Ever thought of clearing an acre of scrub bushland by hand? Well, that 'ud be kindergarten work compared with clearing forest. Of course he struck it lucky with the prices in the wool boom but the whole bloody country struck it lucky. Riley Scott wasn't the only farmer by a hundred thousand who found himself rich overnight. And that includes the taxation boys too.'

The expression in Oliver's eyes turned to tender amusement as for a moment he forgot Bernard Coole and remembered the pastoralists and farmers rushing out from the 1949 wool sale and throwing hats, papers and bank-notes in the air. By golly! That day it rained bank-notes all over the country!

Ellison interrupted his thoughts.

'If Scott has a clean sheet then it's more than likely Bernard Coole has a clean sheet,' he said apologetically. 'He's been a magistrate in his time, hasn't he?'

'That's got nothing to do with being a business man in his time too. Not that he'd dream of ranking himself a business man. He's professionally and historically a pastoralist. One of the landed aristocracy. All the same he's dealt in land, houses and pastoral leases all his life. I'll wager he's got half his income now in stocks and shares. And a fair whack of them will be gold and oil . . . if you know of a sweeter gamble. Take it from me, Ellison, no business man's got clean hands by the New Testament all the way. Not in the world of today. Somewhere along the line he's had to kill or be killed. At the top levels of business, it's jungle law.'

Mr Ellison had a slight sense of impending excitement. A fight to the finish in these terms would provide some good fireside politics for the coming winter. But would it be good for the Club? Reluctantly he abandoned the dream which only reluctantly he admitted had a tangy sweetness about it.

'Let's go over the books again,' he suggested. 'We might find some let-out somewhere.'

Privately he wondered why Oliver was prepared to damage Coole and damage himself in the interests of this unknown man. He wondered where the tie-up was. A business deal? Well, it was none of his business.

'If you say Coole's always been solvent as far as the Club is concerned I guess you're right,' Oliver said. 'But let's look at his financial record. It often tells a story all on its own.'

Mr Ellison wasn't sure that this was at all in order, but after all Oliver Harding was a Vice-President of the Club. And far and away the most important man in Club affairs.

He rose from his chair and went to the filing cabinet. A minute later he handed over Bernard Coole's subscription card. Oliver sat gloomily looking at it.

'Golly!' he said. 'What a bird! Subscription due in March every year and blow me down on March thirtieth of every year for . . . for crying out loud . . . sixty-four years, the bloody thing's been paid. Not on the twenty-ninth, mind you. Or the thirty-first. But ruddy well on the thirtieth of March.' He looked up at the secretary sardonically. 'How do you manage it on Sundays?'

'It gets paid in on the Saturday's post but is dated the thirtieth. We stuck down the same date because that's the date above. I suppose we guess the old boy 'ud like it that way.'

'And what are these five quids spattered through the years? Every time there's a levy or the cap's passed round the old boy coughs up a fiver? And he could buy and sell the Club!'

Thank God it was incorporated, Oliver thought. If Coole would do anything to keep Riley Scott out, he'd probably buy the raking Club if it was legal. The way Transome had bought the Golf Club because they'd refused his wife membership.

Oliver laughed. He told Ellison the joke.

'That was a good one,' he said. 'A few of the nobs had made themselves a private golf links on leased land. Transome flicked the thing from under their feet. You'd better see this thing's properly incorporated, Ellison.'

'I don't know there's any evidence Mr Coole will go to great lengths, Oliver,' he said tentatively. 'After all, we haven't done anything much about approaching him and getting him to change his mind.' It was his turn to laugh. 'It seems to me you're the one who's going to shift the earth off its axis if you don't get that nomination through the committee.'

'You're darn right I am,' Oliver said.

'You wouldn't consider ringing Mr Coole yourself?'

'No, I wouldn't. The man's a fellow member. If he wanted to blackball my nomination why didn't he pay me the ordinary courtesy of the Club and let me know? Get in touch with me? Because he's always worked behind the scenes all his life. There are a dozen of them in the community. You never see their names in the paper or on anything except the chairmanship of boards that never have to make their business public . . . they're so straight and above board. But try and put something new into this community of which they don't approve and what happens? Nothing. The thing's ditched at the Municipal Chambers or Government or Legislative Council . . . and nobody's name appears. It's just ditched, like they would have liked to ditch the Narrows bridge and the talk of an Olympic Pool and . . . By golly! I've got it. It's the *promenade*. The raking drive and promenade along the entire north and west line of the river!' Oliver slapped the table with his hand. 'Got it!' he said. 'I've got it! Riley Scott's running for the Council to push the plan there. Discredit Riley Scott and the promenade's out!'

He stopped, narrowed his eyes and sucked in his breath.

'Discredit Riley Scott . . .' he said quietly, 'and you discredit the men associated with him. Show me a man's friends and I'll tell you the manner of man he is . . . sort of thing.'

He pushed back his chair and reached for his coat. He began to thrust his arms into it.

'Boy,' he said, 'this is going to be a bigger fight than you ever dreamed of. Assassination of character, they call it in Yankee Land. A fight to the finish and no man making a move in the light of day. Every man in the front pew in church on Sundays.'

He had his coat on now. He took his hat from a side table and turned to the door.

'This,' he said, 'is going to be a gentleman's war! There's nothing more deadly.'

Esther heard Oliver slam the car door and then walk quickly and firmly across the verandah in through the open door of the sun-room. She came to the opposite door to get a drink for him. He stood by the telephone chair, his foot resting on it. He held the telephone to his right ear with his gloved right hand and leafed through the pages of the telephone directory with his other hand. His hat was still on the back of his head as if his forehead, weary of its load, had dismissed it to the rear of the premises.

Oliver did not look up as Esther came into the room. He was still waiting for the call to be received and he concentrated on the numbers he was looking for.

'Hallo, sweetie!' he said. 'Make it a double scotch, will you?' Then quickly into the mouthpiece of the phone, 'That you, Riley? . . . Look! Can you get round here for an hour or two after dinner? No, nothing particular. I want to get cracking on those patios and the promenade at the bottom of the cliff in front of the eight houses along here that have agreed to come in on a uniform plan . . . No. Just got the itches to get going. Always was like that, you know.'

His laugh was his usual fun-making crackle but Esther knew something had stirred Oliver. She walked across the room and took his hat off the back of his head. He was dialling the next number.

'Thanks, sweetie,' he said.

He sat down in the armchair, the phone piece to his ear, his legs sprawled straight out in front of him. Esther put his hat on the ledge under the window and went to the chair in the opposite corner and sat down. One hand, long-fingered and delicate at the wrist, rested on its palm along the arm rest. She sipped her own drink and watched Oliver out of calm eyes.

She only half-listened to the conversations he had one after another with his neighbours. She marvelled at the dexterity of his right hand, for he was now smoking a cigarette, occasionally sipping his drink, holding a phone piece under his chin and leafing through the telephone book.

For the first time she noticed Oliver's hair was beginning to recede a little at the temples. For a minute she wondered why it did not touch her. Then she remembered why.

It had been two years after the war when the light in her that had always burned for Oliver, died.

They had gone together by sea around the southern coast of Australia to Sydney. It had been a business trip made into a holiday for both by taking the sea route on a small luxury liner. They had never had a holiday together before. Building the business, having John, the war . . . There had been no time to be together much.

On the third night at sea it happened.

It was a flat calm. The perfect night for dancing. It was early but already there were several young couples dancing.

Suddenly Esther knew she was really on holiday. Years ago she had learned dancing by private tuition. She remembered Jenny Wren and Jamie who had taught her and the lovely gentle abandonment of the waltz steps. The miniature orchestra was playing a waltz tune now.

'Well, how about it?' Oliver said, looking at her. 'Do we dance?'

'Of course,' Esther said.

Oliver danced well. The deck remained horizontal and the moon and the stars and the sea were gentle and kind. Esther's heart danced with her feet though she had never been able to show all she felt in her face. In her eyes, that were level with Oliver's shoulder, was a light. She did not throw back her head, so he did not see it.

The dance came to an end and they went to seats along the rim of the hatch. They did not know any of the other passengers dancing or sitting about and they sat and watched them with the mild curiosity of fellow conspirators. They could not see themselves and did not remember, because of this, that they were forty-odd and everyone else there was twenty-odd.

Oliver danced a second time with Esther and they returned to the same seats. Esther sat, her hands, which were lovely hands, holding her small jewelled vanity case in her lap. Oliver put his hands in his pockets and stretched his feet out in front of him.

The music began again and they sat watching the other dancers. Esther longed to dance again but there was no one to dance with her but Oliver. He did not stir. Perhaps he was tired of dancing. Perhaps he had never cared for it as she had cared for it. There hadn't been any time in their married life for dancing.

The light that had always been in Esther for Oliver was extending its flame like a candle in a mild wind, reaching out to him.

He sat there, silent. His hands were in his pockets and his feet out before him. He watched the other dancers with intelligent amused eyes.

She longed for him to turn, catch her eyes with his eyes and say, 'Come on, my darling, we're wasting the dance.' It was not only that they might dance together, for that really was sufficient to Esther's happiness, but it would camouflage the fact there was no one else to come forward and ask her to dance.

The music stopped and the dancers dispersed. Oliver drew in his feet and took his hands from his pockets. He lit himself a cigarette.

'It's not the same as when we were young, is it?' he said.

'Oh yes, it is,' Esther said. 'The moon and the music and the deck are the same.'

'We're older,' said Oliver flatly.

He turned and looked at Esther and then looked across the floor at a group of laughing girls.

Esther wears well, he thought to himself. Still, we can't sit here doing nothing all night. Doesn't seem anyone about to dance with her but I guess I'd better make myself pleasant to some of those young things. They've got the roving eye that hunts out partners. Can't let the young things down. He smiled to himself.

Esther's happiness was dying hard. Every now and again in her life little prayers welled from her heart without her consciously knowing she was praying.

'Let him want to dance with me,' she prayed now. 'Let him turn and ask me to dance quickly, as soon as the music starts, so we don't sit here in this sad silence . . .'

The music started and two couples immediately jumped up. Oliver dropped his cigarette butt on to the floor and put his foot on it. Esther stirred, half turned to him.

'See that girl over there in the pink dress,' Oliver said. 'The one with the red cheeks? I'm going to dance with *her*.'

He stood up, walked across the deck and spoke to the girl.

The people on either side of Esther were already on their feet. She sat alone, the cold wind of dying youth blowing all around her. She felt as if Oliver had hit her.

For a few minutes she watched him dancing with the girl in the pink dress. He was laughing and the girl was giggling. Both of them had forgotten Esther. It was as if someone had shouted to her, 'You're out. You're finished.'

She sat erect, the frozen smile of the wallflowers on a mouth that had never lost its lovely curves.

The music ended and Oliver took the girl back to her group of friends. He stood laughing and talking with them a moment, then came back to Esther. He sat down beside her, smiling.

'Golly, she's a talker, that one.' he said. 'Make a guess at what she does for a living? A milliner. What do you know!' and he laughed.

'She has a pretty dress.' Esther said. The smile began to make the muscles in her cheek ache.

'The colour's all right,' Oliver said. 'I wouldn't know about the rest. You would.'

'You would too, Oliver.' Esther said. 'You've always known when a woman is well dressed, or not well dressed.'

'Yes. But I don't know what it is about a dress, other than the colour, that makes it smart. What makes that dress smart?'

'The cut,' Esther said briefly, still smiling.

He glanced again at her. She was about the smartest woman on the ship, anyway. Why did he have to worry about who was well dressed? One thing about Esther . . . she always looked good!

He smoked another cigarette in silence.

The music started again.

'This time I'm going to dance with the girl in the blue dress,' he said. 'The one with the curly hair, and damn the cut of the dress.'

He put out his cigarette and went across the deck to the girl in the blue dress.

Esther sat alone for a few minutes. Then quietly she got up and went below.

Now, these years afterwards, she noticed Oliver's hair-line receding a little. She felt sorry, but there was only slight pain in her sorrow.

Oliver ate his dinner in preoccupied silence. Esther asked him if he had anything on his mind.

'Yep,' he said. 'I'll tell you about it when I've sorted it out.'

Esther spent the rest of the meal talking to John about his school affairs. Oliver half-listened. One thing about Esther, he thought, she's a wonderful mother. Always up to date with John's affairs. Wish to God I had more time for the boy myself. Ought to buck in and be a good father. When I start building that thing at the bottom of the cliff I'll get the kid interested.

He didn't have to worry about getting Esther interested, he thought. Esther was always up to scratch on everything. Made a wonderful job of the house and entertaining and that sort of thing. Wonderful how calm she was. Where the hell did she get that quiet serenity, he wondered. She must have depths, but no one would suspect them. Take Laura now. You only had to look at Laura's face to know the bottom of the deepest ocean was her limit mark.

'Got it!' he said suddenly. 'Got it! Got it! Got it!' He slapped his left hand down on the table and pushed his chair back. He let out a crackle of laughter. 'I was thinking of something else, damn it . . . or wasn't I? . . . and all of a sudden the solution throws up like Krakatoa. Einstein on the bridge – no less.'

'You mean the volcano that made a mountain in the ocean in one night?' John said eagerly.

'Exactly what I do mean, son.' He turned to Esther, forgetful of the fact she knew nothing of the events of the day. 'Old

Man Coole pays his subscription on the second last day of the month so the lousy sum can earn its pittance of interest in his own bank for the month. See it? Pays on the thirtieth. Received at the Club on the thirty-first. Paid in to the bank any time in the next two or three days . . . which makes it one month on.'

'Well, what of it?' Esther asked calmly.

'Subscriptions to the Yacht Club are due on the first of March. His cheque doesn't get credited until the first of the next month. For one glorious summer month Bernard Coole is not financial as a member of the Club. Got it?'

'Does it matter?' Esther asked again quietly. She was spooning ice-cream with a small hand-beaten silver spoon.

'You bet it does,' said Oliver. *'You bet it does.'*

He almost sprang into the sun-room and reached for the telephone.

CHAPTER FIVE

Laura stood at the corner of the Highway and the Terrace, waiting for the bus. The war had killed any sense of indignity in waiting for a bus. Years in Ireland with a car or jaunting car at her service might ordinarily have killed any enthusiasm for bus travelling in Australia. The war had virtually done away with civilian cars and even here in Australia there was still a shortage with a high priority for professional services and business people.

There were all sorts of ramifications to her invested interests, each of which posed a problem . . . to uproot it all and take it back to Ireland, or was this really the land of promise and would it be wiser to leave her interests here? Her father and her sister had their graves here in this strange vast country. Her husband and her home were in Ireland. Here was indeed a dilemma for the human feelings. It had everything to do with the intellect and nothing to do with a certain pair of sardonic brown eyes.

When Laura went to Perth she made a day of it, beginning with the putting on of her hat, the drawing on of her gloves and the leisurely waiting for the once-an-hour bus that ran outside her aunt's residence, or walking around the dark asphalted road between the ancient gums and up the gentle sloping hill to the Highway where she might catch a bus within ten minutes.

Laura liked the walk. She felt alone after the hustle and bustle of her aunt's house where every Montgomery in the world found it necessary to ring up before breakfast wash-up was completed to enquire after Aunt Helen, or demand her presence in child sickness or to tell some funny anecdote about someone who was met the night before. There was no end to the comings and goings and ringings-up of the five Montgomery cousins.

Why can't they stay still in their own houses? Laura, who hated noise of any kind, asked herself. But she knew the answer. They were a gregarious lot and their mother was one . . . if not the very centre . . . of their curious community life. They had a positive fever to know how Aunt Helen was getting on every day.

'For goodness' sake,' she once said to Theodora. 'Why doesn't one of you ring up and then pass the news around? That telephone is a positive tyrant.'

But Theodora had laughed and shaken her head.

'That's what Mama says but she doesn't really believe it. She likes us all ringing her up. It reminds her she is not forgotten.'

'Forgotten! Good heavens! Let one of them have a sore throat or a cut on the finger . . . Ring up Mama. Let one of them give an afternoon tea party . . . Ring up Mama and tell Mama "to wear the blue hat with the pink roses and not that abortion of a thing she made in the millinery school, but don't say I said so".'

They were all mad, Laura thought, but didn't know whether she envied or deplored that particular form of community madness.

Aunt Helen would impatiently call her house 'The Nunnery' when they foregathered there, which was several times a week, but Laura felt the calm quiet and solitude of the convent only when she went through the front door and walked quietly up the gum-scented road, through the tree-bowered park to the bus stop.

Laura was not thinking of these things as she stood, one toe pointing down over the concrete edge of the footpath and one gloved finger unconsciously drawing a little pattern on the polished surface of her handbag. She wore the tailored blue linen dress and the wide-brimmed hat that made her look as if she had just stepped out of *Vogue* and not a madhouse at all.

Her eyes wandered down the lower part of the Terrace which

turned into the river drive . . . the way to Oliver's house.

Even when thinking with irritation of her cousins, or with businesslike consideration of her Australian investments, there was an underflow of thought that really governed her whole life at the moment.

Oliver. If only she could get rid of him from her mind. Uproot him. Cast him out.

As Laura stood, one toe pointing down over the edge of the footpath, one finger polishing the cover of her handbag, with unseeing eyes looking down the street that led to the one place on the map of her unconscious mind, her head cried out against herself. 'He is brash, bold, vainglorious. He is ambitious and uses other people ruthlessly and without conscience to achieve his personal ambition. What have I, Laura Montgomery, to do with a man like that? A deep gulf divides our two existences. He is not a person for me to cultivate.' Thus her head. But her heart knew a secret relationship that was rich in hope yet heavy with dread.

There was suddenly the pressure of unshed tears behind her eyes. For one second she had a glimpse into her own secret being. She was proud, independent, selfish, and she could not still the rapid beating of her unquiet heart.

She sacrificed herself with her pride. He was common, bold, cruel. Ah, that she had come to such a pitch; such a place and time. Dear God, if she could only wrench her thoughts away, and keep them elsewhere.

Others standing there waiting for the bus might have remarked the beautiful young woman, dressed in the ultimate of quiet good taste, a shadowed loveliness in her incredibly dark-blue eyes, might have chosen her as one of the world's darlings, the privileged chosen few who toiled not neither did they spin.

One of deeper perception might have noticed the troubled mobile mouth, the toe that pointed down over the edge of the footpath, and the white-gloved finger that moved ceaselessly over the surface of her handbag.

As it happened a dozen times a day Laura, having gone down into the pit, slowly climbed to the surface again. She shook her head slightly and looked diagonally across the road to the pine tree that grew behind the Council Chambers. When she was a little girl it had been a small tree tied to a post to keep it straight during the years of its willowy sapling youth. How all the trees in the park had grown! How long ago was it? Dear heaven! she thought. Don't *count*. One will be old enough soon enough.

The bus was coming down the big hill a quarter of a mile away. She hoped there would be seating for all those standing about waiting for it.

Her eyes strayed again down that street. The big blue car swept around the distant corner and soared up the rise, towards the place where she stood, as effortlessly as if the car was not with high power but without it altogether. Her heart stood stock still, it seemed not to beat. Then it hammered as it began to beat again.

As Oliver swept across the cross-roads he saw her. The car screamed to a braking stop half a dozen yards beyond the corner.

Laura had to turn that corner and meet him. The bus was two stops away. To lower her eyes and turn away would be a coyness so out of character Oliver would have known what was in her heart.

He leaned across the vacant passenger's seat and opened the door for her.

'I'm just going up to the post office,' he said. 'Then I'll drive you into Perth.'

His brown eyes smiled with their mesmerising challenge. Laura wanted to strike out at him with a frenzied hand; instead she too smiled as she got in the car.

'Thank you, Oliver,' she said. 'A much more comfortable way to go to Perth than in the bus.'

Neither of them saw the thickset man with a brown shabby suit, thick-soled shoes and thick-lensed eye-glasses standing against the wall of the chemist's shop, watching them. Nor Miss Martin, a lady totally unknown to them, approaching the shabby thickset man.

'Good morning, Mr Firmingham,' Miss Martin said, at her birdlike best. Then she turned saucy, not a pretty sight in a drab little woman of fifty. 'Now just what were you watching with such interest then?' She wagged a finger at him. 'Oliver Harding's very swagger car, was it? Or could it have been the dashing Laura Montgomery?'

Mr Firmingham did not have to answer or return Miss Martin's salutations for her voice sped on, pouring out the chicken feed of gossip that she constantly garnered only to spill forth uninvited as fast as her overcrowded mind could operate for her.

'Well, of course I don't blame you looking. That's the second time this week I've seen her in his car. One would think she waited for him here rather than round the river there where Mrs Harding might see them. And did you read in the paper she was at his house at that big party he had a fortnight ago? Dear me, Mr Firmingham, what is the world coming to? Right in Mrs Harding's own house too. Under her eyes. The goings-on in Pepper Tree Bay since the war! My word, Mr Firmingham, times have changed. Just imagine Miss Lacey Coole going to parties round at those flashy houses on the East Side. Mr Coole must really be getting on . . .'

· Not once did Mr Firmingham speak or stem the flow by a gesture. Instead he watched the little poison-tongued lady through glasses so thick it made his eyes appear to her no bigger than pin-points.

'Mrs Simmins . . .' Miss Martin continued at so rapid a pace Mr Firmingham knew she did not wish her flow to be inter-rupted until she had eased her mind of its burden. '. . . the housekeeper, you know. She's my best friend. Well, she told me Miss Lacey had a new dress for the party. She must have wanted to go if she wanted to make an impression, didn't you think? Mrs Simmins was quite sure Mr Coole didn't know where she was going. Not that she's not old enough to please herself, of course. But really that Oliver Harding now, he's a rich man, thinks he can do anything he likes with people like the Montgomerys and the Cooles. How can they be taken in? What do you think, Mr Firmingham? Running the whole town, that's what they say, Mr Firmingham.'

Mr Firmingham never told anyone, not even his wife, what he thought but at the moment he was well aware that Miss Martin was not interested in what he thought in any event. She didn't want to be interrupted by any comment from him. She wanted to go on and on . . . the babbling brook.

'He's just a Casanova . . . it is Casanova, isn't it, Mr Firming-ham? The man who went round collecting all the ladies' hearts? Of course I'm not as educated as all that but I did see a picture called that. It was about a man who was just a common lady-killer. That is a wonderful car, of course, and it may be that and not just Oliver Harding himself. And dear Mr Firmingham, did you hear the new preacher at the Gospel Church has seven children? Seven children to keep on that stipend. Well, I ask you . . .'

Mr Firmingham was not interested in the preacher, his seven children or his stipend. Miss Martin had finished the interesting part of her discourse as far as he was concerned.

'Excuse me, Miss Martin,' he said in his cold antagonising tones. He did not lift his hat as he turned and walked heavily but purposely down towards the corner and around it into the Highway.

'What a boorish brute that man is,' Miss Martin muttered as she turned into the chemist's shop.

There she immediately encountered another acquaintance. She began to talk at once, this time of Mr Firmingham. 'A positive miser, you know . . .' she said.

Oliver set Laura down in the main street of Perth. She turned and retraced her footsteps about thirty yards to enter an arcade.

Oliver put up his hand and adjusted the rear-vision mirror so that he could watch her retreating figure. In the bevy of people hurrying or sauntering hither and thither along the city pavement Laura's figure was quite outstanding. She had well-set shoulders, a long narrow back with beautiful legs and ankles. The blue linen suit fitted her exactly and she walked like a model, without swaying. It seemed as if, for a fraction of a second, she hesitated before she turned into the arcade. Almost as if she would turn round first to watch Oliver drive away.

She did not turn and Oliver readjusted the rear-vision mirror and released the brake as the car went into movement automatically. There was a touch of ironic humour in his eyes as he smiled to himself. Then he wondered irritably why watching Laura walking away along the footpath had had a touch of sadness about it. Something to do with himself doubtless. The old nostalgic memories of a bunch of kids in Pepper Tree Bay a hundred years ago. Or was it only twenty-five or thirty? What a missy Laura had been with her disdainful airs and her English-Irish accent! She would never speak to him, Oliver, except when she came down to the back of the Rectory garden to demand over the fence into the caretaker's garden that Danny come home to tea. Then she'd married Danny. Well, Oliver supposed, it was on the cards even when they were kids. He allowed himself the cynical wonder as to what sort of bedmates would Danny and Laura be.

The sight of Harvey backing his car into the car-park behind the administration block took his mind off Laura.

He was going to lose Harvey. He could tell it by the way Harvey walked as he got out of his car, let the door slam itself shut, and go towards the staff entrance. Harvey hadn't looked to the right as Oliver swung his car in.

'I guess he'll tell me this morning,' Oliver thought. 'I hope it hasn't gone to his raking head. I might lose my temper and tell him I got that raking job for him at Banfold and Co. Then that 'ud spoil the whole bloody works. I only got it for him because he deserved it, and even I don't like breaking a decent man's heart.'

When he went upstairs to his office his secretary was waiting for him.

'There were three calls for you shortly after nine o'clock, Mr Harding.'

She never allowed herself to smile back at Oliver the way he smiled at her when he came in. He always smiled as if together they were a huge joke; as if business was a huge joke; as if, in coming in, he was about to set the whole joke-works into operation again.

Miss Weston knew, however, that Harding Motors and all the other concerns in which Oliver was interested were not jokes. Many a time she took pleasure in thrusting under his glance an item of information that would have the effect of wiping that smile from his face. It was like pulling down a blind against the sunshine outside the window.

What's more, she knew that two people in one room can't joke and get the amount of work done that Oliver expected to be done. One of them had to keep up the appearance of sober interest in affairs. So Miss Weston took this duty upon herself. She looked sober and only occasionally smiled. Which was, of course, the reason why Oliver joked.

'Well, you run along and get on with your knitting, Miss Weston, while I do a spot of ringing up,' he said. This was Oliver's standard witticism when the typists were at their most rushed and busiest.

Miss Weston gave him the deprecatory glance he expected so he added sparkle to his smile and she went out of the door.

She put her head back inside.

'Harvey Dalton's waiting to see you,' she said.

'Okay, send him in.' Oliver, hat now on the peg in the corner, was already reaching for the phone. As he dialled a number he nodded to Harvey. 'Take a seat, old man,' he said. 'I'll be about five minutes on this job.'

The voice at the other end of his line said 'Hallo!' in the tones that sang through the wires and addressed even Harvey's ears.

'O. Harding,' Oliver said into the mouthpiece. 'Listen, feller,

I've got Ellison at the Yacht Club to call a special committee meeting at the end of the week. I'll tell you why. I'm going east on Monday and if we can get those orders for the steel for the slipways through in time I can see about them personally while I'm over there. I'll guarantee to get a twenty-per-cent cut . . . or bust. How about it? . . . Right! Incidentally, Ellison can tag on to the agenda one or two other small items that might have stood over. The next meeting won't be so damn cluttered up then . . . You bet! That next meeting will take all night. We've got to map out the plan for next season's ocean yacht races. Best get rid of the fiddly stuff at a short one like this one coming up. Okay? . . . Oh, I don't know there's anything important. Two or three new members voted in. I've got one up myself . . . the rise in wages for the bartenders. We got to do that; the basic wage has gone up. Just a matter of form. Formally appoint that new chef. Just routine stuff to clear the agenda and get rid of the tag ends. Okay? . . . Right, feller, I'll see you Friday night.'

Harvey sat on his chair watching Oliver's broad strong hand with the faint down of red hair on the back as his pencil doodled on the blotting paper while he talked into the mouthpiece. Harvey was glad Oliver was doing some telephoning. It gave him time to control his breathing. His heart had been thumping clumsily when he'd come to the door to see if Oliver would see him.

Harvey had several times rehearsed what he was going to say to Oliver, but each rehearsal had found him saying something different. Anyhow, he was going to get into it all he felt about his service and devotion that had been passed over by O. Harding Esquire. For the first time in his life he was going to make a fool of O. Harding by waving his new job in front of him. A big firm like Banfold and Co. had gone after him. Had, in fact, come to him and sought his services. He was just waiting to see Oliver's face when he, Harvey, told him *that*. He was going to get a whole bloody lot off his chest.

Oliver put down the receiver, put both hands palms down on the edge of his table and tilted back his chair. His smile was friendly and bland.

'Well, what goes on?' he asked.

Unexpectedly, considering all the rehearsals, words dried up in Harvey's throat. He coughed. Then in desperation he hunted in his inside pocket and brought out the final letter from Richard Bardon appointing him as Supervisor of Country Sales for the agency end of Banfold and Co.

Oliver took the letter and read it. Then he looked up directly into Harvey's eyes.

'It's only left for me to congratulate you, Harvey,' he said quietly. 'Banfold and Co. is a big firm. A bigger firm than I'll ever be. Why, man, it's got ramifications through five States.' He shook his head and then sighed. 'Well,' he said sadly, 'I suppose my loss is their gain.'

Harvey was still wordless. The interview was not going the way he had made it go in any one of the rehearsals. Oliver was expected to look staggered, to protest.

Oliver now reached across the table with his left hand. There was nothing left for Harvey to do but shake hands with him.

'I've never made it hard for a man to get a better job,' Oliver said. 'Any time you want a word from me, Harvey, I'm ready to say you're the best salesman I've ever had. That's a promise. If this is a blow to me it's the kind of blow every man has got to take now and again. I'm not going to debate with you. You know how I feel. You go with the best will in the world. Incidentally, I don't give long-service leave by compulsion but I feel morally bound to give it when it has been deserved. You'll take it in cash, I suppose? Banfolds is probably impatient to get you and won't be anxious to wait six months for you. I'll see the accountant about it now. You want to quit now?'

Oliver stood up and walked to the door with Harvey. At the door Harvey spoke his first and last words as a servant of Harding Motors Ltd.

He coughed.

'Thanks very much, Oliver,' he said. He felt hot around the neck band and his knees were inclined to weakness as he walked down the corridor with his late boss and listened to him expounding about the qualities of March weather for ocean sailing.

'An east wind . . .' Oliver was saying. 'Can't get into too much trouble with an easterly when you're under sail. A nor'-wester now . . . Say, Harvey, you ought to join a yacht club some time. With a river and climate like ours . . .'

Half an hour later Oliver asked Miss Weston to arrange his air ticket to Melbourne for the following Monday evening.

She looked at him in surprise.

'But . . .'

He spread his hands, eyebrows raised and the sardonic smile in his eyes.

'There are no *buts*, my dear Miss Weston. I've got to be

94

away as an excuse to get an extra Club meeting in before the end of the month. One of these stylised rigged affairs with only me knowing why. So I've just got to go away some place. I might as well go where I can do a bit of good, a bit of business, and get the Taxation Department to cover the expense. Aren't I cunning?'

Oliver always said 'Aren't I cunning?' when he knew he would be successful over some deal.

All the same, Miss Weston did not approve of his going away in the interests of the Yacht Club. Business, thought Miss Weston naïvely, should always come first.

'That Riley Scott again,' she said in a told-you-so voice.

Oliver nodded lugubriously.

'The things I do for England . . .' he said.

Miss Weston did not know the quotation so she did not see the point. She had not met Riley Scott but already she was tired of him. Mr Harding spent far too much of his time doing things in which the name Riley Scott kept cropping up. She approved of nothing except Harding Motors Ltd and of nobody except O. Harding, Managing Director.

The secretary of the Yacht Club didn't like it, but there was no gainsaying Oliver Harding when he had his feet set on a certain path. Harding was going to travel that way and in his own style. Nothing would stop him.

'All right, we pass these fellows through at a special meeting convened for other matters,' Ellison said. 'Then what? We bury their names in the general membership list. How do I know Mr Coole won't ask me what happened to Mr Scott's nomination; or ask to see the new membership list when it comes out?'

'Coole's not the kind of person to lower his façade far enough to appear anxious for news. If he ever does ask he'll bide his time. It won't occur to him anyone would cross his veto and he'll have to go to a court of law to prove he's still a member though unfinancial. Okay.' He waved a hand to prevent the secretary interrupting him. 'Precedent says we've kept him a member year in, year out, when he's regularly been unfinancial for the month of March. Look up your constitution, old man. It provides for a three-months' dalliance about paying subscriptions but specifically says no unfinancial member may hold office, vote or represent the Club *while he's unfinancial.*'

'I've read it,' Mr Ellison said wearily. 'You're legally right, Oliver. But the rest of the Club is going to ask why you resorted to these tactics. They're going to have a second look at the new member. Oliver . . . for God's sake . . . Coole hasn't got anything on Scott, has he? Any reason the other members would accept as valid for blackmailing a chap?'

'Son of a poor family. No particular background. So what! I fit the same pattern myself and I'll tell you two other committee members who fit it and about half the present membership list. You won't get a sympathetic hearing on that one except from the old brigade. And they can't run an expensive club like this without us. Right?'

'You think those are Mr Coole's reasons?'

'I don't know of any other.'

But did he? Riley Scott's life was an open book as far as he, Oliver, was concerned. But what of those two lost years? God almighty, he'd just have to ask Riley about them. Anyhow, if there had been anything in them Old Man Coole would never have known about it. His kind didn't know the Scotts of Pepper Tree Bay existed.

That ruddy committee meeting would be over by nine o'clock. He'd go round to Riley's house afterwards to congratulate him on being elected. Riley 'ud give him a drink. They'd talk.

It was nine-thirty on the Friday night when Oliver pulled his big car into Riley Scott's driveway. The new house had got its four outside walls well up and Riley's light was showing in the converted four-roomed wooden house on the river side of the block.

It was an old disused house the architect had planned to demolish when he drew the designs for the new brick and stone house. Riley had said no. He'd take out its insides and convert it to a kind of summer pavilion. He'd done this himself with some hired labour for help.

'Don't know why you don't feel you're falling over the cliff in this place,' Oliver said when Riley answered his knock.

Oliver walked to the open window with its propped open shutters.

'Golly,' he said. 'On second thoughts I can see your point, old man. Up here you feel as if you're right out on the river. And this effect is like the deck of a ship.'

Riley pulled up another easy chair and they sat down looking out over the Bay.

'What will you drink, Oliver?' Riley asked.

'Scotch and . . .' Oliver said.

While Riley went to a cabinet and got out the drinks Oliver

96

turned in his chair and watched him.

'You got elected to the Yacht Club tonight,' he said. 'How's that for fast work?'

From where he sat he could see the slight smile that curved Riley's mouth.

'It seems to have been the case of a man who knows a man,' Riley said. 'Nepotism run riot. But thanks a lot, Oliver.'

'Well, don't you grizzle. You're the fellow who's in and not on the waiting list.'

Golly, he's strong, Oliver thought as he looked at Riley's arm and hand as he passed the bottle of whisky. Those shoulders, and his throat. It's a wonder the women haven't got after him. Wonder if he'll marry now he's settled, and the raking war's over.

Aloud he said, 'I guess you got those muscle ripples felling trees down the south-west. Tell me, Riley, did you ever climb one of those two hundred and fifty feet karri trees?'

'Oh yes. You don't work down there in the forestry business without climbing one some time or other. Even if you don't want to, you got to. Prestige with the other fellows.'

'Golly!' Oliver said as he thought of the wonder of climbing without ropes those giant trees. 'How old were you when you went up your first?'

'Seventeen,' Riley said. 'You can do anything at seventeen that you're not game to do when you're thirty-seven.'

'I guess you went up a few trees up there on commando tactics on the island.'

Riley Scott smiled.

'It was my long suit,' he said. 'But then I knew how.'

Oliver nodded.

Riley had said he was seventeen when he'd first gone up a tree. That was one of the lost years. On the casual information Riley had given earlier he'd said he'd gone down the forest country when he was about eighteen.

A feller doesn't always get exact dates and years right when he's telling his life history. And you can't grill a man like Riley Scott. You can't grill a feller who'd spent half his childhood in an orphanage. It was like suggesting he wasn't good enough. The old tag . . . 'An orphanage kid'. You couldn't rub it in.

He'd stake his chips on Riley and ask no more raking questions. If there was something Riley Scott was keeping back . . . and Oliver hadn't dealt with men on the top levels of business and the more adventurous and courageous levels of soldiering without sensing when a man withheld something . . . that it was because it was private, and in the place where it lived it was sore. He'd stake his chips on Riley and stake his own career on his judgment of a man.

'What appeals to you in civic politics?' Oliver asked abruptly. 'It's generally hard to get a good bloke like you to stand for the Council.'

'I guess I like the idea of having roots,' Riley answered.

Oliver noticed that the tablet on which Riley had sketched the ketch was now face down on the table. The back of it was a jumble of miniature drawings. They were the occupation of an idle pencil in idle fingers while waiting for telephone calls. Oliver wasn't the only man in Pepper Tree Bay who doodled.

He had once taken a sheet of his own blotting paper and framed it. It looked like a psychopath's nightmare and it had intrigued Oliver himself. None of it made sense yet all of it was interesting. Cubes, triangles, circles, beautifully patternised. What did it mean, anyway?

Riley's network of pencil wanderings was much more decorative.

Oliver felt now, as he had felt when he had first taken up the matter with Riley, there was a thought-out set purpose in the practical manner in which Riley set about putting his roots down in Pepper Tree Bay.

It was he who had first given Oliver the idea of a promenade. He had discussed with him the architectural plans he had for the concreting of the shore at the bottom of his own cliff and simply stated, 'It's the kind of construction the other houses could easily adopt and with which they could join up. Who knows? In time they might all do it along the Bay frontage. See what I mean?'

Oliver had seen very clearly, and further. He'd seen it running along the river shore from Perth to Fremantle. A riverside drive.

Riley went to get more ice for the drinks. Oliver picked up the writing tablet and looked not at the drawing of the ketch but at the doodling. There was a necklace of miniature fine drawings around the edge of the page. Oliver amused himself interpreting them. There was a palm tree with an anchor at its foot. the anchor chain winding like a snake up the tree trunk. That Oliver interpreted as some dream that one day Riley would sail his ketch . . . or would it be a sloop by then? . . . up into the tropic seas which had been the scene of his activities during the war. There was a miniature schoolroom scene and the silhouette of his own car. There was the unadorned outline of a girl's head and shoulders and oddly enough Oliver found that to be rather moving. There was nothing but the outline. He wondered who, if any, of Riley's female acquaintances had a silhouette so perfect in its symmetry and quite beautiful in its hint of something that was at once pride and meditation and humility.

Riley was juggling the ice in a jug and saying something about the different brands of Scotch whisky a man was now able to buy. Oliver grunted his reply.

The simple single-line silhouette of the girl's head and shoulders fascinated him. Perhaps it was more of a woman than of a girl. Only youth could have so pure and flowing a line, yet the slight inclination of the head implied the downward meditative glance. Oliver tried, out of his ignorance of this particular art, to read what it was that gave the impression of beauty.

Riley came back to the chairs and Oliver pointed to the small drawing with the tip of his pencil.

'The back must be straight for the head and shoulders to be carried that way. That's why she looks proud. Yet she's looking down with only the slightest inclination of the head, isn't she? She's got a beautiful line of the throat and shoulder. This something you dreamed up, old man? Or is she really somebody?'

Riley, the jug of ice still in one hand and a glass in the other, leaned over his chair to look at his own drawings. Oliver, glancing up, saw the expression in his eyes was first one of astonishment and then of an embarrassed curiosity, almost as if he had not known he had drawn that thing and now that he did was finding it incredible, a disturbing mystery, even to himself. It was the drawing of it that was the mystery, not the girl.

Oliver felt like saying a knowing 'Ah!' but Riley's reserve forbade it.

'I'll have a double one, thanks, old man,' Oliver said.

He put the tablet back on the table. As he leaned forward to take up his glass he noticed the bottom drawing of the frieze. It was the top of a walking stick, the head of which was a dingo dog stretched out in the action of running, the head showing the shadings of a beautiful piece of carving.

Now where the devil had he seen a walking stick with that dingo's head? Oliver searched his memory. He'd seen it somewhere.

A man's doodlings were the private excrescences of his soul.

Oliver was already sorry he had examined these as keenly as he had. He decided against asking Riley where he got the idea of drawing a walking stick that way.

'That sort of thing is little short of a Rorshach test,' Riley said as he tore off the sheet of paper, crumpled it and threw it in the waste-paper basket.

Half an hour later, when Oliver was leaving, Riley preceded him out of the door to turn on the outside light. Oliver stooped and picked the piece of crumpled paper from the basket and put it in his pocket.

He wasn't being so scrupulous about delving into Riley's psychology, after all. And he knew it. The man fascinated him in a way.

CHAPTER SIX

My mother leaned back in her armchair, her hands lay stretched along the arm rest.

'I'm tired,' she said. Then with a note of query asked, 'Is it tiring weather do you think, Theodora?'

I was darning Barty's socks and I answered without looking up.

'Everybody's tired, Mama. March finishes everybody off in this climate. Wait till the really cold weather comes . . .'

'But I do feel cold. Is it as cold as all that today, Theodora?'

Mama did look a little tired but not any more than she often did after one of her rounds of enthusiasm with some hard-luck society bent on good works. I looked back at my darning and then looked up again. There had been something odd about Mama's eyes.

I knew what it was then. Way down in them, down long tunnels of thought, was the infinitesimal lurking fear of old age. Mama had never mentioned such a thing. None of us had. But she thought about it. Yes, I could see that. With a pang of sudden enlightenment I, too, suffered for her. For an instant I felt as if I had been hit between the eyes myself.

She must grow old and die. It couldn't be so very far distant. One had simply never thought of it before. Mama was so energetic, so filled with the ebullience of youth. She had so much yet to do. She hadn't finished with life. No indeed, not for a long long time. The world had yet to be put to rights and her five daughters, all hovering round the forties, had not yet had their upbringing finished. They hadn't been taught how to bring up their own children. And there was Gerry without a husband. And Laura needed someone to help her over a certain stile. Mama did not believe any woman should be without a husband. 'It's the companionship,' she would say. If we hadn't been thoughtless we might have pondered on those words. For the greater part of her life our mother had been without a husband. It hadn't occurred to any one of us she might have felt the omission in life. She hadn't mentioned it so we had not thought of it.

Why, I wondered, had Mama had that fear today? Was she any more tired than usual after a special hum of activities? Why should she feel cold?

Suddenly I was angry with her. Mama looked very well. There was going to be no grave-digging in the Montgomery family just because she felt tired. But how did I tell her? How let her know I guessed what that pale spectral light down the depths of her eyes meant?

'Mama,' I said with some emphasis. 'I'm dog tired and I'm stone cold. Everyone is. Life's too energetic these days. Stop being sorry for yourself.'

The telephone rang and Mama got up and went to it. Life and love of life flooded back through her whole being.

'Of course, Mrs Roundell . . . of course. Of course.'

The Women's Aid again! But mother was her old self.

When she came back to her chair it was with paper and pencil, and she sat listing names and addresses and saying to me, 'I feel galvanised into life again when I'm wanted. I feel like a giant refreshed by rain when there's work to be done.' These two expressions Mama had used to exhort us all our lives. Now I knew she was exhorting herself. 'What do you think Mrs Roundell told me? They're thinking of reclaiming part of the river to build that promenade round the Bay. They can't fit it in under the cliffs. They've actually got the impertinence to think they can move the river in order to build a bridge and a road.'

'But Mama,' I said with docility, 'you do know who the "they" is, don't you? Oliver Harding and Company. The Council is in a fifty-fifty vote on it and they're going to run Riley Scott in the new election to push the decision over the line for them.'

'What?'

'You heard me, Mama. What's more, you told Oliver you'd help him.'

'I did nothing of the sort. I told Oliver I'd help him about some stoneworks at the bottom of his own garden. I didn't tell him, nor anyone else, the Bay could be touched.'

I sighed.

'I thought he'd got you on your blind side.'

Mama's back straightened.

'Just where do you stand in this matter, may I ask?'

'Oh, I'm all for the Bay, Mama. I want Barty to play in the fish pools as we did. All the same, you'd better know now, we've all been going to the Bay Improvement group that Oliver's got going on the East Side. And, Mama darling, just let me get in before Mrs Roundell. It's no good calling them communists and saying they're paid by Moscow. They're all rich business men and wealthy doctors. Capitalism is their citadel.'

'Why do you bring politics into everything?'

'So as to prevent Mrs Roundell doing it first.'

Mama said 'Pshaw!' in the extremes of impatience. She went on eagerly listing names and addresses.

'There,' she said at length. 'Now you be a dear and type that list out for me. Could you do it by tomorrow? And I think I need about twenty copies.'

'Listen,' I cried in exasperation. 'I've got a hundred things to do by tomorrow. And how can I go to Oliver's parties and at the same time do the typing that's going to provide the ammunition for the other side? That's treachery.'

'You should mind the company you keep.' And Mama picked up her needle and work. She was young again. The blood coursed freely in her veins and there was the lust for life and battle in her eyes. She dug her needle into her work as if she were impaling all the Oliver Hardings in the world.

'If he comes round here again,' she said aloud because she was in truth thinking of Oliver, 'I'll box his ears. Reclaiming on the river banks! Who does he think he is? Mahommed?'

'It's a river he's thinking of moving, not a mountain, Mama,' I answered.

It was the following evening that we all met at Bill Collings's house. He and his wife, Beth, were already bulldozing the old tree stumps and the elephant grass at the bottom of their block to bring the concreting on Riley's shoreline along their own waterfront.

The boys, as Bill Collings called his other forty-year-old neighbours, were crazy to get going. Dash it all, they'd have something to beat Monte Carlo and the Isle of Capri before they'd finished!

Moreover, they had quickly and readily constituted themselves an electioneering group to get Riley Scott into the Council. The State Government could build a Narrows bridge but the local Road Boards and Councils held the control of their own part of the river. The Government could not act without the will of the local Council.

Oliver's visionary plan was to have its foundation in Pepper Tree Bay.

Those of us who gathered at Bill Collings's house were for the most part those who had been at Oliver's party. Even Lacey Coole was with us. For one thing Vicky was still ordering Lacey's social life for her but for another, one felt that Lacey liked all these comings and goings and bursts of enthusiasm. She had never encountered it before. She had been associated with those whose sole preoccupation had been a maintaining of the *status quo*. Now she was caught in the ebb and flow of a group who wanted to do new things, and who, by doing them, were obviously flying in the face of the die-hards who had pronounced against them.

This meeting in Bill Collings's house was not a party, although I don't know why it wasn't called one, except that no one wore party clothes. That was the only difference between it and Oliver's party. The food, the drink, the gaiety flowed. The meeting consisted of Bill Collings making a speech beginning with 'Well, I say, you people, you know what we're here for . . .' and Oliver making a speech beginning with some remarks that were ripely flattering to the women present. They were true so they delighted the women, and clever so that they pleased the husbands. Then Riley Scott made a speech telling us why he was standing for the Council and that the main aim of his platform would be the river foreshore.

While Bill spoke we laughed at his naïvety which he managed to turn into a pantomime. While Oliver talked we laughed and rolled our eyes at one another and said 'Oh Oliver!' in a deprecatory way but with the warmth of affection flushing our cheeks. Only for Riley were we utterly silent.

It wasn't because we were that much interested in local politics. It was just that there was something arresting about his personality that made one sit in silence in order to digest all the striking things about him. There was his voice that was cast a tone lower than either Bill's or Oliver's voices. It drawled softly too. It was a nice voice. Good, firm and masculine, yet with an odd soft note that betrayed its very masculinity, almost as if somewhere there was an alien spot in the apple of Riley's heart. This was in contradistinction to his eyes which were a warm blue but which had a hard flint-like core. Perhaps it was these unusual paradoxes that made him unusual.

Lacey Coole who was sitting at an angle over to my right had looked up when Riley first stood up and then she sat, perfectly still, her back not touching the back rest of her chair, her hands in her lap and her head inclined a little forward and sideways so that she appeared to be either thinking or listening. Yet her eyelashes rested on her cheek as if her eyes were closed. Oddly enough, when you examined it, her position did not look rigid or strained. She looked like all the dear young ladies who used to sit in their drawing-rooms around Pepper Tree Bay when I was a child. They never leaned back in a chair, they never crossed their knees and they never looked anything but relaxed and very genteel.

Actually Lacey looked rather beautiful sitting there like that. Now that I had specifically noticed it, it occurred to me Lacey always sat like that . . . except she did not usually have her eyes glancing downwards.

'I bet her old granite-hearted father doesn't know she's here,' I whispered to Gerry. 'Who'd have thought Lacey Coole would have played truant from the West Side!'

'Did you see Oliver's face when he came in and saw her?' Gerry whispered back.

I nodded. When Oliver had come in Lacey had been talking with Vicky and Mary directly in front of the doorway. Oliver had pulled himself up short, and blinked. He had made a quite visible effort in recovering himself, and then he'd come on into the room, laughing, and gesturing with his left hand in his own inimitable style.

He said 'Hallo!' to my sisters and then added, 'Well, well, well . . . Miss Coole. And have they given you something heart-warming to drink? Glad you're here. Mighty glad you're here. You going to get a few votes for us round on the other side?'

Lacey had smiled and said, 'I don't know about that, but I'll try.'

Oliver had patted her on the shoulder, calling her a good girl, and then turned away to meet others.

Riley's speech was finished and everyone was laughing and talking together again. The meeting, such as it was, was over and the evening's pleasure was about to begin. Lacey stood up to speak to Beth Collings's mother, and then it was Lacey who was the unconscious centre of interest.

Others did not come up to speak to her yet one could see she was watched under curious and even envious eyelids. She would never, I decided, pass unnoticed in a room. It wasn't just her good appearance. It was her air, the way she carried her head. She had personality and a certain proud simplicity.

Riley Scott was going round shaking hands with each person and speaking to them. A good politician, one thought, because he does it naturally yet never forgetting its purpose. One felt his determination under his pleasant manner and drawling voice.

When he was near Lacey he held out his hand and she lifted hers, but it was as if each was reluctant really to shake hands. Then when they did their hands stayed, clasped in one another's, a shade longer than was necessary.

'Miss Coole, I think?' Riley said, making his salute in the form of a question. His face looked stern and almost forbidding and for Lacey alone he did not smile. Yet his hand held hers.

'Yes. Lacey Coole,' she said. 'I think we did meet at Mr Harding's house, Mr Scott.'

'Yes, of course,' Riley said, still unsmiling, still looking cold and remote from her.

Lacey's head was uptilted that fraction of an inch that was necessary to look at a person taller than herself but it still was held at a slight inclined angle. In spite of the fact it was she who was looking up, the impression was given that she was the one who was proud and distant.

An odd meeting. Probably Riley sensed the impossibility of really winning a West Sider to his cause. He was being polite for politeness' sake. Possibly Lacey felt in meeting a politician she was meeting with a strange species.

Yet there was something more. Did each feel it was an affront to meet the other? Or was there between them the eternal question. Why you? Why *you*?

'This must be a field-day for the Montgomerys,' Oliver said, looking around at us all. 'I'd never have believed anyone could get you all at one moment in time on the same side of the political fence. How come, Theodora?'

'Don't count your chickens because they're in sight, Oliver.' I said. 'I'd like to see Riley Scott in the Council but blow you digging up the yellow sands around the Bay.'

'What ho! Have we got a renegade in our midst?'

'Not exactly. I don't really mind what you do to the Bay

twenty years hence. But right now I'd like it to stay the way it is. And so would Mama. Keep your feeling in rein, dear Oliver, while I tell you I today typed out the list of supporters for the Women's Progressive Association. They're on the war-path . . . and on your tail.'

Oliver roared with laughter. There must have been something of the Irishman in him for he loved a fight.

'The enemy's in sight at last,' he said. 'Don't shoot till you see the whites of their eyes. Mrs Roundell and Company, eh?' The thought of Mrs Roundell made him pass on to the next person, chuckling with delight.

Actually Mrs Roundell was far too self-serious to have provoked a chuckle from anyone but Oliver. When accused of being a militant feminist she had solemnly agreed that that was correct. The price of freedom was vigilance, she constantly cried. And one should not be armed unless one was prepared to strike.

Mama wasn't quite the same as Mrs Roundell. Mama believed in battling but she believed in feminine wiles instead of the tooth and claw. She believed that a woman should go to a women's political meeting in soft chiffons and with roses round her hat.

It was a pleasant party we had that evening, though right to the end it was maintained it was a meeting and not a party.

Meantime the Women's Progressive Association, plus the Women's Aid, had gone into print. Letters flooded the daily newspapers about the bridge over the Narrows, the reclaiming of the river bays. Excerpts from diaries held sacred in the Archives of the Pioneers' Association Library, and memories of what Lord Forrest had said in 1890, were given headlines.

The fight was on.

April passed into May.

The only Montgomery who abstained from the East Side 'meetings' was Laura. Nobody knew why Laura would not go but all five of her cousins guessed. It was all off with Oliver. Well, that was a good thing but who made the break? It would have been nice to know but less painful to remain in ignorance.

Oddly enough a friendship that was clearly and obviously platonic between Laura and Riley Scott burst upon our firmament. Those of us who knew Laura well . . . and don't forget we loved her too . . . marvelled that anything platonic could ever thrive between Laura and any man. But lo and behold, here was someone with whom she talked without once making an attempt to turn on the charm. One had an obscure feeling that there was a fellow feeling between the two. But what it was about no one knew or asked.

Also it had become noticeable in family circles that while Mama was vehement on the subject of the river and even more so on the subject of Oliver Harding, she fell silent when Riley Scott's name was mentioned. When on one occasion it was suggested that as Riley Scott was putting up for the Council and as Mother had a perfectly good vote he should call and see her, she shook her head and said quietly, 'I don't think he would want to come. It is better not.'

'But Mama,' we protested, 'you're against the river schemes but not against Riley for the Council. He ought to know that.'

Mama was biting her under-lip as she sewed. This time it was lampshades she was making. (One for each of us, she promised.) She did not look up.

'No,' she said. 'I don't think he'll come. And I don't want him to come.'

'But why? Are you afraid he'll convert you to the river road idea?'

Oddly enough this made her angry.

'He'd know better than to try.'

Now was not the time to be funny and ask her was he on Mrs Roundell's dossier of communists.

Gerry made the next comment.

'He's been out and about dining with Laura,' she said. 'Laura might bring him home to dinner any time now.'

'It's time Danny came and took Laura home,' Mama said, quite sharply for her.

'As if Danny would ever come for Laura,' we scoffed. 'He's too busy turning Magillicuddy into a really lucrative farm. One thing the war did for the Irish . . . it made agriculture pay.'

'Don't forget Danny offered his life even if the good Lord didn't see fit to take it,' Mama said. 'And you're quite wrong about Danny not coming. He always does the most unexpected things. When your Uncle William died he came all the way back from Ireland to take your Aunt Sheilagh and Laura back . . . and he had no obligation to do so. They were cousins . . . not dependants.'

Yes, we remembered that about Danny. Funny though, how we didn't expect him to do anything so romantic for Laura alone. Anyhow, why should Mama think Laura ought to go back to Ireland now? Had she guessed about the Oliver affair? Or did she put a wrong construction on the Riley Scott friendship?

'Danny ought to come for Laura,' Mama repeated. Then she looked up sharply at me. 'And Sam ought to give away that calculating machine and come home to you. As for David . . . if he doesn't stop home more often instead of dedicating his life to work he'll find Vicky cooking for somebody else's sweet tooth.'

'Mama,' we shrieked in unison, 'what a dreadful mind you've got. What put all these evil thoughts in your head?'

'I never did like a nunnery,' Mama said doggedly. 'As for Gerry . . .' Suddenly she turned belligerent. 'Why don't one of you girls find a husband for her? You're all selfish. Full of your own affairs.'

We were flabbergasted at this strange and wholly foreign aspect of Mama's character. What did she mean? And why?

Then, while we were still looking at her with curious and somewhat bewildered eyes, Mama looked up at the Greenway oil painting over the mantelshelf and said, 'I don't know why I left that picture to Vicky in my will. She doesn't really like it and all the rest of you, some time or other, have asked me for it.'

'Mama,' I said, almost purple with fury, 'if you mention your will, or old age, again I'll go away and never come back.'

A futile threat but there were tears behind it. A minute later I knew I should have laughed. It would never do to show Mama we took her seriously. She just might get old and ill, and even die.

It was stupid to take notice of these momentary moods. The next day she was out and abroad on the affairs of the Bay. And that afternoon Mr Coole came to see her.

Mr Coole had known Mama nearly all his life. In the heyday of pioneers' society in Pepper Tree Bay they had called and counter-called. First by cab and then by car. At parish functions he and his wife had always put in a proper appearance . . . very much dressed up and like royalty coming late and going early. Then death and misfortune had struck in both the Cooles' house and in the Rectory. Each family had gone its way and the meetings between them dwindled to nothing.

It was through Vicky that we had got friendly again with Lacey. We had barely known her as a child because she was younger than us all.

Thus, for Mr Coole to call on Mama was as good as un-

precedented. When she went to the door she could hardly believe her eyes.

'Why, Bernard Coole! she exclaimed. Then remembering
that he had always been the secure one she straightened her
back and reduced her welcoming smile to one that was polite
and pleasant whereas really she was quite delighted to see him.

'Do come in,' she said. 'Leave your hat and stick there on
the hall chair.'

She preceded him down the short passage into the drawing-
room.

I was filling in the afternoon while Barty played with rock
crabs and talked to his angel in the river below Mama's house,
so I was there to witness this old reunion and make the tea for
them.

Mr Coole was no sooner sitting in the armchair and looking
at me icily out of those rheumy eyes of his when I thought tea
would have a definitely warming influence on the atmosphere.

Mama was asking what wind of chance had brought 'Bernard' to see her, as I went through the door . . . carefully leaving it open, of course. There was no such thing in our family
as anyone dreaming of keeping anything privy from another.
The business of absenting oneself was merely a gesture to the
caller. It was perfectly understood as that, and no more, by
Mama, or whoever in the family happened to be playing
hostess. So automatic is this habit in any Montgomery that I
wasn't even thinking about deliberately leaving the door open.
I was thinking it was quite fabulous that anyone had ever
called Mr Coole 'Bernard'. If Mama had done so in some
distant aeon of time then there must have been others. His own
mother . . . his wife. It seemed equally fabulous that he had
ever been a baby . . . a small boy . . . a young man. And had
a mother. He'd had a wife all right, not only on account of
Lacey and the two sons killed in the war, but because I remembered her. A lovely smiling gracious lady with pink cheeks and
dresses that always had lace fichus round the neck line.

Mama and Mr Coole were talking about these new ideas
about the river front and each was agreeing with the other that
it was an iniquitous thing to think of changing the contours of
the Bay to build a road and promenade. They had both arrived
at the stage of saying they didn't know what the world was
coming to, and that the younger generation had no sense of
responsibility, when I came back into the room with the tea
tray.

I suppose it was my Irish father who was responsible for the fact I never could help defending the losing side in an argument. I was quite sure I didn't want Oliver or the Council or even God to do anything to the Bay until Barty had grown up but somehow on this afternoon I found myself saying:

'Everything has to go forward. I remember you telling us, Mama, that the river used to be right up to the Weld Club . . . and that you remember quite well when they reclaimed the swampy edge of the river to make the esplanade.'

Goodness me! I thought as I carried Mr Coole's tea to him and offered him the silver milk jug and sugar bowl. The impudence of them! Why, they must have reclaimed quite a hundred yards of river bank there on that esplanade. How nicely we could turn the tables on Mr Coole's generation by bitterly reproaching *them* for stealing from us . . . posterity . . . some of the river Captain Stirling found for us in 1827.

Mr Coole, however, was the kind of man who had a testy answer to everything.

'That was a health matter,' he said coldly. 'The land was swamp and there had been a typhoid outbreak.'

I thought sadly of the esplanade which was the City of Perth's only triumphal garden adornment. All it was, then, was a strip of preventive medicine. I must tell the Lord Mayor that next time he held a civic reception on it.

'You women,' Mr Coole was saying, 'you should take measures to curb this sort of thing. Do you know it is likely to become policy unless there is a substantial demonstration from the residents?'

After a little while it was quite clear, even to Mama, that Mr Coole had not come to call on her at all. He had come to incite the only woman he knew who was active in women's association to action and protest. I was sorry for Mama's slightly deflated air. She was on Mr Coole's side and she was going to do all these incendiary things anyway, but it depressed her to think he'd come only for that reason. These women's organisations that he had formerly despised suddenly appeared to him to have their uses.

I felt like saying, 'Well, it's not such a bad idea that the place of all women is not in front of the kitchen sink and over the family stove after all, Mr Coole.' However, since Mama's bleak look the other day I had developed a certain reverence for old age so I said nothing. I only wondered why I found it so hard to be sorry for him . . . because he was old. Old and joyless, and probably didn't matter any more.

When Mama had seen him out of the door she came back

into the room pretending she didn't know he had only come to make use of her.

'Very nice of the poor old fellow to call,' she said, moving one pot of maiden hair fern along the window ledge to get more sun and turning the other two pots about so the new fronds would grow towards the light. She picked up the teapot and watered them with the dregs of the tea.

'These things do love tea,' said Mama, putting a period to any discussion of Bernard Coole. So I couldn't say what had been on the tip of my tongue to say.

As I went to the window to see if there was any sign of a small boy with fat legs and very blue eyes coming up the river bank . . . accompanied by an invisible angel . . . I felt a little sad-struck myself. Why did Mama make me feel like this these days? I felt angry with her because she couldn't grow young instead of old and because she made the future seem so short to us all. There wasn't any future without her.

When Barty did come up from the river he had Laura and Riley Scott with him.

Barty between them was talking vociferously. His fat hands gesticulated in the air as he struggled to make clear his pronouncements about whatever it was that was filling his childish head with ideas just now. Over that head Riley and Laura spoke to one another. Riley laughed and his face showed laughter creases at the corners of his mouth and eyes. His teeth gleamed in his bronzed face, and I thought how very handsome he was. Laura, too, was beautiful. I wondered why she always had the luck.

Then as they came nearer to the little gate that led into Mama's side garden I knew Laura was not only bringing Barty home from the river, but also was bringing Riley with her. Mama, in an early conversation, had said something about thinking Riley was not likely to call on her . . . almost as if it was advised that he should not call.

Yet there was nothing reserved about the manner Riley greeted us this afternoon. Laura brought him in through the french door on to the balcony overlooking the Bay. The smile he gave me was one of cheerful conspiracy; the right kind of smile for a young politician to give someone upon whom he was banking for support. The smile was still there when Mama came back into the room yet there was a subtle change in it. What was it? It was almost affectionate, surely; it was a gift to Mama of something that could only be given by one who knew a person well and had reason to have deep and kindly feelings for that person.

Yet how could this possibly be?

Barty was engaging my attention and for once I wished he was somewhere else. Laura stood, her hands dug in the funny slanted pockets in the side front of her slacks, watching Mama and Riley shake hands and exchange that strange smile as if she had known it would happen. Indeed there was a depth of feeling shining behind Laura's eyes.

These two were like old friends, sharing things from long ago; and Laura knew it.

What, I thought with indignation, had Mama been holding up her sleeve about Riley Scott? No one, not even Mama, in the Montgomery family was allowed to hold out against the others. I was almost bursting for Riley to go in order that I could catechise my mother.

'Well, Riley,' Mama said, 'how well you look.' Then she stood back a little and surveyed him. 'Well and healthy. Are you happy too? That's the great thing.'

He was smiling widely now.

'I couldn't be better, Mrs Montgomery. It is a long time since we met, isn't it? I wasn't sure whether I should call.'

'I wasn't sure you hadn't forgotten me. It was a long time ago, wasn't it? In another lifetime . . .'

We sat about, talking of politics and the civic life of Pepper Tree Bay. The river road was not mentioned. Riley, having his finger on the pulse of the Bay affairs, must have known that Mama was associated with the Women's Progressive Association and the Aid in the veto against touching the contours of the Bay. Good manners, one supposed, kept him quiet on that subject. Mama, no matter how fierce was her defence of the Bay as it now was, evidently had some deep respect for Riley Scott. Knowing Mama so well, one could not imagine her in any other circumstances losing the opportunity of castigating the villains who were behind the alteration plans. Wasn't she going to box Oliver's ears when next he came calling?

She showed no signs of wishing to box Riley's ears. On the contrary she was looking at him with a mixture of wonder and, it seemed, pride. Why should *Mama* feel pride in Riley Scott?

She asked him questions about how things had gone with him and listened with curiosity that was genuine when he told her of his saw-milling days down in the forest, the sheep farm he had there now; of the house rapidly rising in its modern architectural glory round the East Side of the Bay. He listed these things more as if he wished to please Mama by relating success than that he was boastful. In fact he spoke of himself cautiously and with a very limited explanation, almost as if he was standing before the Recording Angel giving an account of himself but being careful to remember that pride and vanity were not worthwhile attributes nor were they likely to recommend him to the recorder in the Book of Judgment.

When Riley rose to go, Laura and Barty went with him to the door. It was quite clear that Barty had a proprietorial attitude to this tall friendly man who went walking along the foreshore of the river and clearly understood what it was small boys saw in rock pools.

'Mama,' I begged when he had gone, 'when and where did you know Riley Scott? And why haven't you told us about him before?'

Mama was gathering the wine glasses and putting them on the small tray.

'I can't remember to tell you girls about everyone I've met in my lifetime . . .'

'That won't do. You know very well everyone's agog about him. We've done nothing but talk about him for weeks. Laura goes out walking along the beach front with him. Yet you've said not a word.'

'I should have thought you girls would have remembered for yourselves. How did I know you didn't remember? His family lived over by the swamp. They were very hard up in the days when your father was the Rector of Pepper Tree Bay. We helped them . . . nothing much that I can think of. Just the usual Parish duties. I'm surprised that Riley Scott even remembered me.'

And with that she left the room.

Yet I knew that by the use of understatement and omission Mama had lied in her teeth.

I had never known her hold out on her daughters before. It must be something really interesting. Perhaps his family had all died of tuberculosis or insanity. Yes, it would be something like that. Something you do not hold against a man to influence people against him.

Good old Mama, I thought. Loyal to the death. She'll box Oliver's ears about that river road but the same cause will not drag a word from her lips that would put doubt in people's minds when they looked at Riley.

'The only thing I'm thankful for,' Mama said, coming back into the room and gathering up her silks and ribbons and wires and organdie. 'I was nearly having butterflies for fear you'd mention my other caller.'

'You mean old Mr Coole? Why shouldn't he be mentioned? Or doesn't Riley Scott like people who talk only to God?'

Was that why he had greeted Lacey in that cold, yet lingering manner at Bill Collings's house?

'Just don't mention his name to Riley, that's all. In those days . . .' meaning that other lifetime of which she had spoken to Riley '. . . people like the Scotts were not exactly *persona grata* in the same parish as the Cooles.'

CHAPTER SEVEN

It was Mr Firmingham's turn to call on Mr Coole, if one can put in terms of nicety this strange intercourse between the two men.

Never had Lacey seen him around the West Side or down near the river front.

To her he was a strange unprepossessing man, with an air of finality, almost doom, about his manner of dressing and walking, who was sometimes seen but never really noticed.

She did not know his name or his business. He was just 'that man'. She would have found it hard to describe him and impossible to name his business.

What, she wondered vaguely, was he doing around here? She was quite astonished when he turned in at Meenon's side gate and proceeded towards the front door. Lacey looked up at him and offered her faint, slightly embarrassed smile.

'Good morning,' she said.

'Morning. Your father in?'

He stopped and looked at her, but he did not raise his hat. Lacey had never seen him without his hat so it would not have been hard for her to believe it was rooted to his head. She wondered what his head was like under that hat. Was he bald, for instance? When her father had visited Mr Firmingham in Bannister Street it had been Mrs Firmingham who had shown Mr Coole to the door when he left. Lacey had not known whose was the house they had called at on that morning.

'Yes . . . yes, he is in . . .' Lacey said hesitatingly.

She stood, the clippers in one hand and a spray of wind-damaged chrysanthemums in the other. She couldn't imagine her father being pleased to see this gloomy, ill-bred, broad-shouldered, heavy-footed man. What business could he have with her father? And how did he know who she was?

'If you wish to see him I think you had perhaps better ring the door bell. Mrs Simmins will open the door for you.' She bent over the next plant that needed cutting back and thinning out.

Lacey had no idea of snubbing Mr Firmingham. His calling at the house was something outside her experience, and therefore preceding him to the door and announcing him herself would have been a gesture outside her experience. She acted in character with her background in leaving him to the housekeeper.

Mr Firmingham looked at her through his thick-lensed glasses. If he was not in the habit of being treated like this it was because he was not in the habit of calling on the West Side of Pepper Tree Bay. His plod towards the verandah and the front door was a shade slower. If anyone could have seen enough through the thick lenses of his glasses to read the expression in his eyes he would have seen that it was baleful. Knowing Mr Bernard Coole's politics Mr Firmingham had quite enough in his dossier against Lacey to punish her for that snub.

Mr Coole received Mr Firmingham seated in the old-fashioned leather chair with the button-studded back rest and the padded arm rests his own father had once sat in.

He did not rise and he did not shake hands. Mr Firmingham would never have been able to misconstrue just where he stood in the regard of the Cooles, father and daughter.

'You have some information for me?' Mr Coole did not delay with polite expressions of greeting.

Mr Firmingham sat down in the twin armchair across the room. His hat was off and since no one had taken it from him or told him what to do with it he put it on the floor beside his chair. Behind the veil of his thick glasses he was able to look at the room and give the impression he was looking at Mr Coole.

If his fingers tightened on his knees as he looked at the room in which he sat, it was not from admiration but from rapacity. He knew what he could fetch for its contents. A shrewd guess would be that every other room in this large many-roomed house contained equally marketable treasures. The hall, the glimpse of the drawing-room, had been enough to prepare him for Mr Coole's study.

He brushed the thick stubby fingers of his right hand through his thin greasy matting of hair and made a sound that was half a cough and half a grunt.

'You can't get anything on O. Harding,' he said, paying Mr Coole his only compliment. He came straight to the heart of the matter. 'The only land he owns in Pepper Tree Bay is the block he lives on and that old garage he started his business in, round the corner from the Bank. Searching the records doesn't get us anywhere because his people never owned anything. They either rented or were given rent free that house they lived in next the Parish Hall. His father was the church caretaker.'

Mr Coole watched Mr Firmingham with expressionless eyes.

'I didn't want anything on the man,' he said with cold dislike. 'I wanted his history. I did not necessarily want discreditable matters. I have no reason to imagine there are any. I want to know where the man stands, what his strength is. How much he's got to stake in this idea of his in building a road and promenade around the Bay.'

Mr Firmingham ignored Mr Coole's statement of his good faith.

'He's not trying to push land values, I'll tell you that. He doesn't own a riverside block on the Swan though he's got about two acres, ready to be cut up, on the Canning. That's where he'll figure to make his money in land.'

'I imagine he's probably making enough in motor cars,' Mr Coole said drily. 'However, he must have some kind of a power pressure. Where is it?'

'Could be he just happens to be a man the people like. Maybe they trust his judgment.'

'A common fellow like that?' Mr Coole's drooping eyelids opened a fraction of an inch. His voice was acid. 'What is his judgment? How could he possibly know what was intended for the future of the Bay and the river environs? A caretaker's son who's made a lot of money undercutting other men with the sale of motor cars in a post-war boom?'

'He made a lot before the war, racing them,' Mr Firmingham said.

Mr Coole felt that curious frightening sweep of pain up through his diaphragm and pinning itself in a vice-like grip in the centre of his chest. His left arm ached intolerably. He drew in a deep breath and the pain was released. It ebbed back from where it came, in the regions of the abdomen. For a moment he felt the chill of fear. His lips were cold. He sat immovable as a statue, then gradually and imperceptibly released his breath.

Why had he gone to this man for information? Never in a long life of affairs had he approached a man of Firmingham's class. The man was making it clear to him, Bernard Coole, that he thought this scion of an honourable pioneering family was stooping to digging in drains and ditches to discredit a man. How did he explain to such a man there was a difference between finding suitable matched weapons and scooping up mud?

One did not explain oneself to men like Firmingham.

Mr Coole moved his feet.

'I am sorry I troubled you,' he said. 'I can see that no useful purpose can be served in making the kind of enquiries you have evidently been making. You have told me nothing about O. Harding that I did not know. I merely wish to come to grips with this man on his own ground.'

'It won't be in Pepper Tree Bay,' Mr Firmingham said doggedly, and making no attempt either to defer to Mr Coole's cool disdain or drop the assumption that what this man really wanted was the kind of weapon that is never used in the open, but behind the back.

In actual fact, until this minute, he did Mr Coole a grave injustice. Mr Coole had wanted to know how much land Oliver owned in Pepper Tree Bay because in terms of his own history and arithmetic it is the man who owns land who wields the power. Money in the bank or in investments was one thing, but land was another. To have power one had to own land. This was the first axiom in Mr Cooke's book of Euclid. To suggest a man could sway people by mere popularity was sheer puppy talk; a high-school exercise.

No. The man Harding had power. Where was it and what was it? How had it come about that Bernard Coole had not known such a star was in the firmament, let alone in the ascendancy?

The movement of Mr Coole's feet should have been a sign to Mr Firmingham that the interview was over, but Mr Firmingham sat studiedly on.

'The man's like Caesar's wife,' he said. 'Beyond reproach, unless you call a few light-weight love affairs a matter for research. If the man himself was standing for the Council we could use them effectively enough. There's enough in them to set people talking. Not enough in them to pin anything special on him. But it's the other fellow who's going up for election.'

A faint choleric colour rose in Mr Coole's cheeks.

'Thank you, Mr Firmingham,' he said. 'I am not concerned with Mr Harding's love life, or that of his minions.'

Unconsciously he had given his visitor his cue.

'You're concerned with Mrs Laura Montgomery and your daughter. They're seen together at his house, at other houses round there where they're planning this man Scott's election campaign.'

At the mention of his daughter's name Mr Coole knew a rage which he had not before known existed. He was stone cold, yet inside him something was burgeoning that was frightening in its intensity and in its anonymity. It could have been the will to murder, except that he was stone cold in his heart as well as in his hands.

'My daughter's name does not enter these discussions,' his voice said for him.

Never touch pitch. If you do it will soil you and yours. How do I get rid of this man?

'I'll bid you good morning,' his voice added.

Mr Firmingham, unknown to himself, had waited many years for time and opportunity to put a weapon of revenge in his hand. Coole was a rich man but Firmingham could probably buy and sell him. He had suffered the implied indignities dealt out to him by that dry voice, that stiff condescending manner. The girl out there in the garden had treated him as a servant. Coole had never raised his hat to him, never shaken hands, never stood for him. Yet he, Firmingham, had put many blocks of good riverside land in Coole's way. He had made his profit, of course, but he'd paid the price of the man's limitless snobbery.

Coole wasn't the only one in Pepper Tree Bay whom Mr Firmingham had quietly tumbled. More than one of them he had attacked from the ambush of the landlord's rent book or the mortgagee's stamped document. He had never had that hold on Coole. Coole had come to him under cover of asking for a confidential report and thus he had put himself in Mr Firmingham's hands. The worm would wriggle but he would never get off the hook. Assassination of character was the most deadly of all blackmails.

Mr Firmingham was not prepared to believe that Mr Coole had not had that in mind when he had sought for information about Oliver Harding. Mr Coole might deny it in the innermost recesses of his soul, but the cold fact was he had not wanted information that was reputable or that would enhance

Harding's prestige. He had wanted something else, though he would probably deny this on the very doorstep of the tomb.

Well, he had got something else.

Firmingham had not said that one of these 'affairs' of Harding's had coupled Lacey Coole's name with his. That was a seed of doubt that Coole, if he was strong enough and had faith enough, could tear out from his own heart. If he gave it breeding ground then it was because he had it in his heart to do so.

Laura Montgomery's name coupled with both Lacey Coole's and Harding's was enough. Laura Montgomery as a young girl, a growing woman, and now a married woman, had been notoriously attractive to men. And had dealt notoriously with them.

Lacey Coole could be the reflection of the stronger character. 'Show me a woman's friends and I'll tell you the manner of woman she is,' Mr Firmingham misquoted to himself. He was quite satisfied in his mind that the champagne-drinking, yacht-sailing, car-driving, philandering gang of well-to-do people on the East Side were godless and immoral. If Lacey Coole went to their houses she, too, was one of them. The taint of high living was on her like the mark of a social leper.

Mr Firmingham went to church twice on Sundays. He knew sin when he saw it.

Mr Coole sat, his back stiff and upright, his drooping lids closing his eyes until they were no more than watery grey slits. The long silence was due to his waiting for it to subside. It took longer this time.

'I bid you good day, Mr Firmingham,' he repeated.

'Those are the facts of the matter,' repeated Mr Firmingham, still not rising. He had more to say, more to divulge. Mr Coole was going to hear it whether he liked it or not. If he wanted to get at Harding he could only do it through the other fellow. Mr Firmingham, like Mr Coole, was indifferent to the existence of Riley Scott. Nevertheless it was the existence of Riley Scott that could be the means of shifting the earth from under Harding's feet. In other words, it could be Riley Scott who would put O. Harding back where he belonged, spawn of a caretaker's cottage.

Mr Firmingham did not believe in the Cooles of this world dominating the social hierarchy, but he believed even less in someone jumping up from his, O. Harding's, class to take over that rôle. Mr Firmingham was temperamentally not a builder up. He was a tearer down.

'Mr Harding is an open book,' he said. 'Except for the matter of those love affairs of his. And I'm sorry your daughter has got involved with him. However, he is not a good judge of men. He's behind a candidate for the local Council whose record is not so clear. Very doubtful as a matter of fact.

'They rented a house of mine over in Ratcliffe Street, by the swamp. A byword in the district, they were. I had to get rid of them in the end. They polluted the air . . .'

His voice was going on but Mr Coole's mind, which had never wavered before, now failed to grasp all he was saying. For a minute he wasn't sure whether he was talking about Harding or Scott and somehow his daughter and Laura Montgomery were mixed in the back of his mind with this story of a house of doubtful reputation. He felt too ill and too cold really to suffer as he knew some time later, when he'd sorted it all out, he would suffer.

'Of course the boy had to be taken away from them and went up for custody in the care of the Child Welfare Department. He went into an orphanage. He broke out. That's where he caught up with Harding again. They'd been companions. They put him back of course. But this is where he's hardly eligible to stand for a civic body. There was a police-court case. He was convicted . . .'

He went on, his cold, cruel, flat, insinuating voice not once desisting from its attack though already it was patent that Bernard Coole was already brought down from his high and mighty place amongst the law givers. He sat there, a stricken man.

Well, thought Mr Firmingham, Coole had wanted to pull Oliver Harding down. There was his ammunition. Let him get to it. If he, Firmingham, had played a part in this affair it was to root out pride in the one, and immorality and petty crime in the other.

Let both men, Coole and Harding, take the consequences of their actions. Pride shall be brought down to the dust and only the humble shall be called on Judgment Day.

Mr Coole sat in silence. His blue lips were closed.

Mr Firmingham stood up.

'Well,' he said, 'that is all I can do for you. It is I who bid you good day, sir.'

Mr Coole's eyes followed him to the door. The blood was beginning to course freely through his veins now. His mouth, a better colour, showed his contempt for his visitor.

The girl at the bottom of the garden was stripping leaves

from a spray of flowers in her hand. Her back was turned to him. He gave her no chances of heaven and salvation whatsoever.

He went down the stone steps, down the path and out through the gate. He turned left and walked, the pace never altering in its timing by a second, along the footpath towards the hill road where he would catch a bus back to the Terrace. He walked out of the lives of Bernard and Lacey Coole, but his odour remained on the air, a foreign thing in a world of sunshine, clear cold skies and blue diamond-dancing water.

2

Lacey had retrieved the last of all the chrysanthemums and came up the path and up the steps on to the verandah with the large bouquet clasped in her arms.

Whether it was the flowers or the fresh air, the sunshine or the sparkle the rain had put on things, Lacey did not know, but she felt young and happy. For some extraordinary reason life was happy, burgeoning with undefinable things that made her wish she was very young indeed so that she could dance.

Perhaps it had something to do with the fact she had a morning free from driving her father into the city. For some reason he had elected not to go to his Club till the afternoon. Perhaps his remaining at home had something to do with the visit of that odd, very unpleasant-looking man she had occasionally seen about in the Terrace when she had gone shopping. Some business, she supposed, her father was executing.

Perhaps her own sense of glad anticipation was because she had so much she could look forward to this week.

There was afternoon tea with the Misses Renshaw. They were funny old-fashioned things but they were always so delighted to see Lacey it was a pleasure to visit them. Besides, they had been amongst her mother's dearest friends. When Lacey visited them she always felt she was in her mother's shoes. She was doing a little duty that was also a pleasure on behalf of her mother.

Then, next week, she was going to Denney Montgomery's house. It was Denney's turn to have a meeting, which was never really a meeting but rather a party, of the 'gang' that was going to put Riley Scott into the Council.

How life seemed to have changed since Vicky Montgomery had first taken her to one of those parties! How vital were all those people! Their loud voices had troubled Lacey at first, but already she had got used to them and no longer heard the strident tones or the murdering of their vowel sounds. And they had the most interesting houses, full of gay things and modern colours and wonderful time-saving gadgets. Many of them Lacey had not known existed. It was a change as good as a holiday to get away from the dark tones of Meenon, and the everlasting Victorian furniture of all her acquaintances on the West Side. But the thing that attracted Lacey most was the sense of living at a gay and energetic pace. Everyone had so much to do. They played golf, they served on Parents' Committees at schools; they shook boxes for the Red Cross Appeal, and they collected magazines and books for the Maimed and Limbless Soldiers. In addition they had parties in their own houses and went to other people's parties. They never missed a mannequin parade or the opera at the Playhouse. They went swimming in their family-laden cars to the beaches on the hot summer days and already they were planning picnics to the hills in the winter week-ends. Their children had joint birthday parties where one child's guests would be a cricket eleven and the other child's guests would be the opposing team. The mothers would provide afternon tea from baskets on the park oval where they played and the fathers would be umpires. Everyone from the youngest child to the oldest male would be immaculately dressed in cricket whites and the umpiring would have been a credit to a Test Match.

In and out this back-drop of a different way of living drifted the key characters of her own current drama.

There were the Montgomerys. All somewhat older than herself, but it was strange how, when one had got to thirty, the differences in age that had seemed insurmountable when one was ten no longer were noteworthy. Moreover, all of the Montgomerys, including their mother, were invested with the kind of zest for life that took the years off their shoulders if not from the fine wrinkles beginning to form under their eyes. They were young in spirit.

Even the Montgomerys, however, were more back-drop than stirring characters to Lacey. The two people who occupied her thoughts, who, much as she tried to banish them, came back again and again to play some living part in the waking world of her mind and the dream world of the subconscious, were Oliver Harding and Riley Scott.

She had never met anyone like Oliver before. At first he had shocked her and inclined her to sad criticism. He seemed to personify megalomania run riot. He dominated any scene in which he had a part with his single-toned yet slightly drawling voice; his laugh which was as constant as it was loud and brash; his clothes which were exceedingly well cut but which had the hint of the sporty about them; and his car which was luxurious and downright flamboyant.

The other figure in that scene was Riley Scott. His very existence caused Lacey's world to tremble on its axis. In looking at herself in the mirror of her own standards she was astonished and a little afraid to perceive herself one minute in an infinitely alluring dream, the next to find her feelings verging on a delicate ecstasy and then almost immediately afterwards cast back in an iron mould of self-discipline that reminded her she was not of the chosen to whom these things were permitted to happen. She was pressing her nose to a window pane and watching the gay party inside. But she may not enter. To try to enter meant rebuff and the bitter sting of the cold winter air outside.

When one was used to the weather in the streets one had accommodated oneself to it. One could even enjoy its bracing loneliness.

None of these things did Lacey say to herself because she had never been able to formulate the abstract in terms of the concrete. She merely felt them all. It was only when she *forgot*, as she had on this late autumn morning, that there was a certain unusual joyousness in her eyes and step, and that she had invested the land, the trees, and the river beyond, with an even greater beauty than that with which they had already been endowed.

She came up the steps, across the verandah and into the hall with her arms full of golden chrysanthemums. She paused in the doorway of the study as if addressing her father in the language of flowers. The light from the window was shining full on her face, her lips and eyes, and on the golden flowers.

Mr Coole, who had not stirred from his chair, looked at his daughter. He perceived at once there was some aura emanating from her, yet he looked beyond this, and the outer wrappings of her physical person and saw only the skeleton; an edifice dedicated to deception and the temple to a man whom Mr Coole would never have permitted to cross his threshold. It was beyond his understanding that his daughter . . . his *daughter* . . . should conduct an affair with an up-jumped guttersnipe who had raced cars; a man who, until he had identified himself with the *hoi polloi* on the speedway tracks, had never been heard of before.

Alongside this terrible discovery and parallel with it in its emotional force came the experience of fear. He had been shut out from the life of his daughter. He had been dispensed with and did not exist in this life of hers. He knew it, in the terms of what Mr Firmingham had told him, yet he could not believe it. He was looking not at his daughter but at two separate persons. The daughter who had abided obediently by his side and the woman who trafficked with apples and the serpent.

'Look!' Lacey said, thrusting the flowers forward a little. 'You wouldn't believe it possible so late in the season, would you? But they were protected under the shrubs in the centre bed.'

All she read in her father's eyes was cold indifference, something to which she was accustomed. She gave a small sigh and turned away.

'I'll put them in water. I think they'll look best in the dining-room. There might be one bowl for the drawing-room.'

Mrs Simmins, passing backwards and forwards on her affairs, noticed not only Lacey's preoccupation but also the bemused and happy smile that flitted about the corners of her mouth.

'Are you expecting visitors, Miss Lacey?'

'Not unless someone calls unannounced, but it is lovely to have flowers in the house. Aren't they beauties, Mrs Simmins? Who'd have thought we would find as many as this at this time of the year? All those in the open beds are finished.'

'It was your father who had a visitor, this morning. Mr Firmingham from the agency in the Terrace, it was, by the look of him.' The last remark was added to emphasise she, Mrs Simmins, had not been prying. Just seen Mr Firmingham from the distance, as it were.

'Oh,' said Lacey, without interest. 'I saw someone come to the house. Business, I suppose.'

Lacey put the flowers down on the table.

She looked at the housekeeper with a little worried frown between her brows.

'You don't think my father is looking a little unwell lately, Mrs Simmins? It is most unusual for him not to go and attend to his affairs himself. And I had thought . . .' She broke off. 'I had thought he looked a little grey in the face . . .' She could not bring herself to add 'and that old-man's walk', but it was in her mind.

'Well, we all feel our age at the end of a long dry summer. We haven't had any rain to speak of for six months, Miss Lacey.'

'Yes, I expect that's it.' She picked up the flowers and went on with her arrangement.

When she had put the flowers in the dining-room and drawing-room she went to her bedroom to try on yet another new dress with shoes that had been sent to her on approval from a city store.

It was a simple day-frock but it was gayer than Lacey's usual taste. She liked the look of herself in the mirror and she liked both pairs of shoes. As she always dealt with the same firm they had been able to fit her exactly. She slipped on the plainer of the shoes and went down to lunch in her new dress.

Her father entered the door as she was about to sit down and he noticed the dress at once. He said nothing. He knew that in the fullness of time Mrs Simmins would make what comments were necessary. By a great effort of self-discipline he had brought himself to the point when he doubted the authenticity of Firmingham's accusations. The case, for Mr Coole saw it as a case, was that his daughter, his *daughter*, was suspected of consorting with a common upstart, the very one who had the temerity to interfere with the shoreline of the Bay. Mr Coole found it incredible, after proper reflection. He now believed it incredible, although Lacey's dress, the flowers in her arm when she had come into the hall and the curious smile that made her younger and even beautiful did stab him with anxiety.

Mr Coole was unfolding his napkin when Mrs Simmins came in with the soup.

'My, Miss Lacey!' she said as she set the bowl of soup before Mr Coole. She now stood back and looked at her. 'You must be going places. Or are you having visitors after all?'

Mr Coole presented his spoon to his soup and looked down at it. His heart thumped unpleasantly as he waited for Lacey's reply. It came evenly, almost merrily.

'Neither, Mrs Simmins. But it is nice to wear a new dress on a lovely day. It might be new but it is really a very simple one. Not at all a dress for visitors or visiting. I'm not going out to-day.'

Mr Coole might have been relieved at the reply but his spirit remained sombre. The indignity of being suspicious of his daughter! Lacey had never done anything in her life without his knowledge and permission. He accepted her statement that the dress was for the day and not to impress a certain motor magnate who had made a lot of money but had no manners.

She was not leaving the house. She had said so.

In the evening Mr Coole played bridge with his elderly neighbours. This was a weekly routine and Mr Coole went to the next house by a small footpath from one side garden to another. The Perry family left the light burning over the side door to light Mr Coole on his way. The habitués of this part of Pepper Tree Bay were always reminded it was Tuesday because of the light burning on the Perrys' side door. On Tuesday nights, they knew, Mr Coole played bridge with his neighbours.

Mrs Simmins had asked permission to visit her friends Miss and Mr Martin immediately after dinner and Lacey was left alone in the big house.

She had changed for dinner but now, because she was alone, and would spend the evening reading, she changed back to the pretty day-frock she had worn for lunch.

She had barely finished combing her hair back into place when the telephone bell rang. She hurried down the hall. The postman, the door bell and the telephone bell for the first time in years sounded the clarion of thrilling things that could happen. Nearly always the calls were meaningless and routine but because one or two had come commanding her to the other side of the Bay every other one was fraught with that possibility.

As she lifted the receiver she made a small moue at herself in the hall mirror. Behaving like a seventeen-year-old at my age, she thought.

It was Vicky.

'You can just come down here and do a spot of work,' Vicky commanded in the voice that cannot be denied. 'We're going through the electoral roll and the men have all gone and left us to it. How about it?'

'Of course I will,' Lacey said. She wondered if Vicky noticed that though it was autumn outside there was spring in her voice. Try as she would, she could not suppress it.

She was glad the men would not be there. Yet to be with and near those who knew Riley Scott was like being with him. To work on electoral rolls for Riley Scott was like dining intimately with him across a domestic table.

Try as she would she could not banish him from her mind. Vicky's telephone call had brought back the whole sequence of events to her mind and as she put on her coat, saw the house was locked up and pulled out the car from the garage she began going through them again. Unexpectedly her spirits took a downward turn. She was tired of going through past events. Her mind was weary, even bored, with the burden of this train of thought . . . yet there were times when she could not discipline it.

She had seen *him* standing on that block. That was the first time. As he had passed her he had looked at her and there had been the faintest smile. Just one stranger greeting another. It was that image that rose in her mind more than any other. The polite easy half-smile of one human being to another. Yet it had been years since any man, other than her relatives and her friends' husbands, had smiled at Lacey at all.

Then in the Terrace that morning when her father had come walking out of the Bank with that strange old-man's walk.

Riley Scott's appearance and her father's old-man walk could have no possible connection. Yet in Lacey's mind they were connected. Perhaps because both had had some impact on her. Riley Scott had looked directly at her as she sat in the car. He had looked at her as if to see who she was and what she was doing there. And this time there had been no smile, only something cold and implacable. Yet there was an interrogation. What could he have meant by that glance? Had he been asking of the air who she was? What she was doing there? But of course not. Yet he had looked at her with intention, as much as to say, 'So there you are, and that's who you are.'

Then at Oliver Harding's house . . . and later at the Collingses house . . . and at Vicky's house. Always he had shaken hands, looked right at her, noticing her, barely smiling. His eyes cold yet faintly troubled.

Ah, what did it all mean?

Nothing, of course. He would have no feelings about her. He probably looked in this disturbing way at everybody. And even if it did mean anything, imagine her bringing all those people home to Meenon. Her father would not tolerate people other than the old families around the West Side being brought to the house at all.

Not in the wildest stretch of imagination could she imagine her father taking to people like Oliver Harding and Riley Scott.

She couldn't now, after this experience, go back to the secluded uneventful life she had been leading before Vicky Montgomery, who was Mrs Browning, had met her and dragooned her into going first to her own home and then to Oliver Harding's party. For the first time in years she was really living. Yet, oddly enough, her life had been satisfactory before. She had been happy. Vicky had jolted her out of it. Would she be, in the long run, grateful or sorry?

Lacey swung the big car into the Highway and ran down the hill, turned south at the church corner and round to the small hall in which the electioneering team was working.

There they were, seated at a trestle table like schoolgirls, with Council rolls in front of them and wielding rulers and pencils as they crossed out names and listed others on tablets beside them.

As Lacey came in, unbuttoning her coat, everyone looked up and smiled. Vicky said, 'Ah, there you are. Come on. Your stool is waiting for you.'

It was the heart-warming smiles that did it. For a moment there was mist behind Lacey's eyes. They were friendly, these people. She wondered why they were friendly to a stranger. She had no idea she was not a stranger to them, that each and all said quietly within herself, 'Lacey Coole here,' and felt socially superior because of it.

At ten o'clock when they had decided they had done enough for one night Oliver Harding came in with Riley Scott. They were carrying an urn.

With Oliver's entrance the room seemed no longer full of tired ladies. They were all energetic and full of spirits again.

'What ho, what ho!' Oliver said in a voice that had that brash laugh just behind it. 'The ladies doing their bit for the country. Well, here comes the coffee, girls.'

The 'girls' were all smiles and they were hustling here and there, bringing out cups and saucers from somebody's wicker baskets and sandwiches and biscuits from someone else's cardboard box.

Riley Scott was going to each person saying something that made that person look up and smile. Lacey felt a chill of apprehension as she perceived he would speak to everyone, one at a time. They had been working for him and he would thank them of course.

Never had Riley Scott spoken directly to Lacey beyond a formal 'How do you do?'

As he came nearer her she found herself, without volition, going farther around the table to help Vicky set out the cups and saucers. As Riley Scott came to the end of the long trestle table Lacey moved farther up the other side and touched the plates of sandwiches as if they needed some further rearrangement. Then as he came nearer she crossed the floor to the small table where the urn stood and where Oliver Harding was already pouring coffee into a jug.

'May I help you?' Lacey said gently.

Oliver looked up with his usual broad grin. When his eyes rested on Lacey's face the smile seemed to have something fixed about it. Then it relaxed into something even more cheerful than ever.

'Whacko!' he said. 'Miss Coole passing the coffee!' He straightened up and looked at her attentively, his brown eyes kind and even fun-making. 'Does your father know you keep late hours with disreputable people, young lady?'

It was his way of joking, of course.

'He's playing bridge with our neighbours,' Lacey said with an answering and purely innocent smile. The innocence of it had some effect on Oliver for a shadow crossed the laughing light in his eyes. It was gone as quickly as it had come.

'My father doesn't know where I am,' Lacey said, bending to the tap of the coffee urn. 'But then he's so busy always. He has so much to do . . . I never seem to catch up with him to tell him where I'm going.'

'I'll pour the coffee,' he almost shouted at Lacey in his hearty voice. 'You slap in the cream next. Right?'

Lacey smiled. Already she had learned to love the way he said 'Right?' Even to love his kindly vulgarity. No. How wrong had she been? He wasn't vulgar at all. He did it all on purpose. Just that manner of his! It was cultivated. It was his way of getting things done because he made everyone cheerful.

Oliver poured coffee and pushed the sugar into the centre of the table where everyone could reach it easily.

Lacey kept her eyes down on the cups into which she gently poured coffee. All the time she had been talking to Oliver she had been thinking about Oliver, but all the time she had known with an agony of embarrassment just where Riley Scott stood in the room at that moment.

As he came and stood beside her and put out his hand to take some of the coffee for the ladies she had to look up at him. To have gone on avoiding him all night would have been like a declaration. She prayed God would be kind to her and leave her eyes to look a normal, pleasant, unfeeling grey.

She didn't know what to say and a protective blanket of a formalised dignity fell on her as she raised her eyes. She would have smiled except there was no smile in his eye.

'Good evening, Miss Coole. It is kind of you to come and help us.' His eyes did not leave her face. She felt her own were looking into depths which held a message but which she could not interpret.

There was no smile, but there was something else. What was it? A question mark? No, something more. Almost recognition and regret.

But she was imagining it. All she knew was that for an unnecessarily long second their eyes held together yet whatever it was he had to say was incommunicable.

'I like being here,' she said lamely.

He had coffee in each hand and he turned away now. He did not speak to her again that evening.

At ten-thirty Lacey drove herself home. There had been a shower of rain and the car made big tyre marks over the damp gravel of the drive round the side of the house and into the garage.

She went straight upstairs to bed, remembering only to leave the side verandah light on for her father. The light penetrated in tunnels into the shadows amongst the oleanders and hibiscus in the side garden; and spread a spangle of pin-point lights over the wet tracks of the car leading to the garage.

Mr Coole, an hour later, stood and looked at them. Then he went in, locked up the house for the night and went to bed.

CHAPTER EIGHT

Laura sat in the lounge of the Karri Hotel and watched the entrance with eyes that were half expectant and wholly sombre. She was waiting for Riley Scott. She had arrived in the forest town the afternoon before and immediately had telephoned to Riley to tell him of her presence. He had sounded pleased and said he would drive in from his farm at ten the next morning and would drive her out through the forest to see his own place. He had returned from the city during the week-end and Laura had arranged to come down, if possible, while he was there as she had now made up her mind she would recommit her investments to Australian ventures, preferably in the timber and dairying business. Riley had promised her expert advice.

He was a man she had grown to like very much. He did not take her mind off Oliver but she sensed a compatibility, and the odd sort of friendship that had developed had been one partly of expediency and partly in the nature of an emotional prop.

He took her away from Oliver yet maintained the contact by the very fact of his own friendship with Oliver. They had talked a lot together. She had confided nothing of her private life to him, nor he to her, yet under the stream of their meetings there had mingled currents that gave her comfort. Something like reading a good magazine while passing through the deadly doldrums of waiting for a train that had no schedule for arrival.

Out of a sorrowing cynicism Laura anticipated that this obsession for Oliver would wane and die and become, like others, the love that hurt only as the one before the last had hurt.

She watched the entrance to the small hotel and wondered why. The best cure for an old love had always been a new one. Why not now? Why not, for instance, dally in a more loverly fashion with Riley Scott? God knows, on the face of it, he had everything. Why, she wondered with a little pang of fear, did she feel no lighting of the love life for him? Age? Did one really grow out of that basic interest in man for woman and woman for man? Was this what was called the doldrum period of a woman's love life? The fearful forties? Was that why she had fought and denied that compulsive attraction to Oliver? But no. That was arguing in opposites. If she had outgrown love then Oliver would not have had the effect on her that he had had. She fought against the obsession, because Oliver was not a man she could love with her heart and mind. Only with the body. It was nothing more than being devastatingly overpowered by a man's physical personality. It had engendered hate as well as attraction and, say what the philosophers would, the two were not one and the same thing. She was caught in the worst web of all . . . conflict between desire and escape.

Laura sighed. She took out a cigarette and lit it. She blew the smoke out into the fire-warmed room.

At that moment the swing doors were pushed open and Riley Scott came in.

How different he looked down here in the forest country! He wore an old raincoat over tweed farm clothes; he had on mud-spattered elastic-sided boots like a cattleman and as he came in the door he removed a wide-brimmed Stetson hat. Until he took off his hat his clothes had given him a different personality. It was a more interesting one, Laura decided as she watched him come towards her. He swung his hat in his right hand and smoothed his hair down with his left hand. He smiled now in the pleasantly reserved way that had first captured Laura's interest. She stood up to meet him, and they shook hands.

'Well,' he said. 'Have you been down here long enough to like our forest country?'

All Laura's surface good pleasant manners were back.

'I'm very impressed,' she said. 'What I'm burning to know is how you *farm* in this thick forest.'

'Oh, we clear and burn and rake and destroy,' Riley said, looking down at her. 'Then out of the ruin a different life appears.'

'That ring barking I saw here and there on the way down?'
He nodded.

'Graveyards of forest giants. Rather hideous, isn't it, in its destruction? Shall we go now or is there anything you would like to do in the town first?'

Laura laughed.

'Will I be offending you if I say there isn't anything very much to do? I mean I've looked at the post office and the trucking yards and the wooden hall.'

'You should be here on Saturday nights and Anzac Day. Well, let's go, shall we?'

Already they had turned towards the door and he now held it open for her.

'We'll take our time through the forest,' he said as he opened the car door for her and saw that she was comfortable. He walked round the car and got into the driver's seat. The Stetson was back on his head and she decided she liked it very much. It turned him into an outback farmer, without taking away anything of his charm of distinction. 'I'm afraid you can't buy a slice of the forest,' he was saying. 'It all belongs to the State. But the Dairying Co-operative Society into which you propose to buy is a good concern. All they need is capital for modern equipment and the State will lease out a bigger acreage to them.'

'It's very good of you to help me this way,' Laura said.

'Why come down on your own when you've got an expert on the countryside within a few miles?' he said with a quick smile.

They drove in a restful silence for a few miles. On either side of the road the trees reared up to heaven forming in some places interlocking branches over the road so that Laura had the fancy they were driving down the nave of a leafy cathedral. The undergrowth was high and almost impenetrable.

The air was heavy with the thick sweet scent of last night's rain on the leaves.

'At this next bend we come to one of the forest farms,' Riley broke the silence. 'You'll see how it has been cut out like a swathe through the valley and up the hill. Giant trees all around.'

They turned the corner and Laura saw this unique sight. It was, as Riley had said, as if some monster swathe had been cut in the heart of the forest. The farmlands were green and brown stubble squares with a red-roofed farmhouse and outhouses in the centre of it. In the stubble paddocks there were cattle grazing. The forest stood, a wall, around it.

'Is this what your farm is like?' Laura asked.

'There's a twin likeness,' Riley said. 'Not identical, mind you. Fraternal.'

They drove on through the forest, passing yet another farm. Presently he pointed out one which belonged to the Dairy Cooperative Society in which she was contemplating buying shares.

'There are four or five of them in this district,' Riley said. 'I think it will save you time if you look at my place. I'm not in with them but we run on similar lines. They're a good show.'

Ten miles farther along the road he turned in to a driveway between high trees that had been scrubbed out at their bases, giving an impression of English parklands. Because the undergrowth and smaller, less picturesque, trees had gone one could see light through the forest and that a quarter of a mile away through the trees the land opened out into a wide valley. When they came to it Laura knew that Riley had a beautiful and well-kept farm.

'Merinoes to the left, fat lambs to the right,' Riley said as they passed the sheep grazing fat and contented on acres of green grass.

'I know,' Laura said. 'We farm in Ireland, you know.'

'You don't say. What do you run?'

'Cattle and horses. The stud is the mainstay of the place as well as the glamour. The cattle provides the bread and butter.'

Riley grinned.

'And the corn provides proteins and fats, I suppose.'

Laura laughed.

'How right you are!'

They spent the rest of the morning looking over the home paddock and the outhouses . . . the harness room, the stores, the engine house and the smithy. Mostly Laura was given to

133

looking out over the warm verdant paddocks. There was wealth in that land. She was satisfied.

After lunch, which they had with Riley's manager in a large square living-room which was furnished for comfort more than for glamour, they took their coffee into Riley's own sitting-room. The manager had clapped on his wide-brimmed slouch hat, a relic from the war by its shape and colour, and gone about the farm affairs.

It was colder, down here in the forest, than in Perth. The fire had been lit in a wide log-burning fireplace and the air of the room was faintly scented by coffee, cigarette smoke and the pungent resin from the tree logs burning in the fireplace. It was a man's homecoming room. Deep armchairs faced the fire, but there were others in the farther corners. A rack of guns stood against a wall and near it a table was neatly stacked with files and business papers that Riley was evidently dealing with on this present visit to his farm. There was a bookcase filled with the kind of books that looked as if they were used. They ranged from philosophical tomes to treatises on sheep-breeding and animal husbandry. Nothing light, Laura noticed. This Riley was a serious man.

They sat in the armchairs, almost side by side, their feet in the fender. When they had finished their cigarettes and coffee Riley brought over pencil and paper and went into figures with Laura relating to the stocking of the co-operative farms in which she was interested. She was getting information at the hands of an expert and she was grateful.

'When did you first get interested in farming down here?' Laura asked him curiously.

Riley let his pencil drift round the edges of the paper, drawing miniature figures as he spoke.

'When I was a boy. I came down here saw-milling. I lived with an English couple on this place . . . it was then under the Group Settlement Scheme. They were battling and didn't like the loneliness. I worked in the mills but I gave them a hand here. Eventually they left, leaving me in charge on a share-farming basis. When the Government released them I bought them out. You might say I got their farm by working it for them, and making it pay. Of course it was the war and post-war prices that made it what it is today.'

'But you went to the war. How did you manage then?'

'I had two men on the place. And I was lucky. I was in the commandos operating off Garden Island so I was home between trips up there in the islands, and for leaves, of course.

I kept an eye on the place.' There was a hint of amusement in his eyes as he looked at Laura. 'How lucky can some people be!' he said.

Laura remembered Oliver had told her Riley had had a wretched childhood. She had never listened very closely to what Oliver said of any of his affairs, or of Riley Scott. Her mind had always been preoccupied with Oliver himself and not with what he said. She sat gazing into the fire now and trying to bring back the details of that conversation.

'You didn't always have luck,' she said at length. 'Oliver told me you came down here alone . . . very young.'

'I was a hefty lad. I was sixteen but my size was right so I got my first job in the saw-mills as an eighteen-year-old. I had to stick to that and when I went up for the war I had to think twice before I could remember I was two years younger than I thought.'

He lit another cigarette and Laura, looking sideways at him, saw the smile wrinkles at the corners of his mouth deepen.

Then she remembered Oliver saying something to the effect that Riley's book read like a record of hard work and service. But there had been two lost years Oliver couldn't account for. Here seemed the explanation. He had been sixteen, not eighteen, when he had come down into the forest.

'I arrived here on the doorstep of this house, looking for someone to take me in,' Riley said. 'I had on borrowed boots and a borrowed raincoat over my shoulder. And not a bean in my pockets.'

Laura loved a hard-time success story. One of the fascinating things about Australia was that it bristled with such examples.

'But why borrowed?' she asked.

'I was on the run. Isn't that a great Irish expression? And doesn't it call for a handout on the road? It does in Australia. I can vouch for it. The truck driver who gave me a lift down scrounged the boots from somewhere and he gave me his own coat. It was an old one. He didn't mind parting with it.'

'But why were you barefooted?' Laura asked, incredulous.

'That's the way I left the Home. You know when you clear out from a Home you have to do it *when* you can, not *how* you can.' He looked at her with gentle raillery. 'Didn't you know that?'

Laura smiled.

'You are the oddest man,' she said. 'But do tell me, why did you run away?'

'At sixteen I was a grown man. I wanted to work, and I

wanted my freedom.[1]

'Of course,' Laura agreed. 'But I thought in Homes or Orphanages they put them to work much earlier than that.'

'We worked all right. On the place. That's where I learned farming. I owe them that much. But I wanted my freedom too.'

'Wouldn't they give it to you?'

'Not me,' Riley said.

Laura was not looking at him now but she was aware that the lightness had gone out of his voice. The way he said 'Not me' was profound with meaning. She wondered what sort of a boy he had been there in that Home.

Then another small memory of Oliver's remarks sprang to her mind. Hadn't Oliver rescued this Riley Scott some time when he had run away from a Home? But surely Oliver had said the boy had been caught and sent back?

What a strange though interesting person he was. There was no edge of bitterness in him, nor any evidence in his manner and manners that there had been anything unusual about his upbringing. What did it feel like, Laura wondered, not to have any roots? To be someone alone in the world . . . no parents, no people? Nothing but oneself?

He would probably marry . . .

Laura glanced sideways to where his pencil was scribbling on the paper which he had used a few minutes earlier to tabulate farming figures for her. In miniature, with expert draughtsmanship, he had drawn the head of a walking stick. It was a dingo's head, with the tongue hanging out. Beneath it lay a pair of handcuffs locked together. Laura's startled eyes went to Riley's face. His lids were lowered as he watched the tip of the pencil as it worked. He was thinking. He had forgotten his guest. His hand moved over to another corner and he drew the silhouette of a girl's head. It was a beautiful head, poised perfectly on a smooth slender neck. The slight inclination of the head gave the effect of pride that was not to be confused with arrogance. Rather there was an uncomplicated simplicity about it.

That is either the person he'll marry, or the type of person he will seek out to marry, Laura thought. She's got what he wants. Personal pride and good breeding. That dynasty means to be well founded.

Then she marvelled that in a few lines he had so easily portrayed the head and shoulders of a lovely, proud, but simple person. As it was only a silhouette Laura wondered why it reminded her of someone she had seen . . . or perhaps seen in illustration.

Riley, tired of doodling, tore off the sheet of paper and threw it into the fire.

'The trouble with a midday meal and a fire,' he said, 'it makes one lethargic. Would you like to see something else now?'

'No, thank you,' Laura said. 'I'm afraid the pleasant wine we had for lunch and the fire have made me drowsy.'

'Then I suggest we have a rest here for another quarter of an hour, then I'll drive you across to the main Co-operative Store.'

They sat in silence, relaxed back in their chairs, their lids lowered but not closed, their eyes gazing into the coals and flames engendered by the mightiest log Laura had ever seen burning in one fireplace.

The permission to rest from her host released her from any train of thought that necessarily related to him. Tired, her will lost command, and she was treading back again that thorny course of her own private Calvary. In the deep coals she saw a lean brown face and dark fire-darting brown eyes. She saw the challenge and the sardonic laughter in those eyes. Only sleep would really wipe that face from tormenting her.

Riley stirred and leaned his head back on the head roll at the chair back. The flames in the fire leapt here and there and coals quickened and died.

A young woman's face, her head and shoulders faintly tinged with the glow of the fire in which they were mirrored, leaned towards him. The long slender throat that carried the head so well and gave it its air of pride yet simplicity pulsated with the glowing of the embers. The tender blue veins rising above the collar bone spoke of life rising from a heart that in beating must beat for some purpose not quite related to pride and position. From her place in the mirror of the fire she put out her hand towards him in a gesture that had a touch of style in it. He took the hand and drew her towards him.

His lids dropped over his eyes and he took his midday nap.

A week later Laura entered the Pepper Tree Bay bus on its Perth run. Today she would see her lawyer cousin, Mary, and have the documents finalised that would transfer some of her investments to the Dairying Co-operative Society.

When she took a seat she bent her head over her handbag

as she extracted her fare. She did not see, nor would she have recognised, the two ladies who now got in and took the seat behind her. When she had found her fare she turned her head a little to gaze out of the window; thus her ear was inclined, quite accidentally, to the chatter of her fellow passengers.

She listened without hearing for her thoughts were elsewhere, though if anyone had asked her later she would have been able to say that one lady kept up a persistent chatter about identities of her acquaintance, most of whom had offended against the common cause of community living in Pepper Tree Bay. The chatterer was just a common little woman with too much to say about her neighbours.

'Then there's those other people round the other side of the Bay . . .' the thin toneless nasal voice went on with the relentlessness of a nut-cracking machine. 'The goings-on!'

Laura, despite her unwillingness to hear, could not help a small ironic smile. So that was how the *vox populi* spoke of the East Side.

'Parties,' said Nutcracker. 'And such parties. Drink, you know. The children round there drive their fathers' cars and play that game chicken. You haven't heard of chicken?' Laura and the other lady now listened to a technical description of attempted car-crashing on the part of teenage children of rich parents. Did they really do this? Laura wondered, her attention now fully devoted to Nutcracker.

'Even the decent families, the good families, haven't any standards any more. It's the age, they say, but when people like Miss Lacey Coole go round there to those drink parties that's an end of things in Pepper Tree Bay.'

Laura was so astonished she sat bolt upright. Lacey Coole!

'Not that her father would allow it if he knew,' said Nutcracker. 'That's one gentleman left in the Bay. She goes out at night, so I've heard, and never a word to him. Mrs Simmins, you know she's their housekeeper, told Miss Martin all about it, As for that crowd round there thinking they can fill in the Bay and build a pleasure resort on the foreshore! My, they've got another think coming. Mr Coole and some of his friends are going to put a stop to that. They've already told the Members of Parliament what to do about it, and Mr Coole, they say, is not a man ever to be crossed. I believe he's Chairman of Directors of a whole lot of companies who've got their senior executives living round there on the East Side. Mrs Simmins told Miss Martin they'll all get told to pull in their horns or find themselves another job. They'll get the shock of their lives when they know Mr Coole is just as hard at work as they are. Mrs Simmins said . . . you know, she told my friend Miss Martin . . .'

It went on and on, all the way to Perth.

At the bus terminus Laura stood up and turned round. She gave the two ladies the kind of eye-piercing look that must have told them she not only had heard their entire conversation but that she had her own ideas about it. The owner of the nut-cracking voice shrugged her shoulders, gathered her shopping bag and pushed past Laura. The second lady, looking embarrassed, followed her.

Laura was shaking with rage, as she, too, stepped down and walked along St George's Terrace. She could see the two women gathering speed in front of her. What did one do in a case like this? One couldn't accost people and accuse them. It just wasn't done. A scene in the street, with Laura Montgomery in it? Impossible. But how to silence those dreadful slanderous mischief-making voices? Lacey Coole? A game called chicken? The drink parties?

Well, upon my word, said Laura, the sooner I go back to Ireland the better.

As her temper cooled down she began to sort out just what it was that had been said. It was the East Side of the Bay more than people who had been slandered, surely. Who Mrs Simmins and Miss Martin were Laura neither knew nor cared. But old Bernard Coole she did know. She had known him years ago when she had lived with her own parents in Pepper Tree Bay. And she knew he had very much been a power in the land then. By and large, what really came out of that overheard conversation, apart from the impudence of mentioning Lacey by name, was the fact that old Bernard Coole was setting the works going to obstruct Oliver and his party from their schemes for the river foreshore.

Laura wondered how much she really cared about the troubles of Pepper Tree Bay. She felt detached in the sense one cannot belong to something to which one has given only half one's heart. She had no particular inclination to be a carrier of news to Oliver. She wished him well but felt . . . alack, only too well . . . that Oliver was capable of looking after himself. He had strength and a certain ruthless purposefulness. He also had money, power and, on the East Side, position. He probably was very well aware of the moves made by the Mr Cooles of the world.

The last remnants of her indignation now simmered solely on

Lacey's behalf. Lacey going to drink parties and consorting with undesirable people! Lacey with her cool, shy dignity; her pleasant nature and her carefully correct but attractive manners!

Laura shrugged. Slanderous tongues could not really touch anyone like Lacey Coole. She was walled by the circumspection of her life and the protection of that even more solidly walled society, the West Side.

Laura shrugged as she turned down a small arcade, and went about her business. When people had position, she knew, they were there to be sniped at by the ungenerous and the ignorant. The price of being at the top. The Nutcracker and her companion, Mrs Simmins and Miss Martin . . . whoever they might be . . . could never really touch Lacey Coole.

As for Oliver and his earth-moving projects along the foreshore . . .

Laura felt again the old anger she had for those power-conscious attitudes and ambitions of Oliver. She wanted to treat them with contempt as she wanted to treat him with contempt. She disliked him, even while she was so compulsively drawn to him. His civic endeavours fed her dislike, while his sardonic brown eyes, his laugh, his tall lean figure and the broad-brimmed hat he wore lashed her heart and filled her sleep with dreams that wore her out. It was the slight scar above his temple, the gloved right hand, the quality of tenderness that sometimes undermined the scepticism of his smile that were her undoing. His civic endeavours and practices left her utterly disinterested.

As she turned into Mary's office she was no longer thinking with anger of the Nutcracker and her companion, but of Oliver. Her eyes had the strained look of one who was tired of battling.

Of the whole gang of them the only one who touched her heart happily was Riley Scott. She knew, with that extra feminine instinct so lavishly debunked by the psychologists, that he was a fine man.

That afternoon, when she had finished her affairs in the city, she returned to her aunt's house in Pepper Tree Bay to find Esther Harding taking afternoon tea with Mrs Montgomery.

As Laura came into the drawing-room, drawing off her gloves and then throwing her hat on to the sofa beside her, she first noticed that Esther, though simply dressed, was immaculate, and that her aunt had a grey tired look about her face that was quite unusual. Aunt Helen was always bright, always full of verve and activity. In fact as the 'girls', her five cousins, were wont to say, Mrs Montgomery could do more in a day's march than any one of them. To sit there, talking quietly, and holding in rein that effervescent spirit, her face tired and her mouth with a blue-grey tinge, was very unusual. Laura dragged her eyes away from Esther whose perfect appearance always fascinated her, and watched her aunt. She wondered if something had happened to upset her.

But no. The conversation flowed along gentle chattering paths with Esther showing her pretty even teeth between those naturally red lips when she smiled. Mrs Montgomery smiled out of those very blue eyes that were tired and . . . yes, just a little frightened.

Laura wondered if Esther noticed. Then she decided that no one would ever know what Esther noticed. She was as calm as the river on an autumn morning when it lay like a mirror without a single ripple on its surface. And as beautiful too, Laura thought. The two things that fascinated Laura about Esther were that she always looked perfect, and that she was married to Oliver Harding. Would she, for instance, know she was sitting in the same room with another woman for whom Oliver's existence meant so much heartbreak?

'I'm so sorry, Mrs Montgomery,' Esther was saying, 'that you don't agree with us about the river road and promenade.' She smiled as she spoke and her grey eyes had the faintly tender, appealing look of all very feminine women whose eyes are widely spaced and darkly fringed in spite of the fair curly hair crowning the head. 'But everyone to their own way of thinking . . .' She made a little deprecating gesture with her narrow, small-wristed hand, as if she regretted the difference but not the cause.

Laura had crossed her knees and showed quite a quantity of slim leg. She leaned back, rumpled her hand through her dark luxuriant hair, then reached for a cigarette from the box on the small table beside the sofa.

Mrs Montgomery's eyes went from the fair to the dark. They lingered longer on Laura. She knows, Laura thought. But Esther doesn't know. She hated herself hideously for her rôle. It was not the rôle, but Oliver's position in it, that made it distasteful to her. She had flirted with many another married man in her adult life.

'Is this no more than a political call you're making, Esther?' she asked, not unaware there was the prick of a barb in what she said.

Mrs Montgomery drummed her fingers on the arm rest of her chair. A faint colour crept up Esther's cheeks but she still smiled.

'Why yes, perhaps it is,' she said ruefully. 'I did want Mrs Montgomery to think our way, especially as she is such a leader in the women's organisations. That wasn't altogether my purpose in calling, though. We're old friends, aren't we?' She looked at Mrs Montgomery for confirmation.

Laura blew out smoke and watched the spiral idly.

'As long as politics is not the sole topic of conversation . . .' Laura said. 'I suppose, not belonging to Pepper Tree Bay, they bore me.'

'Laura, would you like a cup of tea?' her aunt asked.

Laura smiled.

'All right, Aunt,' she said. 'I'll be good. Let's talk about some-one else. Who in the whole of Pepper Tree Bay is Miss Martin? And Mrs Simmins?'

Both Esther and Mrs Montgomery looked surprised but shook their heads.

'Someone *you* know?' Esther asked.

'Very well, I should say. They have expressed the opinion that they are a debauched lot living round on the East Side.' She looked at Esther sideways. 'And when I say that that's what I mean. Drink with a capital "D" is the main trouble round there evidently. Living there, would you think so, Esther?'

Esther's delicate eyebrows rose but her mouth smiled.

'Oh dear!' she said. 'I suppose it's all the parties.'

'People who live in glass houses are bound to be talked about,' Mrs Montgomery said. 'And you know there is a frightful amount of glass round there. The service must be worth a fortune to the window cleaners.'

'I think some of them will regret those glass walls,' Esther agreed.

'It was an American fashion, wasn't it?' said Laura, pinning Esther as if the other was responsible for the people who had preferred glass to brick and stone when building their houses. 'Suitable to the American climate?'

'A mixture of Swiss and American, I think,' Esther said. 'A queer mixture, but some of the houses are really lovely inside.'

'Laura,' said her aunt, 'will you get a cup of tea for yourself or will I get it for you?'

'No, thank you, Aunt dear. And I won't say another word to imply criticism of Pepper Tree Bay, if that is what is worrying you. Let's talk about the weather.'

Laura was being exasperating and Mrs Montgomery looked as if she would like to get up and box her ears. You can't box the ears of a beautiful young woman who is forty years of age, however, and one who is so obviously troubled that her irritability should be forgiven her.

Well, as the senior lady present it was her duty to take the edge out of the conversation.

'Have you heard the latest about Gerry?' she said. 'She's been doing some welfare work for the Government Travel Agency. She had to make a booking for some nuns who were going east and another one for the boys' football team. Just like Gerry . . . the football team was booked into a convent in Melbourne and the nuns into a boys' school.'

The old laughter so particular to that room which over the years had had its walls ring and ring again with the misdoings of the Montgomerys trilled from Esther's lips and broke in an involuntary way from Laura.

'Aunt, you can always tell a good story at the expense of the girls but what about the time you invited a young man to the house, thinking he was someone else. When he arrived you all called him by the wrong name and then had to confess the error in order to find out what his own name really was.'

The grey look faded from Mrs Montgomery's face as she laughed. The more she thought of that long ago incident that had resulted in twenty years of friendship with the 'wrong man' the more she laughed, and presently the laughter tears were in her eyes.

As Esther later went away they could see Vicky turning in at the gate. Immediately Mrs Montgomery began bustling about in the kitchen, biting her under-lip as she went, as if tiredness had not sat upon her like a warning of things to come. Laura, helping with putting away the tea things, could see the conscious will straightening the shoulders. Only one small escaped strand of hair told the tale of a woman fighting to convince a loved daughter that all was well in the best of possible worlds.

'Aunt,' Laura said suddenly, 'I'm sorry I was snipperty with Esther. You were cross with me, weren't you?'

'Not cross. Just sorry you had had a tiring day.'

'I nearly spoilt your little tea party,' Laura went on.

Her remorse burgeoned from her at the sight of those tired yet straight shoulders and the little strand of grey hair that had escaped its proper place. Suddenly she felt desolate. Then Vicky came in the door and she could see from Vicky's eyes that she, too, saw that her mother was playing a part. Yet Vicky, too, must join in this game of making believe that life went on for ever and Mrs Montgomery would never grow old . . . and tired.

'You must be bursting with energy, Mama, rattling those pots and pans about. I could hear them outside. Don't you ever rest? I'm just worn out . . . poor me.'

It was all designed to comfort her mother.

Vicky put her handbag on the dresser and a parcel on the table.

'Open that when I'm gone,' she said. 'Just a new gadget, but useful.'

'Vicky's a great one for gadgets,' her mother said. 'All the same I'm going to open it now.'

Her fingers were struggling with the string but neither Laura nor Vicky offered to help. They knew that a present was a present and even the untying of the string and shedding of the paper was the privilege of the one presented.

'I saw Esther driving off,' Vicky said. 'Why don't you cut the string, Mama? Was Esther visiting?'

'Yes, we had tea together. Oh, Vicky! A telephone directory. How does it work?'

'Push the index down to the initial. Look, D for Denney, press the button and the directory springs open at Denney's number. See?'

'What a clever thing. Yes, dear, Esther was here and Laura was irritated.'

'Not really irritated, Aunt. It's just that Esther is so impeccable. I always want to scratch to see how deep it goes. But I said I was sorry.'

Vicky looked up at Laura with amused eyes.

'Sorry for scratching Esther? I don't think you need worry, Laura, Esther is just what she looks . . . untouchable. But I like her and I wouldn't be in her shoes married to a man like Oliver for a million pounds.'

'Why not?'

'Too fascinating.'

Mama was holding up her new directory to examine all its praiseworthy points.

'Fascinating? Oliver! Oh, I never heard such nonsense in all my life. He's a *good* fellow. But fascinating! With those shoes and that dreadful laugh of his!' she exclaimed emphatically.

Laura leaned against the sink, her arms folded. Was Vicky, or her aunt, lecturing her? She would not spoil her contrite mood by saying anything now. She would move the conversation one step west of the dangerous point.

'Are you in league with old Mr Coole, Aunt, about that river road and the promenade? I believe he's getting all the powers behind the scenes to work against Oliver.'

'Gossip,' said Mrs Montgomery, putting the telephone directory up between the flour and the tea tins . . . a position from which Vicky immediately removed it to its proper one on the telephone table in the hall. 'Mr Coole is quite out of public affairs now. Besides, he is not a man anyone can work with. Too autocratic.'

'And where did you hear that gossip?' demanded Vicky, coming back from the hall.

'I forgot you were in on this thing,' Laura said. 'You're on Oliver's side, aren't you? Then you'd better tell him old Bernard Coole is on the war-path, and in spite of what Aunt says he has got some powerful friends in the hierarchy.'

It was on the point of Vicky's tongue to ask, 'Why don't you tell him yourself?' but something in Laura's manner caused her to hesitate. Laura was being very co-operative. It could be that Laura wasn't really the most fortunate person in the world. It was so easy to lift one's eyebrows at a socially illegal love-affair and feel smug when the lovers suffered for their follies. Stolen fruit was bitter, Vicky decided, from the first bite.

'Mama,' she said, sitting down at the kitchen table and putting out a hand and taking a piece of the cut cake left on the afternoon tea tray. 'You know that awful old short-sighted man in the brown suit that's tramped the Terrace ever since I was born? What's his name? Yes, Firmingham. Always gives me the willies to look at him. Grim old snooper, I would say.'

'Not a very pleasant person,' Mrs Montgomery said, rescuing the cake from the table and putting it away in a tin. 'That . . .' referring to the cake, 'is in case the other girls come in, and besides, you're putting on weight round the middle, Vicky.'

'Well, I like that,' Vicky said in her offended, eldest-of-the-family voice. 'I'm not an inch thicker or a pound heavier and you really want that to stuff that wretched little Barty. And I've never heard you tell Gerry to stop eating.'

'You haven't been listening,' Mrs Montgomery said. 'Well, what about Mr Firmingham. Is he dead?'

'You sound as if you think he would make a useful funeral, Aunt,' Laura said. 'But he's pretty well in, is that same Firmingham. I can't imagine him leaving anything to charity when he does die.'

'I've been having afternoon tea at the Crockers', round on the West Side. I saw him coming out of Meenon. What do you suppose old Mr Coole would let that leper in the gate for?'

'Really, you girls are uncharitable, the way you talk of other people,' began Mrs Montgomery.

Vicky said in her voice which she occasionally pitched high, 'Well, I like that. You just wanted to know whether he was dead or not yourself. There weren't any tears in your voice.'

Mrs Montgomery dusted the tea tray, folded up the tray cloth and put it away. She turned down the gas under a saucepan and said, 'Let's go out of the kitchen, anyway. It never was big enough for the whole family.'

'Evading the accusation,' Vicky said sententiously to Laura. Then as she followed her mother into the drawing-room she said, 'To be quite frank I don't care whether Mr Firmingham lives or dies, Mama. I just got the shock of my life to see him coming out of Meenon. Perhaps he has truck with the gardener or something.'

'Quite likely,' her mother said. 'Sit down, Vicky, and don't look as if you've arrived in time to go. Where is Laura?'

Laura had gone out of the kitchen down the short passage up the path that led to the road. She didn't want to sit and talk to her aunt and her cousin. She wanted air, space, escape. But one can never escape from oneself. One can dream of going away, of taking train or bus or ship. Yet one takes one's own self along. There is no escape.

A big clump of oleanders on both sides of the path hid the approaches of the road from either side. She was within a few feet of the gate when Oliver turned in. They were face to face, neither expecting or prepared for the other.

Oliver lifted his hat and then replaced it on the back of his head. It looked slightly rakish that way.

'Well,' he said. 'Imagine seeing you.'

'Who did you expect round about this garden, Oliver?'

'Esther. She was going to call on Mrs Monty this afternoon. Have I missed her?'

Laura leaned on the low stone fence. Oliver stood, his feet slightly apart, and looked down at her quizzically.

'She's gone,' Laura said. 'I think I spoilt her *tête à tête* with Aunt by asking her if she had come lobbying for that wretched promenade of yours, Oliver. Why do you rope everyone into your schemes? Even Esther? And I suppose John too?'

Oliver was barely smiling now.

'These things are bigger than a game of politics in a riverside suburb.'

'I know. I once worked in a stockbrokers' office. Big men deal in big ventures, don't they? It's a kind of personal competition on national levels when they've outgrown marbles at the schoolboy stage. Did you play marbles, Oliver? Is that where you learned to outwit your opponents?'

She knew she was bitter . . . showing her hand, as it were.

Oliver looked at her steadily. Then he nodded his head in the direction of the gate.

'Get in the car, Laura. We'll go down to the Bier Garten and blow that one out of your head.'

A week, a day, an hour ago Laura had been strong enough to say no. Now she stood upright, gave Oliver a lopsided smile and walked through the gate towards his car which was parked a few yards south of the gate.

Oliver closed the car door behind her and walked round the back of the car and got in. He eased the car away from the kerb and let it glide round the corner before he accelerated.

'Wasn't it Esther you came for?' Laura said, fighting to make it sound a light joke.

Oliver's hat was still on the back of his head. His eyes were narrowed against the westering sun and he whistled softly between his teeth. He did not answer.

They drove in silence. He turned north, then west, and drove up the Highway in the direction of the ocean.

'This is not the way to the Bier Garten,' Laura said. 'And I haven't a hat or a coat. Where are we going?'

'Just up the road,' Oliver said.

Up the road was a mile over the hill and three miles along the coast road. Then he swung the car into a place that looked west into the sunset and the blue ocean. He braked to a stop. He threw his hat off on to the back seat and took out his cigarettes and lit two. He handed Laura a lighted one.

'Talking about promenades and politics,' he said evenly. 'There's three ways of looking at those schemes. It could be personal prestige for the promoters. It could be improving the country. It could be giving decent people something decent to keep them together.'

Laura was leaning back in her corner and at a slight angle She could watch Oliver's face. She had never wanted to analyse any of Oliver's motives. It had helped her to think the worst. It gave her dislike ground to feed upon. She didn't want to overcome her dislike. If she found that Oliver was a saint she would be lost indeed.

'You tell me about it,' she said. She tried not to sound sceptical because she knew she was giving herself away if she did. She wanted to sound natural, just an ordinary person taking an ordinary late afternoon drive with another ordinary person. It would be heavenly to be just ordinary and pass unnoticed in the pack.

'Some of those chaps round there . . . not all of them by any means . . . were flying bombers. Twenty thousand pounds and a crew at stake. Never mind who won the war. Some of them were prisoners under the Japs. A lot of them were crawling about, commando style, with no one to take responsibility, but themselves in the island jungles. There's one chap spent his time delousing mines and unexploded bombs. They've come back home. Money's easy. Too easy. There's no real decent percentage for them in just accruing more money, more blocks of land, bigger launches and bigger cars. With their background in the war . . . and the money they've made . . . they can make a decent ruling class for their State or country. Or they can make a degenerate one. Men like that can't go slowly. Can't settle down. Do you get me, Laura?'

'You're giving them something to do to eat up their energy, their responsibility and their money.'

'After a fashion. I include myself in the gang, you know.'

'So you build a road and a promenade. Why don't you call it a war memorial and be done with it?'

'Just what we might do. We've got to call it something.'

Laura's eyes searched in Oliver's.

To her dismay she believed him. Oh, Oliver, her heart cried. Don't turn out to be a hero. So long as you're a stinker I can manage.

The pain showed in her eyes and her lids drooped over them for a moment. She stubbed out her cigarette in the ash tray and Oliver threw his out of the window. His left arm could slide now along the back of that seat so that though it did not touch Laura it seemed by its very presence to encompass her. From it there radiated a magnetic impulse that had the promise of sweetness and rest; all of an opiate.

Laura's shoulders were stiff with the pain of withholding from it. With a terrible effort at concentration she forced herself to think, to conjure up an interest in Pepper Tree Bay and its energetic young men. By energy, she could see, they were saved from anger. They would go forward . . . upward and onward . . . if only the old men would let them.

'Riley Scott . . .' she said. Somehow the very saying of the name took the tension out of her physical being. Here was a man who had everything to command attention, yet she didn't seek to seduce or be seduced by him.

'Well, what about Riley Scott?' Oliver asked. 'You've been down there in the forest seeing his place, I hear. What did you think of it? What did you think of him?'

Laura leaned back easily now, her shoulder blade touched his hand and he cupped it on her shoulder.

'I liked him. By the way, didn't you tell me something about two lost years in your account of him? I found them.'

She turned to look at him now and saw his raised eyebrows. 'You found them?'

'Yes. Aren't I clever? He got his first job saw-milling when he was sixteen. Not eighteen. Do you know why he stuck to the eighteen? He got so used to saying that was his age. He ran away from the Home he was in . . .'

'When he was sixteen?'

'Yes. Don't you see, Oliver? He was supposed to be in that Home till he was eighteen, so that's why he stuck to the fact he was eighteen when he was only sixteen. Do I sound as if I'm repeating myself?' She laughed.

'Yes you are, my sweet. It still doesn't account for two years.'

'But Oliver, it *does*. Look, you send Esther lobbying round the town. You rope in all the people, like my cousins, round and about. I've no doubt you pull strings like old Bernard Coole. And you're not even grateful when something comes your way from a totally disinterested person.'

'In what way does Bernard Coole pull strings?'

'Don't tell me you don't know just who are Bernard Coole's contacts. And don't tell me you don't know he'd save the Bay from your marauding friends with his body, if necessary.'

Oliver was looking thoughtfully into Laura's eyes as if he was examining their depths and not fully conscious of what she was saying. His face was very near hers. So near she could feel his breath on her lips.

'Oliver,' she said slowly, her will fighting him off again, 'I have it straight from the horse's mouth. Miss Martin and Mrs Simmins, no less. Town gossips and well informed about certain households on the West Side. Bernard Coole is moving behind the scenes, if I may use an expression so melodramatic. So I had it from Nutcracker sitting behind me in the bus . . .

who had it from Miss Martin . . . who had it from Mrs Simmins who is somebody's housekeeper. Am I telling you anything interesting? Even informative?'

'Yes, my darling girl, that's just what you are telling me.'

'Then why don't you look grateful? You even disregard two whole years when Riley Scott was lost . . .'

Oliver's face was close to hers.

'He was not lost, my pet. He was at large.'

'At large? What a way to put it. What do you mean exactly, Oliver?'

'I mean that Homes or Orphanages, whatever they call them, do not keep their juvenile inmates, guests, clients, whatever you call *them*, after fourteen or sixteen years of age. Not in the State of Western Australia, anyway.'

'Oliver! What do you *mean*?'

'Only that you still have not resolved a certain riddle.'

'You don't think . . . ?'

'No, I don't think. I never stake a hand on a man unless he's a good man. And I'm staked on Riley Scott.'

His mouth was within two inches of hers.

'Oliver . . .' Laura implored.

'The riddle is . . . what is the connection between Riley Scott and Bernard Coole? There is one, you know. Do you like being kissed square on the mouth, Laura?'

The hand on her shoulder, the whole arm encompassed her now. She was gathered to him and his mouth came, no not to rest but to ravish her own beautiful and troubled lips. The right, gloved hand that could not feel rested on her breast.

'Laura,' he whispered through parted lips. 'Go back to Ireland.'

'Yes,' she implored him. 'Yes. If only I could go *now*.'

CHAPTER NINE

The river had its summer glories but they were not to be compared with the illustrious beauty of a sunlit winter's day. On such a day there was no wind. The water shone with a still serene surface and the distant colour of the far reaches merged from grey mists on the water's surface and over the hills, through pearl and amethyst until there was nothing above the great expanse of bay but the piercingly blue dome of sky.

In the foreground the yellow beach shone with diamonds of moisture. It and the dewdrops on the grass beside it was a very field of gems. At the Yacht Club the yachts rode at anchor, painted ships on a painted sea; their reflections riding upside down were perfect in every minute detail.

On such a June day Mr Coole sat on the verandah of Meenon, basking in the sun, if one might ever use such a word as basking in connection with such a person as Bernard Coole.

Now and again he raised his binoculars particularly to pin some point of interest on one or other of the boats.

There were two strangers riding at anchor there, a ketch and a very fancy-looking launch with its bow too snubbed for Mr Coole's liking; and the paintwork glittering in an unseemly way.

The launch, to Mr Coole, smacked of the *nouveau riche*. It was pretentious, in spite of that snubbed bow. The wireless mast, the small promenade deck with its gleaming brass rails, the glass superstructure of the deck house, the Reckitt's blue of the paint on the cabin roof, shrieked money and bravado. There were new-fangled bits and pieces which Mr Coole could see through his binoculars and for which, since it was many a long day since Mr Coole had sat in a launch, he had no name. The whole told a story of a launch that had *everything* in marine gadgetry.

As Mr Coole watched he saw figures clamber aboard from the dinghy, and activity begin. There were three men in the whites of yachtsmen, their peaked caps bearing a recognisable likeness to the badge of the Pepper Tree Bay Yacht Club. The man with the white cover to his peaked cap must obviously be the skipper. As he worked, Mr Coole adjusted his binoculars to pick up greater detail. Yes, it would appear his cap too bore the insignia of the Club. Yet the man was a stranger.

A new member surely. Mr Coole felt again the pang of the old man being left behind in the stream of events, Time was when he knew personally every man who attained membership in that Club. Later he had at least been acquainted with them by reason of the binoculars. But always he and his binoculars were several weeks, even months, behind the event of new membership.

Feeling the pang, Mr Coole also felt distaste over the blackballed nominee introduced by the man Oliver Harding.

He had not been able to bring himself to broach the subject of this man to Lacey. He would not have admitted to himself there had been in the reluctance a fear of that nervous seizure he had had more than once since his seventieth birthday, when his whole chest became inflamed with its agony.

The very thought of that man Harding, nowadays, brought on the suggestion of that nervous seizure. His mind winced away from the rôle his daughter was playing in Oliver Harding's love life, as a wounded limb will wince away from contact of any kind. More than pain and fear was the terrible knowledge that he could no longer rule the comings and goings of his household. No longer could he, with a glance or a word, veto activities of which he did not approve. The tyrant in his chest held a rule and sway against which there was no appeal.

Ever since Mr Firmingham's second visit, when he had declared himself indisposed and not available to the visitor, his head had joined league with the chest tyrant. His head had moments of fuzziness, always associated with the thought of men like Oliver Harding, up-jumped get-rich-quicks with no colonial background, interfering with the geography of Stirling and Forrest's Bay, backing a Government that would put a bridge across the Narrows and thus defile the natural bushland, that was the Swan River's heritage, with playgrounds for ice-cream vendors.

And now his daughter. 'How sharper than a serpent's tooth it is to have a thankless child.'

It was Saturday afternoon and Lacey was doing something in the garden outside. Mr Coole got up and walked around the verandah and watched her. He knew he was consciously testing himself out. Until such a time as he was in the ascendancy, and not the tyrant in his chest, he knew he would be rendered powerless in the State of which Lord Forrest, then Sir John Forrest, had said to him as a small boy: 'This will be your land. See you look after it when I am gone, boy.' Even in his age Bernard Coole remembered the hand on the head of the small boy that had been himself; the deep full-throated voice with its overtones of human kindliness.

Lacey wore gardening gloves as she took the first ripe apples from the back-garden tree.

The red of the beautiful cider-smelling apples Lacey picked was reflected in her cheeks. There was a glow of soft pink beneath the skin. As her father watched her, he perceived the physical difference in Lacey. Almost, he felt disgustedly, a fecund difference.

Love, if that was the terrible emotion she felt for the man Harding, had softened the light in her eyes, brought a certain fullness to her arms and breasts. A new unnameable something shone delicately from the very pores of her skin. Her mouth had attained a mature beauty that was full of promise.

The whole sight was tragic to Mr Coole. Yet he remained calm. The beasts in his chest and the wraith in his head did not stir. His spirits rose, within proportion to his restraint, that is.

'Lacey,' he said, opening the wire door and standing there looking at her and not seeing the verdant winter-loving garden. 'Lacey, bring the car round. I want to go down to the Yacht Club.'

'Why yes,' Lacey said, tumbling the last of the picked apples into the basket she carried on her arm. She looked up and smiled. There was pleasure in her face and a sudden startled mobility about her mouth. Mr Coole thought the colour deepened in her cheeks.

Anything to be in the vicinity of that man, he thought. But she shall stay outside.

He was safe. His binoculars had told him Oliver Harding's pretentious car was not outside the Club House.

Lacey was surprised her father asked to go to the Yacht Club. She thought with real pleasure that it was a splendid idea. He really ought to go out on Saturday afternoons; specially in such glorious weather. It would do him good. The Yacht Club must surely be an infinitely better place in which to sit than the stuffy smoke-ridden rooms of his city Club.

To sit there, right by the water's edge, and smell the water and the peculiar odours of boats . . . the leather, the salt-soaked timbers . . . and see men who sailed, why, that would be good for him indeed. He had worried her lately. His colour had not been good and when his eyes had met hers they seemed to have a sombre lifeless quality.

'To the Yacht Club,' she almost sang as she drove the big car through the drive gates of Meenon, along the waterfront to the Club less than half a mile away.

She did not mind sitting outside while her father went in. She, too, was thus on the water's edge. She could sit and smoke a cigarette and dream. If her thoughts stole occasionally to a tall man who rarely spoke to her, who had ambitions in civic politics, whose blue eyes though cold and forbidding held some inexplicable message in their depths, then on such an afternoon it did not matter. The river was made for dreaming. In a dream, and not reality, cold blue eyes could become tender, and a message be spoken and not merely implied in a certain darkness deep within them.

Mr Coole entered the Club. There were a few Club members about. Some of them were in ordinary street attire and there merely for the Club facilities and the pleasures of social intercourse with fellow human beings. A few wore boating whites. It was not the sailing season but those devoted to the sport spent the winter lay-up of their boats in attending to the tasks of careening, painting and general maintenance. There was more life outside on the slips, and in the boat yard than inside the Club.

Mr Ellison, on seeing Mr Coole enter, came forward, making an effort to hide a certain tremor of nervousness. Mr Coole had never been to the Yacht Club on a Saturday afternoon in Mr Ellison's period of service. Remembering that extra meeting of Oliver Harding's and certain incidental items that had gone through that committee . . . 'just to clear the decks of trivia' . . . Mr Ellison's physical heart took a slight plunge in the thoracic cavity. How on earth would he, Ellison, ever explain to Old Man Coole that for purposes of slipping certain matters through an unsuspecting committee O. Harding Esq. had declared Bernard Coole unfinancial and therefore ineffective for the month of March.

Mr Ellison had the curious feeling that he had known all along there was such a thing as an axe, and that now it was about to fall.

'Good afternoon, Mr Coole,' he said, doing his best to seem pleased.

Mr Coole, who knew all about detecting the emotional state of a man from that man's mannerisms, knew that the Club secretary had misgivings at seeing him there on such a day and at such an hour. Mr Ellison was making a great ceremony of adjusting his handkerchief in his breast pocket. Mr Coole noted it and put it away in the corner of his mind for reference later . . . should it be needed.

'Afternoon, Ellison.' Mr Coole nodded and handed him his hat and stick as if he, Ellison, was a steward and not a professional administrator. Mr Ellison put the hat correctly on the stand and the stick in the corner.

'Would you like some service, sir? Or are you just paying us a social visit?'

Mr Coole walked on into the annexe to the bar lounge. He took a seat overlooking the river and the activities amongst the boats below.

Ellison was torn between a desire to please the old man, in terms of custom, and a sense of outrage that anyone had the effrontery to treat him thus. Custom and tradition prevailed, however, and he followed Mr Coole to his comfortable chair.

'I'll take some tea presently,' Mr Coole said. 'You might tell the steward, if you will. Tell me, Ellison, who owns that gaudy-looking launch down there on the port side of *Nicolene*.'

As a non-sailing yachtsman Mr Coole liked this single-worded hint of a knowledge of the marine highway.

Mr Ellison might have gone pale if, in the last minute or two, he had not been indignant with Mr Coole's off-hand treatment of him.

'That is *Satire*, sir. Oh, excuse me. I'll catch the steward and let him know you would like service.'

He sped in the direction of a steward who fortunately was in the act of leaving the lounge. It gave Mr Ellison excellent excuses to leave Mr Coole in the first instance and the lounge-room in the second instance.

'Tea presently for the elderly man in the corner by the bay window. And I don't want to be disturbed by him or anyone else for the afternoon. To all enquiries just say I'm not available.'

He retreated to his office and shut the door.

The steward when he took Mr Coole's tea to him was asked to bring the Club's boat list to him.

Between cautious sips of tea that was a little too weak and a little too hot, Mr Coole perused the lists. *Satire*, he observed, was owned by R. Scott. On the list of sailing craft he learned that the stranger ketch was also owned by R. Scott.

Reading the name on those lists for the second time a bell rang. He saw the general office of the Bank, a tall man writing out a cheque form and a Bank clerk saying, 'Mr Radford will see you at once, Mr Scott. He was hoping you would come in.' Scott was the name of the man with the striking blue eyes who had preceded him on that day when the beast in his chest had first lifted its head. The man . . . so important he had preceded Bernard Coole . . . had come out of the Manager's office and had stooped to pick up his, Bernard Coole's, walking stick. The cold animosity in that man's eyes had changed the colour from definite blue to sea grey. Or had it been because the man had been looking into the light streaming through the open doorway? Had that animosity been no more than the man's inability to relax a naturally stern expression?

Mr Coole cared nothing for the unknown man's animosity. He cared only that the Manager of the Bank had seen fit to call him in first. It was like reading a sign written across the skies of Mr Coole's own horizon. He was preceded, and by an unknown.

This man, then, was a member of the Pepper Tree Bay Yacht Club. He owned that gaudy abomination of a boat, the *Satire*. He also sailed a yacht. When had he come into the Club?

Then the second bell rang, loud and clear with the intonation of a single toll.

Nominee . . . Mr Riley Scott. Introduced by Mr Oliver Harding. Seconded by Mr Stanley Redfern.

The notice on the notice board.

The man he himself, Bernard Coole, had blackballed. Riley Scott had been elected. He was a member of the Club.

Mr Coole sat frozen cold with his anger and astonishment. A minute later he recorded that nothing had stirred in his breast or his head. In spite of the anger a secret elation mounted his heart. Beyond this immediate matter that would get his immediate attention was the preoccupation with the fact he had conquered those nervous spasms. All he now had to do was rein in all emotional unrestraint. A cool head and a cold heart. These would give him back his health and with health he would put affairs in Pepper Tree Bay in the place they belonged . . . the care of those who had inherited them from the first colonial pioneers. The men who knew best. The men who had first loved the strange south land inhabited only by black primitives.

Carefully, coldly, he would deal with Oliver Harding. Of this man Riley Scott he knew nothing and cared nothing but Firmingham had told him something about him. What was it?

Now with this return to health and restraint he would be able to deal with Firmingham on his own terms. Distasteful as it might be he would see the man again. He hadn't listened when Firmingham had begun to tell him some tale about Oliver Harding's front man.

He stood up and walked to a full-length side window that gave a view on to the beach beside the Club where the slips were a hive of industry. He saw the man Riley Scott sculling in the dinghy from the ketch to the shore. On the shore he saw his daughter Lacey standing watching the men working at the slips. She was smoking a cigarette. He revised his decision that what he must do would be for his daughter as well as for the safety of the bushland and the shoreline. In Lacey he saw that most terrible of all sights, the fallen woman. If she had not actually slept with Oliver Harding her spirit had consorted with his. It was enough.

Lacey was quite innocent of the personnel on the ketch *Cathleen Moy*. She watched the men careening a racing sloop nearby and marvelled as she had often marvelled as a child on this very beach at the wonders of a boat when it was high and dry above water. She knew exactly what the men were doing and why they were doing it. She had no occasion to ask questions so she spoke to no one. She stood aside, a little aloof, her slim body quite still where it leaned against another beached boat. The smoke from her cigarette spiralled away lazily and though she looked up with interest at the incoming dinghy she did not recognise at that distance who was its occupant. If when she had dreamed over the river she had dreamed of a tall man she did not dream now that in another minute she would see him in all actuality.

Riley Scott jumped out into the shallow water and dragged the dinghy inshore to the waterline. When he straightened up he saw the girl, and she saw him. Astonishment leapt too quickly to her eyes for her usual carefully trained manners to hide it.

Then she smiled. It was a careful polite drawing-room smile yet the astonishment in her eyes and the nervous movement of the little muscle at one corner of her mouth gave to her quickly withdrawn proud air the really human touch.

Riley Scott appeared surprised, then it was as if he gathered himself together, remembered this young woman was one of the team of helpers in his electioneering campaign. He saluted but did not smile. He took a few steps towards her.

'Are you interested in yachting or yachts, Miss Coole?' he asked pleasantly. There was a formal reserve about his manner that made it quite clear he was speaking social nothings because he would not talk of deeper things, for there were, somewhere, intangible barriers which could not be overcome.

'Both . . . really,' Lacey said. 'Can you be interested in one without the other?'

He did allow himself an amused smile now.

'There are those who go yachting who know nothing about boats,' he said.

Lacey listened to the resonant timbre of his voice. It was a good voice, soft yet firm, masculine but not unmusical. So seldom had he actually exchanged words with her, or near her, that his voice was still a stranger to her. She liked it, with a feeling that was actually much deeper than 'like'. She was long past the stage when she forbade herself forbidden fruit. It was, after all, better to have loved unloved than never to have loved at all. She would, however, have given up her life before she would have uttered a word, or spoken with a glance from her eyes, to tell anyone in the world . . . let alone Riley Scott . . . that for a little brief while her life was illumined by a dream.

It had flickered brightly when he had come those few paces across the sand and addressed her. It subsided at the uncommunicating politeness of his words.

He turned now and stood, the flats of his hands on his hips, the water trickling down his strong muscled legs on to his bare feet, and looked out at the boats lying in the Bay.

Lacey looked away from Riley Scott's feet. Oddly enough, she who had seen yachtsmen all her life in their water-going uniform, felt a sudden intrusion into Riley's privacy because he stood there in white shorts with wet bare legs and sandy feet.

She looked away but not right away. Her chin had that unconsciously proud tilt that made so fine a line of her neck and shoulders.

'That's the ketch *Cathleen Moy* over there,' Riley Scott said as if it was understood she should know the ketch was his boat.

This Lacey did not know. She did not even know he was a yachtsman or a member of this particular club from amongst the three Yacht Clubs in Pepper Tree Bay.

'Oh yes,' she said with interest.

He turned a little to speak to her again and his eyes took in that lovely line of the throat, the slightly tilted chin and the head carried so beautifully on a soft column of neck and beautiful rounded shoulders.

He looked back at the boat.

'You are staying down here long?' he asked.

Lacey knew the conversation was difficult and it implied there was nothing communicable between them. It was almost devastating in its ordinariness, yet it was fraught with sharp undertones of feeling and each seemed reluctant or unable to terminate it. She was at a loss to know how to dismiss him, for in truth she was loth to do so.

'I am just waiting for my father,' she said. 'He is in the Club.'

'In the Club!' He was startled now.

'Yes. He's a member. He has been a member nearly all his life. I think my grandfather entered him when he was very young . . .'

Her voice trailed away. Why tell him about her father? As if it could possibly matter. And it might sound like laying down one's claim to antiquity . . . the only safeguard to the top layer of the Bay's hierarchical society. Riley Scott didn't belong, couldn't belong that way. He was someone she had never known and never heard of, and alas her life had been circumscribed by those who were known or heard of. To know him now was a release from that family bondage, yet it left her insecure in a society which had no landmarks.

The colour stole up her cheeks as she recognised the tenor of her thoughts.

Riley Scott looked at her curiously. She bore the scrutiny with her head lifted a little higher. In this futile conversation they had eventually reached the ground where there was no compatibility whatever, even though the subject was yachts. Each was in the world of his and her mind and there was apparently no point of contact. Though she felt a sudden agonising pain of regret in her heart its only outward sign was in the remoteness of her manner.

'Yes. Very interesting,' Riley Scott said thoughtfully, as if he was answering his own thoughts.

At that moment Lacey caught sight of that figure standing at the long window on the balcony of the Club House above her. Following the direction of her eyes Riley, too, saw Bernard Coole standing immobile, no expression in that down-drooping mouth or in the grey heavy-lidded eyes. He stood there in the window embrasure and looked coldly down on the two standing on the edge of the beach below.

Lacey lifted her hand in the beginnings of a wave but when she saw her father make no movement to respond she dropped her hand to her side.

'I think perhaps I'd better say goodbye, Mr Scott. My father may need the car.'

Riley Scott had been looking up and he now lowered his gaze to Lacey's face. His mouth had taken on a grim line and his eyes were cold. When she saw this the light in her died altogether.

'Goodbye, Miss Coole,' he said.

He saluted, turned away and walked, warily, because he was barefooted and the beach was prickly with dried seaweed, towards the lower entrance of the Club House.

Lacey, too, turned away. As she sat in the drive seat of the car, waiting for her father, she gazed over the sunlit river and wondered why the glory had gone out of it and the mists that were creeping over it from the farther shore were no longer soft with mystery but were cold, and soon, before nightfall, they would encompass all the Bay.

On the Tuesday following the Saturday when Mr Coole visited the Yacht Club, there was a meeting of the Board of Directors of Banfold and Co.

Mr Coole was a senior member of that Board, being a past Director and now a Vice-President of the Company.

In the report before him he read that the services of Mr Harvey Dalton had been recruited to boost the country sales of merchandise. Mr Dalton, the report read, was an able and experienced executive with former experience of fifteen years with Harding Motors Ltd.

In the regulations governing the administration of the Company the General Manager had authority to employ staff without reference to the Board. The Board however, retained the right of enquiry and the right of veto. Now and again the Board exercised this right by way of keeping its power within the bounds of current practice.

No one, therefore, thought it odd when Mr Bernard Coole expressed the wish that the Board might meet this Mr Harvey Dalton who was to be manager of country merchandise department.

Better still, as someone smilingly corrected Mr Coole, let Mr Dalton come and meet the Board. After all, they were paying him what looked like a prince among salaries: expenses and a bonus to boot.

'Let us look at this man,' the Board agreed. 'He's cast in pound notes, that's for sure.'

'I wonder why Oliver Harding let him go,' someone ventured. 'He could afford to pay what we can.'

'Maybe Mr Dalton wanted to come to us,' someone else suggested.

Conjecture made the case of Mr Dalton interesting so that when he came in at the invitation of the Manager it was to meet a battery of interested eyes. The only pair of eyes that held no interest for Harvey Dalton was a pair of rheumy grey ones worn in a long narrow face with a mouth so scornful and down-turned at the corners that it could be almost cruel. Harvey took no particular anxious interest in this one personality because he decided on the first immediate glance that the owner of that high-bred, discontented, acid face was old, moribund and not a physical ornament to the Board.

'Sit down, Mr Dalton.' The Chairman indicated a chair. 'You have a very important post with us now. We thought that maybe we ought to get to know one another.'

Harvey smiled. He prided himself that he did it easily and that his manner of entry had conveyed in exact proportions confidence, courteous attention and pleasant diffidence. Harvey knew that to give off an aura so paradoxical took considerable business training as well as a touch of talent in the art of being all things to all men.

With the deft handling of the Manager the conversation between the new business executive and the Board flowed easily from pleasantries and generalities to the more specialised subject of just what Harvey Dalton hoped to do in the interests of the firm while in office.

The only man who neither joined in the conversation nor asked a question was the old man at the right hand of the Chairman whose cold grey eyes missed nothing and whose expression did not alter a whisker throughout the interview.

'Well, I suppose you're a busy man, Mr Dalton,' the Chairman said at length. 'We'd better not keep you or we'll have the Manager castigating the Board for interfering with the routine of the firm.'

This was received with the general laugh that was expected. Harvey smiled pleasantly at the Board's little joke. He wished O. Harding could have been here to see him pace off the old boys whose real intention had been to pace *him* off.

Now what about Tomlinson's job, he thought. Chicken feed after an interview like this.

He rose and gave a polite half bow. It was at this minute that Bernard Coole spoke for the first time since Harvey came into the room.

'Just a minute, young man. I think you might answer a further question.'

Harvey was taken aback. To begin with, the clear unexpectedly youthful tones of Mr Coole's dry voice startled him. He had thought the old fellow was probably in his dotage. Now there issued from those proud hard lips a voice that had authority as well as the clipped tones of a man of more than usual culture. Moreover, Mr Harvey had not been 'questioned' by the Board. The interview had taken the form of a pleasant conversation with question, statement and answer exchanged all round.

This quiet cold command issuing from the man on the Chairman's right hand had the suggestion of the inquisitorial about it; almost as if the Board had not arranged this interview merely to have the opportunity of meeting Harvey Dalton, manager of country merchandise, but rather to catechise him and see if he measured up to the post.

Harvey's debonair manner dropped from him. He hesitated and one hand went out to touch the back of the chair near him. He was a shade paler than when he came into the room.

The Manager, to whom Oliver Harding had passed over Harvey, noted the subtle change. There was a slight smile on his lips and he bent his head to shake ash from his cigar.

Harvey's hand, resting on the chair, gave him confidence.

'Sir?' he asked with a too careful look of enquiry.

'You seem to have so many good ideas,' said Bernard Coole's clear clipped tones. 'Your record seems enviable. Would you tell the Board why you elected to leave Harding Motors? Just what advantages did you seek with us?'

The whole tenor of the interview was changed. No one knew why Mr Coole had taken this note and charged the atmosphere with something subtle but unnameable.

Before Harvey could answer, Mr Bardon, the Manager, intervened.

'To be quite frank, gentlemen, I knew of Mr Dalton's work with Harding Motors. I invited him to join the firm. That speaks for itself.'

Harvey had a feeling the Manager was rescuing him. He must appear to stand on his own feet. The men present must sum him up, once and for all, as a prospective director.

'I'm afraid Harding Motors could not offer me the advantages of Banfold and Co. I must confess I'm an ambitious man, gentlemen. There is only one way for an ambitious man to fulfil his hopes. That is to build the edifice that will carry him.'

There were hearty sounds of 'Hear, hear!' from all round the Board. Ambition in a man that carried his firm with him was an advantage to business prosperity, provided, of course, the ambition remained within bounds. This fellow had an engaging air.

'And did Mr Harding make any attempt to retain your services?' the dry cold voice persisted.

Harvey's eyebrows flickered. He was thinking fast. Actually Oliver had not done any such thing. He had accepted Harvey's resignation out of hand and had then walked through the door with him, talking about yachts, winds and current drifts.

'Mr Harding is not a man to stand in another man's way, sir.'

'He's not a man to train a man and then give him away either, is he?'

Harvey was silent.

'Mr Harding didn't have the choice,' the Manager intervened again. 'Mr Dalton was invited to join us on a yes-no immediate reply. He had the decision to make. And he made it.'

'And did Mr Harding not protest?'

There was a restless movement of feet here and there under the table. From experience the members knew Bernard Coole had a reason, generally a valid one, for his methods. At the moment everyone was in the dark. Harvey seemed okay to them.

'Mr Harding would not protest once he knew the decision was irrevocably made,' Harvey said, still feeling his way.

'Would you say it was a good business proposition to lose a first-class executive to another firm without putting up a fight?'

'No, I wouldn't,' Harvey said before he had time to see the trap. His feelings and not his head had governed that reply.

The Manager stabbed the note pad in front of him with his pencil.

'Then Mr Harding could make mistakes?' said Bernard Coole.

Harvey was going cautiously now.

'Well, yes. Every man is fallible.'

'Some more than others, eh?' Mr Coole turned to his fellow members. 'You will note that Mr Dalton, late of Harding Motors, concedes his former employer was fallible.'

'Every man is fallible,' he repeated. 'Mr Harding no less than others. His judgment is not always sound, gentlemen. But then, whose is? There is a very fair field for the motor agency this firm holds. I can promise you sales in that direction.'

He smiled on the Board. The Board smiled back on him.

'Very good,' Mr Coole said. 'Very good. And of course, if such is the case, it would all be due to Mr Harding's incapacity to know a good man when he sees him?'

This brought a laugh from the Board and an eager smile from Harvey.

'Mr Harding is a good business man,' he said. 'A very good business man. But since we must concede that everyone has a weakness, then Mr Harding's weakness lies in a lack of discernment when it comes to individuals. If I take some of his country sales, gentlemen, it will not be because I use methods contrary to the code of this firm. It will be because Mr Harding himself has not protected those men who act for him out on the roads.'

Harvey could have patted himself on the back. He had virtually told the Board he would cut into Oliver's sales and given them a good ethical reason for not having a business man's conscience about it on the firm's behalf. At the top level business was the jungle law. The places at the top were for the strong. Oliver was no picker of men. Damn it all, he hadn't picked him, Harvey, for Tomlinson's job. A man who is a bad picker of men has to pay the price. He will lose sales. And this Board, sitting here right in front of him, would feel it was justified because Oliver had a certain flaw in his business make-up.

Everybody's conscience would be at rest.

Harvey beamed on the Board. The Board, rather doubtfully, beamed on Harvey. They would like him to cut into Oliver's country sales but preferred him to say nothing about it. If that old fool Coole had only kept quiet . . .

The Chairman first dismissed Harvey and then the meeting in general. As it broke up and some of them began to drift away, Bernard Coole asked four of them, including the Chairman, to stay behind as he wished to have a word with them.

'What was that interrogation about?' the Chairman asked him.

'That is why I wanted you to remain behind,' Bernard Coole replied coldly. He had not risen from his seat. 'I don't care a fig for that young whippersnapper's capacity to break or make sales records. What I wanted was a clear statement of a weakness of that man Harding's. Now I'll tell you what it is about. I've asked you four men to remain because you've got one thing and one thing only in common. You all live in Pepper Tree Bay. You may not have noticed that is now being run from behind by this Oliver Harding. He has got a nominee up for the Council. A man called Riley Scott. You've heard of him? Good. But what have you heard of him other than that Oliver Harding and a gang of his cronies are behind him?'

'Anything wrong with the man, Bernard?'

'I think so. I'm not prepared to say what yet. I'm inclined to look into it first. I just wanted to demonstrate to you this afternoon that O. Harding is a bad picker. That fellow in here five minutes ago is one of them. Oh yes . . . I know. He'll bump up the country sales. New brooms always pick up the leftovers. We can pass him on when he's served us to capacity.

He'll do for the time being. However, I want you to understand that when O. Harding chooses a man that man is not necessarily a good choice. You'll hear more about this from me later. Meantime don't let people in Pepper Tree Bay be carried away by any eloquence on O. Harding's part. And you might drop a hint to be wary in the Club. Wary of the man Riley Scott, in particular.'

The four men looked interested. Not one of them was particularly wedded to civic politics. At least two of them never bothered to cast a vote, but Oliver Harding stepping off on the wrong foot in a political matter was a subject not without its titillating aspect. Anyone who thought that characters were assassinated by women in drawing-rooms had never been a member of Boards of Directors in big competitive firms. Nor had he sat for long in a Club.

There wasn't a man among them who didn't entertain a wholesome respect for Oliver Harding's capacity as a business man. They knew his war record and knew it was little short of the heroic. However, if he was venturing in the new and higher realms of power politics he'd have to fight his way there. There is no tighter fraternity than that which enfolds the few who drive politics from behind. It didn't let any newcomers in. A man who got in was a better man at jungle tactics than the combined efforts of the members of that fraternity. The five men sitting there in the Board Room of Banfold and Co. knew this, and they pondered.

At the drop of the flag from Bernard Coole there would be a closing of the ranks. And Oliver Harding would pay a dear penalty for his ambition. A venture in power politics had broken many a better man than O. Harding. If you bid and won, the world was yours. If you lost, your business, your wife and family paid the price.

Not one member of such an ambitious person's family can take a step out of line or out of place. And they'd better not have a skeleton in the cupboard.

Bernard Coole and the four men to whom he spoke at the conclusion of that Board meeting knew the rules of the game, remembered each rule and considered each one. There was something a little grim as they said good night to the old warrior. Deep in each the primitive aggressive instinct was stirring. The game was on. Another big-business man had stuck his neck out an inch too far. Queer how they all suffered from megalomania when they got near the top of the ladder!

On the Thursday Oliver Harding and Riley Scott entered

their city Club together. It was not the exclusive pastoralists' Club that Mr Coole favoured but a lively and useful business man's Club. It was the lunch hour and the members' rooms were crowded.

The two men hung their hats on the rack in the hall and stood, side by side, in the wide entrance of the bar lounge. The room was hazed with smoke, and conversation buzzed loudly all around.

At that moment Oliver knew that something was afoot.

What goes on? he said to himself. To Riley he said nothing more than, 'Well, let's find a corner at the bar.'

It would have been impossible for Oliver to tell anyone how he knew something was afoot. Years of experience in business and war had grown for him those extra invisible tentacles that warned him when the atmosphere was not dead right.

The two men weaved their way past tables and chairs. The cheery greetings exchanged were no different from any other day. The jocular welcoming note in the voices of his friends was exactly as it always was. The steward with a glass-laden tray stood aside as courteously as he ever did. The bartender was as eager to take an order and deliver it satisfactorily. Yet Oliver, who had known nothing before he entered the Club, knew with absolute certainty that there had been a veering in the wind. He scented a foreign atmosphere.

The two men stood leaning against the curved chromium gleaming bar, sipped their whiskies and blew out spirals of smoke from their cigarettes. They talked idly because all the time there was a passing to and fro of men to whom they were known and who said 'Hiya!' as they passed, or 'Howzit, Oliver?' One or two stopped and shook hands with Riley because he was so rarely seen in the Club.

All the time they were bland, breezy, friendly.

Oliver, laughing, cracking a joke here and there, watched with slightly narrowed eyes.

What goes on? he thought. What the hell goes on?

When they sat down at a small side table in the dining-room he conducted a first-class intelligent conversation with Riley and didn't once have his mind on it. He was watching that room, wary as a scout trailing Japs through the Timor jungle.

Ellison, the Yacht Club secretary, passed through the room. He lifted a hand in greeting but did not stop. Two Members of Parliament lunching with two heads of Government departments all had their eyes on Oliver Harding's table at the same moment. A minute later each member of that quartet was interested elsewhere.

A member of the Pepper Tree Bay Civic Council left and was shortly followed and joined in the hall by another councillor with whom he had never been known to have anything in common. Through the open dining-room door they could be seen passing out of the main entrance together.

At a table in the corner were four prominent business executives who all lived in Pepper Tree Bay. There was no reason why they should not sit together in the Club at the lunch hour. They had just never been known to do it before.

They were small things. Intangibles. They could mean nothing. Oliver was darn certain they meant a lot.

'The heat's on,' he said to Riley abruptly.

The other man looked at him out of keen interrogating eyes.

'You mean they're going to fight the promenade project? But you expected it, didn't you?'

'Yeah,' Oliver said. 'I expected it. But it's going to come from above. Not below. It's not going to be the public that's going to squeal. The public is always bloody apathetic till someone kicks it in the pants. It's going to be the boys in power. They'll blockade it, if they can.'

'If I get into the Council that'll be my fight, won't it?'

'Yeah. Can you take 'em on single-handed?'

Riley smiled faintly. He had a very firm jaw.

'I'm raring to go,' he said quietly through half-closed lips.

Oliver laughed.

'You bet you are,' he said. Then he stopped laughing, and his eyes were suddenly hard. 'If you get in, boy,' he said. 'That's where they'll go to work. I know this game through and through. They'll begin at the beginning. And nobody will ever know they had so much as a little finger in the pie.'

Riley Scott's eyes were half-closed in thought.

Harvey Dalton entered the dining-room and proceeded a few steps between the tables in the direction of Oliver's table. He saw Oliver and turned away. He avoided him. The four men, top executives, from Pepper Tree Bay saw Harvey and greeted him more enthusiastically than Harvey's position warranted.

'Why doesn't it add up?' Oliver asked himself. 'Harvey's in it somewhere. Harvey's got nothing against Riley . . . only me. And I'm not putting up for the Council.'

The two men finished their lunch, pushed back their chairs and stood up.

Oliver said, 'Be with you in a minute, Riley.'

He walked down the dining-room to the table where the

four Pepper Tree Bay men sat. He leaned both hands on the table and grinned at them, one after the other.

'Well, fellows,' he said. 'What goes on?'

Yes, there was the tiny flicker in one pair of eyes after another. The infinitesimal tightening of the muscles at the jaw-line.

'Want to hear a good yarn?' Oliver asked. He told them one that made them throw back their heads and laugh so that everyone in the dining-room looked at them.

'Go home and tell your wives that one,' Oliver said with a grin as he turned away. 'So long, fellows. See you some more.'

He looked up at the room-wide mirror that hung above the tables on the opposite wall. Yes, they laughed, and when he turned away that laugh died and they met one another's eyes.

In the hall Oliver flattened his hair down with the palm of his hand before he picked up his hat.

'It still doesn't add up,' he said to himself. 'Maybe I'll get Esther on to that one. Woman's instinct and all that . . .' Funny how Esther was always right.

He parted from Riley in the Terrace. As he walked along the wide sunlit pavement he thought not of Riley Scott, or whatever it was that was cooking up in certain circles in Pepper Tree Bay, but first of Esther, then of Laura Montgomery.

'I wish that girl would go back to Ireland,' he said.

He turned into the small corner florist's and sent Laura flowers. Then he went into the chemist's and bought his wife a bottle of French perfume.

'It's not conscience, young lady,' he told the girl across the counter. 'I just like giving women presents.'

'You are a one, Mr Harding.' She smiled and fluttered her eyelids at him.

'Not you, sweetie,' said Oliver, grinning. 'Wait till you grow up.'

'I'll still be around.'

You bet you will, Oliver said to himself as he went through the door. You, and some more!

When he walked into his house through the side verandah door that evening, Esther, who had heard him coming, was pouring two drinks at the cabinet against the wall.

Oliver's hat was still on the back of his head.

'Hallo, pal,' he said. 'At it already?' He leaned forward to plant a kiss on her forehead.

'I heard you coming,' said Esther. 'They had their Women's

Meeting in the Parish Hall today. There's going to be a petition to the Council. We'll be canvassed from door to door for signatures.'

'And was Mrs Montgomery making speeches?'

'She made one, and a very good one.' Esther turned and handed Oliver's drink to him. He threw his hat, cart-wheeling it across the room to rest on the floor under the chair by the telephone table. Esther smiled. 'I'm afraid she coined their slogan for them . . .'

'Halt me if I'm wrong?' Oliver said. 'I bet it was "Hands Off the Bay!"'

'Darling. How did you guess?'

'That's the one I'd have thought up myself if I'd been on their side. Listen carefully and answer correctly, my sweet. This is the sixty-four dollar question. Did they stick exclusively to reclaiming and building round the Bay? Or did they mention a certain rising young politician we hope to plant like a thorn in that particular bunch of roses?'

Esther had gone across the room and she sat down in a small armchair, neatly crossed her legs and looked at the drink she held in her hand. She shook her head.

'They didn't mention politics or Riley Scott. Unless Captain Stirling and Lord Forrest were politicians. Were they?'

Oliver sat down in the chair under which rested his hat, stretched out his legs straight in front of him and smiled sardonically.

'Why do you suppose they don't come to me for their arguments?' he said. 'They're standard ones. A hundred years ago someone raised them when they reclaimed the land below the Weld Club. Sixty years ago someone raised 'em when they replaced the plant track across the Causeway with a metal and bitumen road. They said it all over again when they built a breakwater at the foot of the Mount. Shall I tick 'em off for you, Esther?'

'No thank you. I know them by heart too.'

The telephone at Oliver's elbow rang imperiously.

'I forgot to pull that ruddy plug out,' he said, then lifted the earpiece. 'Hallo, hallo! . . . Yeah, it's me.' He listened to the voice on the other end for a long time. Once he said, 'Okay. Go on,' and the voice went on. Oliver's face was expressionless as he listened.

Esther gazed idly out of the window and wondered how late John would be coming home. Now it was football. Not so long ago it was cricket, and then junior rowing. Perhaps in the holidays they would be able to go away together. She and John. Up to the hills, or even up the coast where it would be warmer. John had never seen a sheep station . . .

Oliver's voice broke the silence now.

'Okay, Ellison, so the old boy knows. All right. He can't do a darn thing about it. I was inside the regulations. He'll know that, so quit worrying. Bet you won't hear another word from him. I'll be the goat . . . What? . . . Anyhow, thanks for the story. I knew it round about midday today . . . What? . . . No, no one told me in words You did when you came in the dining-room in the Club . . . Okay! I'm not going to lose any sleep so you'd better not. So long!'

Oliver, when he finished a telephone conversation, always banged the receiver down on the stand. Esther, as she always did, winced.

'Bernard Coole . . . and the Yacht Club,' Oliver groaned. 'Don't they ever give up, those old boys?'

Esther did not answer because her ears were listening for John.

Oliver leaned over and pulled out the telephone plug.

'I want one short cat-nap,' he said. 'Then after dinner I'm going to give you and John a sum. See if you can figure out the answer.'

Esther moved across the room and picked up his glass, then went to the door.

'Not John,' she said. 'He's too young for politics.'

'He can do long division of algebra, can't he? I never could.'

But Esther had gone through the door. She quietly closed it behind her.

'Hell, that woman's always calm,' Oliver thought to himself. 'She looks as if she has just stepped out of a bath . . . all softly powdered and scented . . . Damn it all, I forgot to bring home that perfume!'

Then he thought about Bernard Coole until his lids dropped over his eyes and he took his cat-nap.

On Friday night, after dinner, the first telephone call Oliver had was from Richard Bardon, the General Manager of Banfold and Co. Would Oliver be in for a private talk if he came round?

'I certainly will be in,' Oliver said. 'You're probably the man I want to see. How's Harvey making out?'

'It's about him I want to see you.'

'Don't tell me I sold you a pup, Dick. That feller's a real

salesman if you give him his head.'

'I'm half-way to seeing that already, old man. And he's got ideas. I can see why you couldn't give him Tomlinson's job though. He gets himself into a trap on the top level and never knows he's in it. I'll see you in about half an hour. Right?'

'Right!'

Oliver put down the telephone and pulled out the plug.

'Say, John,' he said across the room to his son, 'do you think you could throw ink about somewhere else? I've got a business talk coming up.'

'Why don't you use the study, Dad? That's what Mum had that room fixed for. So you could do all that telephoning and talking in private.'

'Yeah, I know,' Oliver said. 'Trouble is I like this room, old man. It's nice and big and airy. And there's a river view. Not to mention the proximity of the whisky cabinet.'

'It was to get you out of this room Mum fixed that other room.'

'Oh, did she indeed?'

'She certainly did,' the boy said with emphasis. 'This way we got to live with your business all the time. Say, Dad, can't you leave your business behind in Perth, like other chaps' fathers do?'

Oliver watched his son collect his books.

'So she wanted to shut me up in that corner room, did she?' he said gloomily.

'No. She just wanted to get rid of you out of here. All the same I guess we can move in there.'

Oliver had been drumming the fingers of his left hand on the arm rest. They lay still now.

What had the kid said?

He watched the boy go through the door, and watched him shut it quietly behind him.

His mind went back over the years to the time when Esther used to bring her sewing in to be with him. Sometimes it was her painting materials with bottles of water and palettes and a stack of pencils and brushes. When had she stopped doing that? For crying out loud, now he came to think of it, it must have been years ago. Why hadn't he noticed?

He sat, his eyes sombre, staring into the roaring log fire in the grate until Dick Bardon rang the door bell.

'Come on in, old fellow,' Oliver said heartily as he opened first the front door then the door to the sun-room. 'Golly, I'm glad to see you. Just feel like a yarn.'

171

Not even Richard Bardon, whose business in life it was to know by the flicker of an eyebrow that something ailed a man's nervous system, could have detected that Oliver was anything different from what he had ever been. There was the quick laugh, the flash of teeth and the expressive brown eyes so full of intelligence and life. There was the almost adolescent eagerness to get that whisky poured out before 'old Dick had time to thaw out.'

'Pull in that chair over there,' Oliver commanded. 'It's usually Esther's . . .'

He stopped short then and Richard Bardon noticed the break. He wondered vaguely if Oliver and Esther had had a few words, the way husbands and wives do. However, she came into the room at that moment. Bardon stood up and Esther shook hands with him. She always was a bit old-fashioned, he thought.

'I can see you two are going to have a session,' she said. 'I'll bring you in some sandwiches and leave you to it.'

'Say, Esther . . . it's warm in here,' Oliver said.

She smiled. It was a clear unaffected untroubled smile.

'It is in our room too,' she said. 'No, I won't spoil a stag party. I'll come back and have supper with you later. Besides, I want to help John.'

She smiled again at Richard Bardon and went out through the door.

Bardon scratched one ear and squinted at the fire through his glass of whisky.

'You know what,' he said as he sat down. 'Esther's the prettiest woman I ever saw. And she's as nice as she looks.'

Oliver grinned.

'I always pick the best,' he said. But the smile faded a little quickly. 'Reckon I put too much water in this whisky. How does it go, Dick?'

'Just right, thanks.'

They sat in their deep armchairs, Oliver's chair across the corner and Richard Bardon's chair dead in front of the fireplace. They stretched their legs and sat, a glass in one hand and a cigarette in the other.

Esther came in again and put small tables beside each and a plate of sandwiches on the mantelshelf. She lifted down two ash trays and put one on each table. Bardon was on his feet again and he went to the door with her and saw her out.

'Either she's a man-spoiler, or you've got her well trained,' he said with a laugh as he resumed his chair.

'Bit of both. Well, Dick? Let's to it. What's cooking with Harvey?'

'It's what he's cooking without knowing he's in the same room as the kitchen stove. Listen, Oliver, why's old Bernard Coole gunning for you?'

Oliver looked at the other man but did not alter the expression of his face.

'Is he?'

'I've got a feeling for atmosphere. And there's atmosphere all round and about just now.'

'You're dead right,' said Oliver. 'You tell me about it, and I'll finish the story for you.'

Bardon told Oliver about the meeting of the Board of Directors of Banfold and Co. and the part Bernard Coole played in it.

'I'm certain he had no more interest in Harvey as a servant of the firm than any other man in the place. He wasn't interested in Harvey but in the place Harvey had come from. Harding Motors Ltd. You're a Limited Company, Oliver, so I know he's not interested financially.'

'Only personally.'

'I got that impression.'

'I've got ideas about shifting a few million tons of riverside dirt in Pepper Tree Bay and he doesn't like it. He wants the Bay to stay the way it is. I don't. That's all there is to it.'

Bardon stared into the fire. He flicked the butt of his cigarette into it.

'Could be,' he said. 'Those old die-hards die very hard. But as I said before, I got a feeling for atmosphere. There's more in the air than just opposing a man on a civic issue.'

'I think you're right, Dick. I'd like to know what it is. I had a nomination up for the Yacht Club and Coole tried to blackball it. I intervened by ruling Coole unfinancial at the time of the committee meeting.'

'Yes, I know. You rigged that committee meeting.'

'How the blazes do you know? The only other man who knows is Ellison. He's scared white about it but I'll stake my life he'd keep quiet.'

'Harvey.'

'Harvey?'

'He overheard a telephone conversation you had with Ellison in your office. He didn't know it involved Bernard Coole, I promise you that. Coole found out in less than five minutes at that Board meeting that Harvey was easy to pump.

He took him out to lunch the day after the Board meeting. To the Pastoralists' Club. You know what going to that place with a Vice-President of the Company would do to a fellow like Harvey? Specially one who just didn't get Tomlinson's job. It would make him feel good. Justify him in the conviction you were wrong not giving him that job, and passing him out so easily.'

'Don't tell me,' said Oliver. 'I can see it all. And Old Man Coole just sat like a spider in the corner and sucked Harvey dry. How did you know what was said between them?'

Bardon gave a deprecating laugh.

'Harvey told me,' he said. 'He didn't want to get on the wrong side of the fence with me over wining with a Director, and a Vice-President to boot. He was anxious to satisfy me he wasn't sucking up. He faithfully recounted the whole interview. The trouble with Harvey is . . . besides not being the Tomlinson calibre . . . he's transparently honest. He thought this line of Coole's, taking a new executive out to lunch, was part of the initiation routine. The chat about Harding Motors Ltd a pleasant way an old-fashioned gentleman had of putting him at his ease. He was, I imagine, strictly faithful to you. He was giving you a bit of a build-up when he told Coole how deftly you can handle a committee meeting to get your own way. By quoting the Yacht Club incident he was keeping away from business secrets.'

Oliver was silent. Then he got up and poured out a whisky for himself and handed the bottle and jug of water to Bardon. He sat down and lit another cigarette.

'Harvey had to think that way,' he said. 'He had to think that way to prove to himself he didn't get passed out because he wasn't good enough. Human nature running true to form.'

'That's how I see it. But it was a hell of a giveaway.'

'Do you want to off-load him?'

'Hell, no. He's a good salesman. He'll pay his way. I'm not worrying.' He looked at Oliver through the cigarette smoke. 'I just happen to be a pal of yours. And I know old Bernard Coole.'

They were silent. Neither mentioned the fact that either of them could have broken Harvey Dalton. Run him out. It didn't occur to them to think about it. They had met Harveys all the way up the ladder of success. They'd met them coming down or tumbling down but neither had ever given another man a push just because he wasn't lucky when the natural gifts were given out on the day of birth.

'To tell you the honest truth,' Oliver said, 'I still think there's more than just the promenade business in the Bay that gives old Coole that sense of animus. You can always fight a man over a business deal and shake hands a week later.'

'It's the social snub or the prod in the prestige that brings out the dirty streak,' said Bardon.

'The Yacht Club business was neither. The feeling was there then. It was that feeling that made him blackball my nominee.'

'He didn't know your nominee then?'

Oliver narrowed his eyes and whistled faintly between his teeth.

'It's an odd thing, Dick,' he said at length. 'I'd say Bernard Coole doesn't know Riley Scott from the next man. But Riley Scott knows him.'

'Then he probably knows the answer to it. What does he say?'

'I haven't asked. And he doesn't give.'

'Then how do you know he knows him?'

'Like me, he doodles on blotting paper and writing pad. And every time he doodles he draws the head of Bernard Coole's walking stick.'

'Maybe he just saw it somewhere.'

'Yes,' said Oliver slowly. 'He saw that stick in some place and time that it means something to him . . .'

'Why don't you ask him?'

Oliver shook his head.

'There are some things you don't ask Riley Scott,' he said.

He reached down Esther's plate of sandwiches and passed them over to Bardon. Then he took one himself. Suddenly he laughed. His eyes had in them again the old sardonic gleam.

'The cloak and dagger game, eh?' he said. 'Well, it certainly makes life interesting.'

'Interesting as long as you don't get hurt . . .'

Oliver held up his gloved right hand.

'That's all the hurt I'm taking from this particular life,' he said with a grin. 'You watch. I got ears and eyes open.'

Bardon looked at his friend. What on earth had made him think Oliver couldn't look after himself?

CHAPTER TEN

Mama and the women's committees were having the time of their lives making out rosters for canvassing and knitting their brows over the right wording for their circulars. They'd got a signwriter to paint a beautiful banner on which stood out in red paint on a white background that unique slogan:

HANDS OFF THE BAY

The elections were two weeks away, and seven days hence would be the rally in the Pepper Tree Bay Main Hall at which each of the candidates for the Council would speak.

Usually it was a soul-destroying business trying to beat up enough people to fill the front seats for such an election rally. Nobody cared very much who sat on the Council so long as the public park was well cared for and the swimming baths kept free of barnacles. Pepper Tree Bay was not very much interested in community facilities. The people were well-to-do and could provide all those things for themselves. They liked the town to look nice and the rubbish to be cleared regularly. When they had too much rubbish to burn at the end of the block they rang up the Council and the Council came and obligingly cleared it away for nothing. So the people were satisfied.

When a vacancy had occurred through a Councillor's death, Riley Scott might have been elected unobtrusively and unopposed, if it hadn't been for the fact the women's organisations and Bernard Coole, on the West Side, had decided that no one should touch the Bay. Riley Scott was openly and frankly for the building of that promenade.

That rally was going to bring out the entire citizenry of Pepper Tree Bay. The man who was putting up against Riley had had HANDS OFF THE BAY printed on his personal stationery.

Mama was having a whale of a time ringing up and being rung up. In between bouts of addressing envelopes and talking on the telephone Mama would make teapots of strong tea . . . the way we all liked it . . . and address us on the subject of Oliver Harding. Oddly enough she never said anything about Riley Scott. She seemed to omit from reckoning the fact that it was Riley who was standing for the Council. She was just sorry for him that he wouldn't get in.

'Such a pity! Such a pity!'

'If you feel like that, Mama, why don't you let him get in?'

'And ruin the Bay? Certainly not. What a pity he's misguided. That's what I mean.'

Then she would go on about the impudence of Oliver Harding having swollen ideas about what he could do in a place like Pepper Tree Bay.

'Wants his ears boxed,' she said more than once.

We had stopped going to the electioneering meetings that were parties organised by the pro-Riley faction round on the East Side. Mama was a Public Figure and we had to pretend to be loyal to her, whatever we thought or felt.

Anyway, I still wanted the rock pools, the baby crabs, the lovely trailing seaweeds dancing in the sunlight and shadow under the Judge's old boatshed, to stay there till Barty was grown up. So I didn't go to the meetings and didn't agree with Mama, but got sore, instead, from sitting on the fence. You see, except for Mama, we all wanted Riley Scott to get in. He was a very striking man and in a mild kind of way managed to promote tendencies to hero-worshipping on the part of the female population.

He was a born leader, we sighed. Then added, like Mama, 'Such a pity he wants to interfere with the Bay.'

And we wondered, not without a sigh, who would be lucky enough to marry him, one day. Someone, we thought, who was beautiful, who could stand beside him to receive the Governor on grand occasions. Someone with an *air*.

On the last night we had attended one of these committee-cum-party affairs on the East Side, Riley Scott had arrived rather late. He had motored up from his farm down in the forest country and came in trailing a huge bunch of wild flowers, the way a man will, which he brought for Esther Harding.

Oliver had said these were too many flowers for Esther and he had broken the bunch up and given some to various of the ladies who had done most of the work. By work he meant, of course, those who had spent most of their time making Pavlova cakes and brewing cider cup . . . from Riley's orchard-grown apples . . . for the committee meetings.

All the ladies gave little cries of delight as Oliver, playing Lothario, gave some to each.

When it was Lacey's turn to receive a bunch it was odd how

Oliver first hesitated to give her some and then Lacey hesitated to take some. When she did take them she might have been receiving a bouquet like royalty for her back seemed straighter than ever and the beautiful way she carried her head made her look to have more pride than she really had. She covered that momentary hesitation with her usual clever good manners.

'Perhaps it is selfish of me to take flowers when we have our own farm down in the south-west . . .'

She looked past Oliver at Riley standing with a half smile watching the distribution of the spoils.

He gave a grave kind of bow and said, 'Please take some, Miss Coole. I don't suppose you have any in the town house at the moment.'

It was all so civil and formal in the middle of a group that was almost notorious for its informality.

Oliver went on being the grand fellow with Riley's flowers, but Lacey and Riley stood the full width of the room apart, Lacey with the flowers in her arms as if holding them close to her, but her head at that beautiful angle that always made her look so distinguished and well-born; and Riley looked at her out of eyes that were so veiled they were expressionless.

Thus, these weeks later, as I sat on the floor in Mama's drawing-room and put circulars in envelopes, in between drinking tea and snatching a puff at a cigarette, I thought of Riley marrying someone who could stand beside him on grand occasions . . . and I thought of Lacey Coole standing in that room with the flowers in her arm and her head so beautifully set on her shoulders.

Not Lacey Coole and Riley Scott! The well-born darling of the West Side and the orphan boy from the swampland! That could never happen in *Pepper Tree Bay*. But what a pity!

Ah, but another thought nudged me, Oliver Harding married Esther Hillman and she was well-born and delicately educated. In that case *she* had been the orphan.

Well, here I was playing my hares and hounds game of thinking with sympathy of my friends on the East Side and sticking flaps down on envelopes for Mama which contained letters instructing the citizens of Pepper Tree Bay to vote for another man; who *would* keep his hands off the Bay.

I did not know it then, but much later, that those flowers of Riley's had not brought Lacey happiness. When she had taken them home her father had looked coldly on them as they graced the dining-room table.

'Has someone come up from the farm?' he asked, looking at the flowers. 'And I don't like the smell of boronia in a closed room.'

'Oh no. Oliver Harding gave them to me,' Lacey said. 'I'll take the boronia out if you don't like it, Father.'

'Oliver Harding?' Bernard Coole's face was grey and his mouth was a line.

Mrs Simmins was in the room to carry away the soup dishes.

'Just leave it, Miss Lacey,' she said. 'I'll take the whole vase away and bring another.'

It was in the middle of that night that Bernard Coole was taken seriously ill with a terrible pain in the chest and shoulders. Mrs Simmins who assisted Lacey to attend to him said it was the mixture of boronia and the name of that dreadful man Oliver Harding that had given him such an attack of indigestion he might have been having a heart attack.

In the morning he was all right so the brief illness was put down to boronia, Oliver Harding and indigestion. Mrs Simmins told Miss Martin who told the grocer's delivery boy who told Vicky's cleaning woman who told Vicky . . . amongst others.

Mrs Simmins also reported that Mr Coole had taken such a dislike to his daughter these days, he could hardly bear her in the same room.

'He's getting old and difficult, probably,' we all said. Poor Lacey. We didn't mention this theory to Mama because Mama didn't like the mention of old age these days. We rather blessed the digression of the promenade and civic affairs, for she once again forgot she was 'old' and soon would be useless. *We* were able to forget it too.

That is until the Saturday morning before the Saturday of the Election Rally.

I was cleaning celery over the kitchen sink in my own house when Mama came in.

On this particular Saturday morning she brought tomatoes. She had grown them against a brick wall and they were so large there were only two to the pound. But it wasn't the winter crop of tomatoes over which I marvelled. It was Mama.

She came into the kitchen and I turned round. She stood there in the doorway, a wide-brimmed red hat, which she had made herself, on her head and a blue dress that I had helped her make. In her hands were the red tomatoes.

But it was her face and her eyes that were so beautiful.

'Why, Mama,' I said, 'you do look well!'

179

She did look well. She looked young and gay. The colour in her cheeks was kinder than that in the tomatoes and the blue of her eyes shamed the blue in her dress. Her lips were red and she smiled like a young girl.

'Mama,' I said again before she could reply, 'you look marvellous. Has something wonderful happened?'

'No,' she said gaily. 'I just meel marvellous. I haven't felt so well for years. It must be the sun shining.'

'Golly,' I said. 'You do look so *young* . . .'

'Do I?' she said, tossing her head as sprightly as a yearling. 'I feel young. Well, here are some tomatoes. I grew them all by myself. I'm off, dear. Can't stay for a minute. I want to get to Vicky's before twelve o'clock.'

'Do stay, Mama,' I said, feeling I wanted to cling and examine the young girl that was burgeoning out of Mama's eyes and indeed the very pores of her skin.

'Can't,' she said, fairly bolting off through the living-room and down the passage. 'I've such a lot to do.'

And away she went.

Later in the day I had to ring Vicky up about something and I asked her had Mama called in.

'Yes, she was here before lunch. She wouldn't stay on. Wanted to get home because she was going to spring-clean the house. Just imagine . . . on a day like this . . .'

'Didn't she look *well*?'

'I thought she looked marvellous. I asked her had she got a boy-friend or something. She just said she felt so well she was bursting with energy.'

Somehow Mama's radiance was shed about my own house all that day. And the wonder of it too.

At seven o'clock in the evening, David, Vicky's husband, rang me.

'Theodora,' he said in a voice so carefully quiet I knew something had happened. 'I'm at your mother's house. She's not well. Now don't panic. She is just not well. We've got the doctor coming in a few minutes and I thought you and Mary might be here.'

'But, David . . . what is it?'

'Some pain. Just take your time and come quietly, Theodora. It may not be anything serious but I think you might come.'

That was all. But I knew. That radiance!

At Mama's house there was nothing to break the deathly quiet but Mama's painful breathing. She lay on the sofa, partly undressed, in the drawing-room. Vicky, in her dressing-gown, sat on one side of her and the doctor sat silent in a chair on the other side. One glance at Vicky and I knew what had happened. Laura was out. Somehow Mama had got to the telephone and rung Vicky. Vicky had come as she was, half-dressed for a party. David still had not put on his shoes. He had picked them up in his hand and run for the car.

Mary sat frozen upright in a chair in the corner and a minute after I arrived Denney and Gerry came in. No one asked a question and no one said anything. We stole in and sat there and listened to Mama's groaning, and watched the doctor's dark intent face as he made a second injection into Mama's arm.

After a long long time, and when Mama had quietened, he got up.

'I will ring an ambulance,' he said. 'Your mother has had a heart attack. A very bad one, I'm afraid. I'm going to put her into hospital.'

Mama opened her eyes.

'No,' she said. 'No. I want to go home with one of the girls.'

The doctor looked from face to face. Which of these? he seemed to be thinking.

We all wanted to take Mama home. If she was going to die she was going to die in the home of someone who loved her. In the end my house was decided on because I had a spare room ready now, and because Vicky had too many children around and Mary and Denney and Gerry all went out to work.

By Monday morning Mama was sitting up and trying to pretend she had never had a heart attack. But her face was grey and there was a fine blue line around her lips.

On Tuesday she got up and nothing I could do would prevent her. I rang up the doctor about it and he said, very sombrely, 'Let her do what she wants to do, Theodora. She hasn't long. You should let her be happy meantime.'

It wasn't easy to let Mama get up and move about the house. If the others knew I let her do this I knew they would be beside themselves with wrath. When they came, carefully, quietly and one at a time, Mama was sitting primly on the sofa, a rug round her knees, pretending that's where she'd been all the time.

On Wednesday she walked round the garden and I cried into the tea cups because I knew that with every step she walked nearer the grave but I couldn't stop her. And the doctor said let her do it. But still I dared not tell my sisters.

On Thursday Oliver Harding came to see her.

'Oliver,' I said, 'don't you badger Mama.'

'I won't mention promenades,' he promised, 'the Bay or civic elections. I just want a little story that only your mother can tell.'

But I wouldn't go out of the room for fear he did get her worked up about his wretched promenade.

'Mrs Monty,' Oliver said gently, leaning forward, 'years ago, as the Rector's wife here in Pepper Tree Bay, you went into a Children's Court and intervened in a case in which a child, a young boy of eight, was being charged with being a neglected child. Your cause was, I think, that no child innocent of an offence should be charged and convicted in a Court of Law because he is neglected.'

Mama nodded. She leaned back in the chair.

'It is not the child who should be convicted – but the parents,' she said. 'That child was Riley Scott. I didn't win my point, Oliver. I never won it. To this day, even a newborn child can be charged and convicted because he is neglected by his parents. When that happens the child is made a Ward of the State and the State finds it a home, often with foster parents, which is a good thing. It was the "conviction" I opposed.'

'Riley Scott then was a Ward of the State, Mrs Monty? Would you tell me Riley's whole story?'

Mama looked at him steadily.

'Why do you want to know, Oliver? What happens in a Children's Court is cancelled when the child becomes eighteen years of age. There is no record after that.'

'I know that. The truth of it is, Mrs Monty, though there is no record there can always be people who remember and who repeat by words of mouth. There is no way of silencing them except with the truth and by using truth as a sword. Someone in Pepper Tree Bay knows Riley Scott's early history and it will be used against him on the night of the Election Rally.'

'Who?' said Mama curiously.

'Noah Firmingham, and possibly Bernard Coole.'

There was a tiny silence.

'Would you tell me what you know, Mrs Monty?' Oliver asked very quietly.

This was the story Mama told:

Riley Scott was a child born in a household of doubtful merit in the only poor part of Pepper Tree Bay, the swampland. The Scotts were a feckless lot and at some time the male members of the family left the town and never returned. What relationship each of the Scotts was to one another could never be quite ascertained. Old Mrs Scott claimed to be the mother of the young boy as she was undoubtedly the mother of the four pretty feckless girls who inhabited the small four-roomed wooden shack with her. The young blades of the West Side occasionally called on the pretty, gay, careless Scott girls.

Time and the neighbours and public opinion finally caught up with the Scotts. They were evicted by the landlord Firmingham, and the old lady herself took the boy to the Child Welfare Department and asked that a home be found for him. To do this the Department, in accordance with the law, had to charge the child before a Court of Law as being neglected. A Justice of the Peace in Pepper Tree Bay sat on the case and the boy was made a Ward of the State and sent to an Orphanage . . . a good one . . . in the country.

The boy, who had lived a free, undisciplined, carefree, barefooted life amongst the birds on the swamp and the horses running free in the sandhills west of the suburbs, was imprisoned within four walls and under a set of rules against which he finally rebelled. Twice he ran away, and twice he was found and returned to the Home. On the third occasion, after five and a half years, when he was nearly fourteen years of age. Oliver had found him behind the church. Oliver had fed and hidden him for three days. Then Riley had been found, by the police this time, while bathing in the river.

The local Justice of the Peace in Pepper Tree Bay constituted a Children's Court to hear the charge, brought by the police, of 'Absconding while a Ward of the State'. During the hearing the boy was asked how he had walked so far from the Home without food or water. The boy answered frankly enough. On the first night he had come to a farmhouse. It was winter and he was cold and hungry and barefooted. He went round to the back of the homestead and found a shed with a very poorly fixed padlock. He removed the padlock and entered the shed and slept there during the night.

The Justice of the Peace then asked the police why they had brought only a charge of 'Absconding while a Ward of the State'. Why hadn't they brought a charge of 'Breaking and Entering'? The astounded police then said they did not think the case warranted it. The Probation Officer from the Welfare Department protested. It was to no avail. The boy had convicted himself out of his own mouth. The Justice insisted and the most the Probation Officer could get was an adjournment.

He took the boy to the Rectory to the care of the Rector's

wife, Mrs Montgomery.

Two days later the case was resumed. The Justice was adamant and he had the book of law on his side. Reluctantly the police changed their charge to 'Breaking and Entering' but put forward a strong plea that they did not wish to press the case. The Probation Officer pleaded, Mrs Montgomery fought like a tigress defending her own.

To no avail. The Justice, who in reality was an Honorary Justice of the Peace with no more than local jurisdiction, was not to be moved. The boy, he said, had a record of running away. He must have a lesson in order to prevent any further such occurrences. He believed that prevention was cure. He believed in discipline. Without punishment the boy might abscond again and break and enter with more serious intent.

The boy was charged and convicted and committed to an Institution until eighteen years of age.

After the conviction, the Justice had no further control over the case. The Welfare Department returned the boy to the orphanage which was more a Home than an Institution.

Riley Scott had his freedom taken from him until eighteen years of age. The conviction would be expunged from the records when he did attain eighteen. Such was the law. He had received a sentence an adult would have had to commit a major crime to earn.

When he was sixteen he left the Home again and was never found. An understanding Probation Officer knew where Riley Scott was, down there sawmilling in the forest. He kept a weather and friendly eye on the boy but he never told the Department, the police or the Home where that boy was. Riley Scott was listed as one more missing child in an age when such was not uncommon.

'Who was that Justice of the Peace?' Oliver asked quietly.

Mama looked for a long time in Oliver's eyes. Then after a silence she added, 'It couldn't happen today, Oliver. Now we have a properly constituted Children's Court in Perth with a Stipendiary Magistrate.'

'Would that boy remember that Justice?' Oliver asked.

'He might. He might not. What he would remember was the walking stick that stood in the corner of the room adjoining the hall where the case was heard. When I took the boy home to the Rectory after they adjourned the case he had nightmares about it all night. He had sat there looking at that stick . . .'

'The handle was a carved dingo's head?' Oliver asked.

'Yes.'

'Then . . . ?'

'Yes,' Mama said quietly. 'It was Bernard Coole.' She made a sad defeated gesture with her hand.

'Mama is tired,' I said to Oliver.

'Yes,' he said, standing up. 'I'm sorry to have come when you are ill, Mrs Monty. It mattered though. It mattered to Riley. If Bernard Coole brings up the story of a conviction on the night of the rally it will ruin Riley. I'm glad you told me.'

'But he cannot bring it up,' Mama said. 'At eighteen years of age all convictions are expunged from the record.'

'It is too late for the law to stop Coole after the event,' Oliver said grimly.

When I went with him to the door I asked him if he knew why Bernard Coole still haunted Riley with his vengeance.

Oliver slapped me gently on the back.

'He doesn't know who Riley Scott is, Theodora. That's the pity of it. He wants to discredit him to debunk *me*. Riley can pay the price for being promoted by O. Harding.'

'But why?'

'Because Coole is old, and can't bear to give up the reins of government. Because he has exaggerated ideas of his necessity to life. Because he loves that river Bay and hates it being changed. Because he's alone and unloving. Because he believes in family and tradition . . . and I have none. I'm just a jumped-up nobody whose people might have come into the colony in the gold rush or as indentured servants. I wouldn't know myself, and I couldn't care less. But a nobody like me, no matter how much money I've made, should not be allowed to entertain ambitions of supplanting the Bernard Cooles of the day. Not while they're alive anyway, Theodora.'

'But Riley Scott?'

'Yes. Riley is the next problem.'

When he had gone I went back to Mama.

'Oliver says he doesn't think old Mr Coole knows he sat on Riley's case.'

'No, he wouldn't know,' Mama said. 'He sat on hundreds of cases in those days and when I once reminded him of it he had no recollection of which boy he had sent to what Institution.'

'How can we stop him, Mama?'

'You can't stop him, Theodora. But I can.'

'Mama, you're not well enough.'

'I'm well enough for that, and no one else can do it. I will go and see him. Before Saturday.'

I literally wrung my hands.

'What could you say to him that I couldn't say for you?'

'He wouldn't believe you, but he would believe me.'

'Believe what, Mama?'

'That he is old and should mind his own business about what the new generation wants to do with the Bay. Only an old person can tell another old person we should be dead and out of the way.'

'Oh, Mama,' I cried, 'don't . . . don't say that about yourself.'

She was looking into the fire when she answered.

'But it is true, dear. We've done all that we can do. It's time now to leave it to the others.' She looked up and there was a flicker of her old smile. 'It will take a long time to build that promenade. Too long for me ever to see it.'

There was almost a thankful note in her voice.

CHAPTER ELEVEN

Five weeks passed.

Lacey had been staying a week with Esther and Oliver Harding. She stood now at the window of the sun-room and watched four people and one small boy walking along the river shore at the bottom of the block.

The tall slim man beside Laura must be Danny Montgomery, she thought. The last of a line . . . Strange, but that was what she, Lacey, was now that her father was dead. The other man with Theodora was her husband Sam. They were walking slowly, the men with their hands in their pockets and Laura and Theodora tossing back their heads against the rush of the wind.

Oliver's idea of a promenade was a wonderful one, Lacey thought. Standing here watching the passing parade she decided that though the river and the Bay were so very beautiful the human interest provided by the strollers was equally attractive.

She remembered the day Mrs Montgomery had come to see her father.

The two elderly people had sat together a long time in the study. Lacey was thankful she had stoked up the fire for them. She wondered what they had had to say to one another. Her father had not told her and the next day he had had the heart attack.

He had been ill a week before he died and not until she had seen the withering flowers on that other grave had she known that Mrs Montgomery, too, had died.

As Lacey thought about it afterwards it gave her a strange feeling of comfort that they should lie there, side by side. Her father, she thought, would not be so lonely with an old friend with whom he might share the silence of that graveyard. When she saw the Montgomery girls, and could speak to them about it without a quiver in her voice, she would tell them about this comforting thought. Then she remembered that her father had said it must be fifteen years since the Montgomerys had any claim to being called 'girls'.

For the first time in weeks Lacey could smile at one of the memories of her father.

Watching two of the Montgomerys, the cousins Laura and Theodora, walking along the foreshore with their husbands, Lacey smiled now.

Already the pain, and loss and loneliness, was beginning to lose its sting. And she was able to think of things that had happened in the last five weeks without feeling the tears behind her eyes.

When Mrs Montgomery had left Meenon that day she had got into the waiting taxi and then turned and smiled who was seeing her off. She had waved her hand and said, 'Your father really loves that river, Lacey,

'Yes, I know,' Lacey said eagerly. 'He always sit can see it.'

Mrs Montgomery had sat back in the corner of the taxi and said,

'Now I think I've fixed everything up. I've sent a cable to Danny to come and take Laura home; and a telegram to Sam to come home . . . without that calculating machine . . . and look after Theodora and Barty.'

Lacey had laughed.

'You sound as if you are putting your house in order, Mrs Montgomery,' she said.

'Yes,' said Mrs Montgomery. 'At my age it is time to put one's house in order.'

She leaned forward then and touched Lacey's hand where it rested on the window frame.

'Give your vote to Riley Scott, dear. He's a good man, and he'll look after the Bay for us when we're all gone.'

The taxi had driven away then but Lacey had thought it was a strange thing for Mrs Montgomery to have said.

Now, five weeks later, looking down on the four figures on the point of disappearing round the bend of the Bay, she understood that Mrs Montgomery had been ill and had known her days were numbered. She had sent for Danny. Even Lacey had known that Laura needed Danny.

Mrs Montgomery was a wonderful woman, and it was rather fun the way she had changed her mind at the last minute about the promenade. And her father too. Just before he had had that heart attack he had rung up some man – Firmingham? – yes, Firmingham was the name, and told him there were to be no obstruction tactics in the civic election. Her father was a good man. He had worked for the well-being of the State just as Mrs Montgomery had done.

Lacey also thought her father would be pleased to know that when the dreadful solitude of Meenon had frightened her, she had gone to the telephone and rung up Oliver Harding. Her father would be satisfied to know she had asked a clever business man to help her with all that property associated with Meenon. Her father had never believed that a woman had any business capacity whatever.

The day that Lacey had rung up Oliver had been one on which she had reached the lowest ebb. Never would she forget Oliver's understanding friendly voice on the telephone.

'You're alone there, Lacey? Put some clothes in a suitcase. I'm coming for you.'

She thought perhaps she had rung Oliver because instinctively she had known that it was round there on the East Side she had known the first real happiness in years.

She had packed her suitcase and gone out from the dark panelling and sombre leather chairs of Meenon into the blue and gold of Esther's sun-room.

'Lacey,' he said, 'you have a caller.'

She turned in surprise. She had not told anyone she was staying with the Hardings. She had wanted that period to get used to the idea of her loneliness and her bereavement.

Oliver stood there, in the centre of the room, smiling and poking the finger of his left hand through his hair.

'He's a gentleman from the Civic Council. I've put him in the study because it's warmer there. Esther has built quite a fire for you.'

Lacey made a slight nervous gesture with her hand.

'The Council?' she said. 'Will it be about Meenon do you

think? Perhaps one of those old trees has come down across the fence. They were creaking badly in the wind the night my father died.'

Oliver shook his head.

'He's a Councillor. I don't think those august personages bother themselves about fallen trees. In fact they're more concerned with whether you've paid your rates.' His eyes were fun-making. 'Have you paid your rates do you know, Lacey? This fellow will be wanting them. He's going to build a promenade round the Bay.'

Lacey walked to the door. She turned back and gave Oliver a puzzled smile.

'I don't know, Oliver. You see, my father . . .'

Oliver nodded his head in the direction of the study.

'He's in there, waiting for you. You'd better make your explanations to *him*. And Lacey . . .' He smiled gently at the girl. 'Be polite to him, my dear. One day he'll be the Mayor.'

Lacey went through the door, across the hall into the study. Standing, his hands behind his back, and his back to the fire-place, was Councillor Riley Scott.

'Oh . . .' Lacey said, and a faint flush tinged her cheeks. 'I don't know why I didn't think it was you.'

Riley held out his hand, and Lacey put her hand in his.

'I hope I have not intruded, Miss Coole . . .'

'Lacey,' she said. 'Nobody here calls me anything but Lacey.'

'Thank you, Lacey,' he said gravely.

Then they both realised that he still held her hand. Lacey looked down at them, then looked up. There was a fleeting tenderness, quickly veiled, in Riley Scott's eyes, and wonder tinged with a great happiness in Lacey's heart.

Esther went into the sun-room and saw that Oliver had poured himself a whisky and soda.

'I suppose old Bernard Coole would turn in his grave, if he knew who was calling on who in our front parlour, sweetie,' Oliver said. 'And tell me . . . what made you turn it into a study?'

'To get rid of Harding Motors from the sun-room. I don't really mind you, Oliver . . . so long as you leave your business somewhere else. And why should Bernard Coole worry about who calls on Lacey? He and Riley Scott had a lot in common, you know. They both wanted the best for the Bay. They both loved the river.'

'They just had different ways of demonstrating a capacity for love, eh?'

'Yes,' said Esther. 'That's all it was.'

'*That's all it was?*' Oliver sounded almost belligerent.

Esther was standing on his left side now and he was able to rub the knuckle of his left hand, even though it held a glass of whisky, against her arm.

How soft and warm was Esther's arm. If only his right hand could feel it. If only his right hand . . .

The telephone rang.

Oliver crossed the room and sat down in the armchair. He let the telephone ring while he put his glass on the small table and then lit a cigarette. He thrust out his feet in front of him, leaned back, and lifted the receiver.

'O. Harding speaking,' he said.

Esther went out of the door and quietly closed it behind her.

Lucy Walker

Love, misunderstanding, heartbreak, tenderness . . . in the unfamiliar, exciting setting of Australia's vast Outback country.

THE OTHER GIRL. Three very different girls find themselves drawn to one man—and each is sure she'll lose him to one of the others.

HEAVEN IS HERE. Every girl within hundreds of miles was chasing Hugh Wilstack, and Jeannie vowed not to join the crowd. But her heart betrayed her. . . .

THE DISTANT HILLS. Angela was forced into a "marriage of convenience" through a cruel misunderstanding—could love grow from such a disastrous start?

SWEET AND FARAWAY. Lesley came out from England for her cousin's wedding—and found herself a virtual prisoner in the hands of the master of a vast Outback estate.

THE CALL OF THE PINES. Cherry came out to Yulinga as a governess, but a strange twist of fate threw her into a struggle for survival—and for the man she loved.

COME HOME, DEAR. Penny's love for John Dean had always seemed the most real thing in her life—then Ross Bennett came home. . . .

LOVE IN A CLOUD. Sonia loved John for his gentleness, Nick for his virile handsomeness—how could she decide?

FOLLOW YOUR STAR. Like many another girl, Kylie discovered the man she loved was an enigma—but she had to follow her star, wherever it might lead. . . .

HOME AT SUNDOWN. Two girls—and ten men—on a dangerous expedition, with feminine rivalry not the least of their perils.

REACHING FOR THE STARS. Ann came to Australia as an honored guest—and then found it had been a terrible mistake. . . .

A MAN CALLED MASTERS. It was Penny's chance for independence—but was she a match for the silent man who needed her?

THE STRANGER FROM THE NORTH. She had to do a man's job—and was doing it well . . . until the stranger rode in and took over.

THE RIVER IS DOWN. She had crossed her own Rubicon—now she was free to be a different woman, with a new life.

THE ONE WHO KISSES. Had Hal changed, or had he always been selfish and cruel? And how did he measure up to someone like Rick?

THE MAN FROM OUTBACK. Mari was whisked off to Australia to mend a broken heart—but as soon as she met Kane Manners, her heart was in trouble again. . . .

DOWN IN THE FOREST. The tragedy of the fire had reached them all—but, in its embers, Jill sensed that her dreams might come true.

WIFE TO ORDER. Her guardian had treated Carey as a child—and now he told her coldly that she would soon be his wife. . . .

THE MOONSHINER. Joan fled the social whirl for life in the vast Outback. She learned much of the ways of the wild—and then she learned to love. . . .

THE RANGER IN THE HILLS. Was he a myth or a man? Now that he held her in his arms, Kate would discover the truth about the man she had had to trust.

SHINING RIVER. They had loved each other as children, but now that life's hardships had torn them apart, could they ever recapture the sweet past?

SIX FOR HEAVEN. Theodora had four lively sisters—and four men to choose from!

THE GONE-AWAY MAN. Heartbreak tore Lisa as she watched the man she loved turn to another girl.

KINGDOM OF THE HEART. Judith had to share her inherited cattle farm with darkly handsome Andrew, who felt that the Outback was no place for an unmarried woman.

THE LOVING HEART. He hired Elizabeth to pose as his fiancee to evade designing women attracted by his fabulous wealth. But the masquerade backfired. . . .

MASTER OF RANSOME. He married Sara out of need—not out of love. . . .

JOYDAY FOR JODI. Jodi Dean came to Australia in search of her missing brother—and found herself in a three-way fight over the same man.

To order by mail, send 80¢ for each book to Dept. CS, Beagle Books, 36 West 20 Street, New York, NY 10011.